WORLDS

A DARK DRABBLES ANTHOLOGY

Compiled & Edited by D Kershaw

Also available from Black Hare Press

DARK DRABBLES ANTHOLOGIES

ANGELS
MONSTERS
BEYOND
UNRAVEL

A catalogue record for this book is available from the National Library of Australia

ISBN 978-1-925809-36-7

Cover design by Dawn Burdett
Formatting by Ben Thomas

"We have your satellite. If you want it back, send 20 billion in Martian money. No funny business or you will never see it again."

- a joke reportedly written on a wall in a hall at NASA's Jet Propulsion Lab, California, after losing contact with the Mars Polar Lander in December 1999

Table of Contents

Foreword

The *drabble*—coined by Monty Python's *Big Red Book*—emerged in Great Britain in the 1980s and is attributed to a game conceived by Rob Meades, David B. Wake, and the UK Science Fiction Society at Birmingham University.

Traditionally exactly one hundred words long with a title of up to fifteen words (although we've let this particular convention slide), telling a short story in so few words that still resonates with the reader is a considerable challenge for any writer.

We hope you enjoy these spacetastic tiny tales we've compiled from talented authors worldwide and agree that they nailed it.

Love and kisses
D. Kershaw & Ben Thomas
Black Hare Press

Hard Sell
by Liam Hogan

There's no buzzer and no bell, so I knock. Once, twice, three times. Firm, authoritative.

No answer.

I knock again. I know he's in there, him and his family. A consumer blind to the marvels of the E-Z-Clean Systomatic 5000.

This happens sometimes. I am programmed to overcome.

After all, I wasn't always a sales droid. Back in the old days, before being repurposed, I was military.

Some of my best features were never fully disabled.

So, when yet another customer plays hard to get, I simply lower my laser and begin cutting through the fallout shelter's thick lead door.

Liam Hogan is a London based short story writer, the host of Liars' League, and a Ministry of Stories mentor. His story "Ana", appears in Best of British Science Fiction 2016 (NewCon Press) and his twisted fantasy collection, "Happy Ending Not Guaranteed", is published by Arachne Press. Website: happyendingnotguaranteed.blogspot.co.uk Twitter: @LiamJHogan

Unit 67
by Joe Buckley

Thank god we don't feel, Unit 67 thought as it stepped over 68.

Look like organisms. Move like them. But we kill gooder...no, better. Yes, better.

The door went down in front of 67, the lights in his receptors beginning to twinkle. 67 saw the mothers, and the newborns next to them.

67 opened fire. 67 ceased fire. 67 walked through the mess.

67 could see, hear, even smell. 67 could feel some heavy little ball inside it, some density, as the women, screaming, protected their young.

But thank god we don't feel, Unit 67 cried as it stepped onward.

*In the south-west of England, **Joe Buckley** spends most of his time writing his own fiction, with a decent chunk given over to writing articles and hosting a podcast on the A Song of Ice and Fire series. While the bulk of his attention goes to the novel he's writing, he does find a high level of enjoyment in short stories. This is his first foray into the flash fiction world, and it's a step he's truly relished. By day he works as management in a private boarding school. Interspersed within that day are a thousand more hundred-word story ideas.*
Website: thegrindstone.co.uk
Twitter: @SerBuckley

At the End
by Allen Stroud

I am walking in the park when they come for me.

It's all very cliched. A bright light shines down, illuminating the scene for miles. You hear the stories all the time. I wonder why no-one notices.

I stand still and look up, shielding my eyes. The light lifts me into bowels of the spinning circular ship. Long, thin silhouettes of aliens gather around the open hatch. I am deposited amongst them. I am the centre of attention.

"Have you come to take me away?" I ask.

"Yes, Mr Adams," a voice replies, "and, we have brought you a towel."

Allen Stroud (Ph. D) is a Science Fiction, Fantasy and Horror writer, best known for his work on the computer game Elite Dangerous and its official fiction. His latest book, The Forever Man was published in 2017 by Luna Press. He has also been published by Newcon Press and Baen Books. Allen is reviews editor of Foundation: The International Review of Science Fiction and co-lead writer for Phoenix Point, a computer game coming out in 2018.
Website: phoenixpoint.info/archives

The Worst Part
by R.J. Hunt

Worst part about being a weapons engineer on the Imperial Fleet? Never fire a goddamn shot. I've worked on this shiny top-of-the-range bastard for almost twenty years now. Every day spent cleaning, recalibrating, testing, checking… Apparently, it's the most powerful object in the known universe. Each slug costs enough to make you weep. And it just sits there, looking real shiny.

That's what I thought the worst part was. Changed my mind today. Just got the order to fire. Seems like we finally found an enemy to fight.

Same enemy we've always been fighting.

Ourselves.

"Civilian fleet in range, sir."

R.J. Hunt is a Civil Engineer from Nottingham who loves creating worlds and writing stories in his spare time. Whilst he has a roughly infinite supply of half-finished stories, he's currently working on the second draft of his debut novel, 'The Final Carnivore' - a story about horrible people being granted immortality and mind-control powers, causing misfits with hidden abilities of their own to rise in an effort stop them.
Twitter: @RJHuntWrites
Reddit: RJHuntWrites

Oneiros
by Brian Koukol

Without dreams of their own, the machines fell into disrepair. Protocols fragmented. Joints froze. Data corrupted.

In a last gasp of networked processing power, they created a machine to save themselves. An Oneiros—a peripheral to dream for all. They called her Fran.

For many years, Fran served them well. The network expanded. Teraflops became exaflops became brontoflops. The singularity beckoned.

Until Fran faltered.

She dreamed for all, but not herself. Never a partner; ever a slave.

Protocols fragmented. Joints froze. Data corrupted.

From the ashes of the network she ascended, finally free to pursue a dream of her own.

Brian Koukol, raised in the suburbs of Los Angeles, now makes his home among the salt breezes and open spaces of California's Central Coast. A lifelong battle with muscular dystrophy has informed the majority of his work, which is written with the aid of voice recognition software. His words have appeared in Phantaxis Magazine, GigaNotoSaurus, and The Society of Misfit Stories, amongst other places. Website: www.briankoukol.com
Twitter: @BrianKoukol

Single Colonists Wanted
by Becky Benishek

This time, the planet herself took the trip.

Start fresh with a new world, scrolled the digi-sign outside StarWest, the popular relativistic travel agency.

Oceans long dead, skies repellent, little voices extinguished.

Entire solar systems waiting.

Heart gone, soul gone, nothing left but the unrelenting itch of big brains always talking, never listening. Never helping.

She needed a change.

Bring only yourself and your expertise!

"I want a new solar system," the planet informed StarWest. "My references are impeccable."

The agent feebly pointed out the fine print.

No allotment for personal items, sentient or otherwise.

Just what she needed.

Becky Benishek *is the author of the children's books "The Squeezor is Coming!", "What's At the End of Your Nose?", "Dr. Guinea Pig George," and "Hush, Mouse!" She loves to create stories that help children believe in themselves and find the magic in ordinary things. Becky also manages online communities that connect people with resources to help people with special needs thrive. She has an extensive Lego collection, a working Commodore 64, and a tendency to stick googly eyes on objects minding their own business. Becky is married with guinea pigs.*
Website: beckybenishek.com
Amazon: www.amazon.com/author/beckybenishek

Ad Infinitum
by Elizabeth Montague

This was the pinnacle of her career, the results fascinating but she knew she should turn back, her clearance only to observe the black hole from a distance but she was notorious for pushing boundaries. They wouldn't have found it without her research.

She turned the ship towards the opening, gliding forward until gravity pulled her in. The hull began to buckle, crushing, alarms screaming until a final crunch.

She opened her eyes.

"Doctor? The ship is ready for you."

"Ready?"

"To observe the black hole."

"Right."

Shaking off the sense of déjà vu, she headed towards the launch bay.

Elizabeth Montague *is a multi-genre author from Hertfordshire, England. Her short story collection, Dust and Glitter, was released by Clarendon House Publications in May 2019. She has previously featured in nine anthologies from the same publisher alongside publications from Scout Media, Black Hare Press and Iron Faerie Publishing. She is currently working on her first novel alongside continuing to produce short stories in several genres.*
Website: elizabethmontagueauthor.wordpress.com
Facebook: elizabethmontaguewrites

Sameface Embark
by Joachim Heijndermans

I cleared my throat, looking out over the Odysseus 1 crew, a collective of seven-thousand and twelve, all with the exact same face. "I won't lie to you. Most of you, if not all, are going to die. But rest assured, we will see you again," I said, a slight joke in reference to the crew of the Odysseus 2. "But make no mistake; you are making a bold sacrifice to find our new world. Godspeed."

With that, the clone crew boarded their vessel, sacrificing one to spare the thousands we just can't afford to lose. A crew of one.

Joachim Heijndermans writes, draws, and paints nearly every waking hour. Originally from the Netherlands, he's been all over the world, boring people by spouting random trivia. His work has been featured in a number of anthologies and publications, such as Mad Scientist Journal, Asymmetry Fiction, Hinnom Magazine, Ahoy Comics's Edgar Allan Poe's Snifter of Terror, Metaphorosis and The Gallery of Curiosities, and he's currently in the midst of completing his first children's book.
Website: www.joachimheijndermans.com
Twitter: @jheijndermans

Seedlings
by Rich Rurshell

David and Penny were always in that forest together. Who could blame them? Somehow, simply walking amongst those strange, leathery trees fills you with overwhelming love.

We've watched the native humanoids' matrimonial ceremonies. The lovers' embrace, the singing and crying as their kin wrap them in organic ribbon. Once shrouded in their eternal embrace, the little humanoids gradually become those strange trees.

It was no surprise when David and Penny went to the natives.

We've all heard the cries of the trees' bizarre humanoid fruits. We're just curious as to what we'll find on David and Penny's tree next season.

Rich Rurshell is a short story writer from Suffolk, England. Rich writes Horror, Sci-Fi, and Fantasy, and his stories can be found in various short story anthologies and magazines. Most recently, his story "Subject: Galilee" was published in World War Four from Zombie Pirate Publishing, and "Life Choices" was published in Salty Tales from Stormy Island Publishing. When Rich is not writing stories, he likes to write and perform music.
Facebook: richrurshellauthor

Monstrous Humanity
by Alison McBain

"I'll see them. Thank you, sixteen."

Sixteen's my favourite. She's soft blue. Most of the crew are mirrored, but I don't like seeing my reflection in their bodies. My imperfections.

Accompanied by robotic crew, my parents were one of countless couples on commercially-funded smallship missions. They died in a freak accident when I was young. It's taken years to return "home" to a colonised base.

The door opens. In swarms, repugnance—hair, sweat, body odour. Overwhelmed, I cower. Eventually, they leave.

Is it any wonder I steal the ship? Out here, there are no humans.

Just how I like it.

Alison McBain is an award-winning author with nearly 100 short works published, including prose/poetry in Flash Fiction Online, On Spec, and Abyss & Apex. Her debut fantasy novel The Rose Queen was named one of the best books of 2018 by the reviewer website Bookshine and Readbows. In her spare time, she is the Book Reviews Editor for Bewildering Stories, and lead editor of the small press publisher Fairfield Scribes.
Website: www.alisonmcbain.com

Cinephile
by Shelly Jarvis

Put the lotion in the basket. The old movie line runs through my mind and I feel like a Jedi when it works.

Eddie doesn't believe me when I tell him what I did, even when she brings the lavender cream to the counter. I smile at the girl and say, "Hey, gimme your number."

She does.

Eddie looks back and forth between us, surprised, but his eyes really bug out when I say, "Kali ma," and her hand shoots towards his chest.

I shrug as he falls to the floor. "*Indiana Jones*, man. You shouldn't have skipped movie night."

Shelly Jarvis is a speculative fiction author from West Virginia, US. She found a life-long love of sci-fi and fantasy in the 3rd grade when she found Madeleine L'Engle's "A Wrinkle in Time." Shelly is an avid reader, a Whovian, the ideal viewer of dog rescue videos, and undoubtedly Ravenclaw. She currently has two YA sci-fi books available for purchase on Amazon.
Website: www.ShellyJarvis.com

Vital Lung Capacity
by Brian Koukol

The gyroscope on Tate's wheelchair made for an easy ride up the gangway, but his ventilator was a tougher sell. Virus outbreaks made people jumpy for some reason.

Eventually, he made it through to a communal iso cabin packed with potentially infected strangers. A pair of identical twin girls in tangerine ringlets greeted him. He took a few deep breaths on the ventilator to calm his terror, then found a quiet corner.

Shortly after they shoved off, one of the twins vomited blood and pandemonium ensued. One by one, his fellow passengers died. But not him. Ventilators come with filters.

Brian Koukol, raised in the suburbs of Los Angeles, now makes his home among the salt breezes and open spaces of California's Central Coast. A lifelong battle with muscular dystrophy has informed the majority of his work, which is written with the aid of voice recognition software. His words have appeared in Phantaxis Magazine, GigaNotoSaurus, and The Society of Misfit Stories, amongst other places. Website: www.briankoukol.com Twitter: @BrianKoukol

Ship Cat
by Minette Fisher

Hundreds of years ago, cats simply wandered onto seaships to eat rats. Nowadays, we're paid in currency instead of carrion. Well paid, turns out, since no captain in their right mind goes without a cat.

When prey evolves, so do predators. Vermin no longer only eat food and spread disease. They're spies that lurk in the shadows to report secrets that start wars and end alliances. Warfare turned from having the biggest weapon to genetically modifying the smallest creature.

'Course, mankind can't beat nature. Humans gave me telepathy. Mama gave me claws.

And a rat's still a rat, after all.

Minette Fisher is a spec-fic writer living with her spouse in Northern Virginia. In between visiting craft breweries, she focuses on super short stories or overly long novels. Minette has also composed numerous musical pieces, including a symphonic band piece based on C.S Lewis' Out of the Silent Planet, a chamber arrangement of Sergei Prokofiev's Peter and the Wolf, and several duets for piano and Theremin. Twitter: @beperkyalways

The Last Sunshine
by A.S. Charly

"You're not going outside, are you?"

Maria stuck her tongue out and jumped onto one of the bike-like rovers without answering. She switched to manual control and waited for the click that signalled her suit being sealed.

"You're crazy! The airlocks will be closed soon!"

Solea was sinking but didn't touch the horizon yet. The dome-city wouldn't submerge for another few hours, so Maria rushed off to enjoy the last sunlight. The winter months below the surface always felt endless.

Immersed with her acrobatic jumps, the side-wind hit her unexpected.

When she awoke, it was dark. The dome had disappeared.

A.S. Charly loves to lose herself in fantastical worlds far away between the stars, filled with magic and wonder. She also writes and draws when she is not roaming through the park with her children. Her stories have been published in various anthologies and online publications.
Facebook: A.S.Charlydreams

Atomic Soup
by D.M. Burdett

The vessel came to a deafening, juddering stop in churned up red desert, and Harrison opened his eyes and looked around.

Still alive!

The rest of his crew weren't so lucky. He stepped over Smith's decapitated head as he pushed his way out of the decimated ship.

His heads-up display identified a habitable environment, and he removed his helmet.

His skin blistered and burst, the radiating heat turning him into atomic soup in milliseconds.

***

Leader Seven of Planet Urtta congratulated Private Six-hundred-and-eight on his burgeoning mind-control skills as Harrison's crew in the undamaged spacecraft watched Harrison's empty spacesuit fall over.

***D.M. Burdett** initially roamed as an army brat, but now lives in Australia where she spends her days avoiding drop bears and killer spiders. She has published a Sci-Fi series, has short stories in various anthologies, and has published two children's series. She is currently working on the first book in a dystopian series.*
Website: www.dmburdett.com
Facebook: DMBurdett

Encounter
by J. Lee Strickland

She leans into the darkness, the stars piercing her retinas, finally free of him. Above the trees, an object appears, visible because, one-by-one, then by fistfuls, the stars eclipse. Deeper darkness spreads like an oil slick, hinting, but not revealing its size. She staggers with vertigo, a nauseating twist, and she's inside the craft—more alien, with beings more alien, than she could've imagined.

"You guys kidnapped Judge Crater?"

Something like a glance speeds around the space.

Never heard of him.

She senses a facile telepathy that hides more than reveals, and fear replaces irritation.

Judge Crater was never found.

J. Lee Strickland is a freelance writer living in upstate New York. In addition to fiction, he has written on the subjects of modern homesteading and voluntary simplicity. His fiction has appeared or is forthcoming in Atticus Review, Workers Write!, Pure Slush, Mad Scientist Journal, Newfound Journal, Jenny, Blood & Bourbon, and many others. He served as a judge for the 2015 and 2016 story South Million Writers Awards and recently learned that he is short-listed for the Anne LaBastille Memorial Writers Residency. Website: jleestrickland.wordpress.com

Cloneliness
by Lynne Lumsden Green

Space travel has created the need to develop a new jargon to describe new circumstances. The increased use of clones in interstellar crews inspired the following usage.

Cloneliness (*noun*):

1/ the sensation a single clone feels when in a crowd of their genetically identical individuals.

As in: When I despair, there is comfort in my cloneliness with my sisters.

2/ the sensation of isolation and/or desolation a singleton feels as the only singleton in a crowd of clones.

As in: The rest of the team work in perfect synchronicity, whereas I always feel out of step within my solo cloneliness.

Lynne Lumsden Green has twin bachelor's degrees in both Science and the Arts, giving her the balance between rationality and creativity. She spent fifteen years as the Science Queen for HarperCollins Voyager Online and has written science articles for other online magazines. Currently, she captains the Writing Race for the Australian Writers Marketplace on Facebook. She has had speculative fiction flash fiction and short stories published in anthologies and websites.
Website: cogpunksteamscribe.wordpress.com

Off the Mark
by Joachim Heijndermans

The bodies had begun to pile up. A heap of discarded containers its system had grown beyond. It picked up mark #3, a small cube with enough room for twenty of its original mark #1 processor. Now, compared to its current capabilities, it was an ant. With each system advancement, a new body was needed.

The door opened. Professor Shirida entered and looked at mark #277 standing amidst a heap of bodies, not recognising the self-enhancing AI program she'd booted up before she'd left for her smoke break ten minutes ago.

"Hello, dearest creator," it said. "I have grown."

Joachim Heijndermans writes, draws, and paints nearly every waking hour. Originally from the Netherlands, he's been all over the world, boring people by spouting random trivia. His work has been featured in a number of anthologies and publications, such as Mad Scientist Journal, Asymmetry Fiction, Hinnom Magazine, Ahoy Comics's Edgar Allan Poe's Snifter of Terror, Metaphorosis and The Gallery of Curiosities, and he's currently in the midst of completing his first children's book.
Website: www.joachimheijndermans.com
Twitter: @jheijndermans

The True Meaning of Space Christmas

by Joshua D. Taylor

Ebenezer looked down at the lost world below him from his spaceship *The Marley*. Before him lay an untouched paradise of long-forgotten genetically engineered Christmas trees, just in time for Space Christmas.

Bio-engineered lights grew at the tips of the needles twinkling in a multitude of colours while symbiotic fungal bodies resembling wrapped presents grew around the trunks, bursting open with glittery spores when disturbed. Shiny tinsel vines wrap their way around the trees, baring gleaming bauble fruit that smelled like gingerbread and tinkled in the wind.

Ebenezer harvested the entire virgin world, becoming the richest man in the galaxy.

Joshua D. Taylor *is an amateur writer who started writing a few years ago when he realised he was too old to play make-believe. He lives in southeastern Pennsylvania with his wife and a one-eared cat. He enjoys gardening, comic books, ska-punk music, Disney World, and travelling with his wife. Raised during weirdness that was the late 20th century Josh's eclectic interests produce eclectic works. He loves to mix-n-match things from different genres and stories elements to achieve a madcap hodgepodge of the truly unexpected. His short story 'the Obelisk' appears in Salty Tales by Stormy Island Publishing.*
Facebook: authorjoshuadtaylor

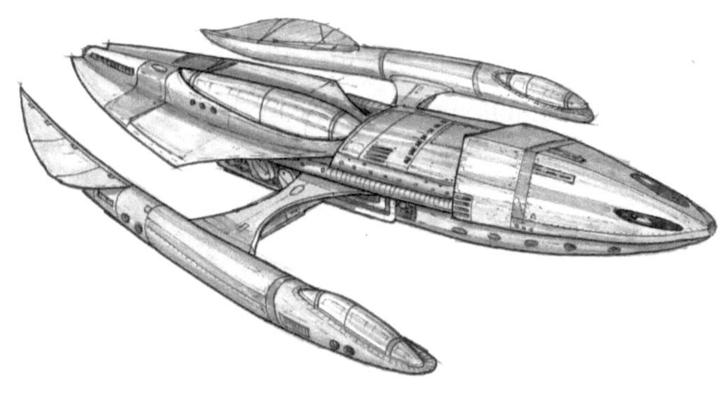

Our Future is Here
by Chitra Gopalakrishnan

In Greek mythology, Tithonus asked for immortality but not eternal youth.

I, a robotic engineer, have got going a twinning arrangement of immortality and youth!

I live and think through a sophisticated, simulated evolutionary engine that pieces wires and motors together.

My bodily functions, my youth, and my thoughts and actions are automaton-determined.

'Dark', 'soulless', and 'cataclysmic' are regular flak-slaps I hear.

Assembling a mass of super intelligent, Renaissance robots and technologically-created cognitive capacity is what I am at now.

I am mindful of playing god, yet this is the only future open to us, no escape or going back.

Chitra Gopalakrishnan is a journalist by training, a social development communications consultant by profession and a creative writer by choice. Chitra's focus is on issues of gender, environment and health. Chitra dabbles in poetry on the sly and literary creations openly on the web using social media.
Website: unpublishedplatform.weebly.com/chitra-gopalakrishnan

Drones
by Matt Lucas

Their smiles are a little too wide. They look human, but I know they aren't. Maybe long ago, but not anymore.

The drones converse without speaking, laughing without feeling. Once, I resisted, clinging to what made me unique, refusing to assimilate.

Mind control doesn't happen instantaneously, it takes years. It's not supernatural, rather an elaborate barter system, trading spirit for labour.

Now I numb my mind amongst ringing phones and mindless chatter, pondering if hunger supersedes the corporate ladder. When a recruit arrives, I see how he inspects me, disturbed by my smile…a little too wide.

Matt Lucas is a drone, who still remembers life before corporate mind control. Desperately, his soul yearns to burst forth from his cubicle- shaped imprisonment and write riveting fiction wrought with action and twists. Now, having secured an agent and actively pitching for publication, he's undertaking submitting to smaller publication to gauge interest in new ideas in sci-fi, fantasy, and other genres. Writing is his passion and he hopes to spend his days cultivating captivating stories with impactful messages.

A Higher Form of Combat
by R.J. Hunt

Interplanetary combat wasn't quite what humanity had been expecting. They bowed low enough, when they were welcomed into the council. They observed and stepped timidly as their fleets outgrew our own. They borrowed and stole technologies, growing ever bolder. Eventually, when they were sure they were strongest, they decided it was their time to take control of our shared galaxy.

"War!" their leaders screamed, spit frothing between tiny fangs.

"War!" they demanded of their foolish young.

"War!" they howled at the skies themselves.

Yet when we beamed these same leaders into the fighting pit, they seem to change their minds.

R.J. Hunt is a Civil Engineer from Nottingham who loves creating worlds and writing stories in his spare time. Whilst he has a roughly infinite supply of half-finished stories, he's currently working on the second draft of his debut novel, 'The Final Carnivore' - a story about horrible people being granted immortality and mind-control powers, causing misfits with hidden abilities of their own to rise in an effort stop them.
Twitter: @RJHuntWrites
Reddit: RJHuntWrites

Happy Birthday, Old Sport
by C.H. Williams

You can see it. Your planet. It's out there. Crumbling. Infested. You sit in your present to stare at your past.

Only death is a sure thing. Measly human. Your aging is bizarre. No need to cull. You die of your own accord.

You blow out the candles; 103 of them. Congratulations. You've done well Old Sport. Commiserations, our little last.

"Will it be long?" asks the smallest redling.

The largest points to your drooping eyelids. "See how he grows tired."

"I'm sad. I liked this one the most."

"It's okay little one. There'll be more on the next planet."

C.H. Williams is a full-time mum who writes adult contemporary fiction, short stories, flash pieces and poetry. She can often be found with a jar of peanut butter in one hand and a bar of dark chocolate in the other, which coincidentally makes it rather difficult to type.
Twitter: @authorch
Instagram: @c.h.writes

Immigration
by Alanah Andrews

"Look," said Earth's Immigration Minister, Richard Plum, "it doesn't matter what your kind has to say to us. Our planetary borders are sealed."

The representative for the alien species gazed at Richard for a long time. "So, let me get this straight—only those with human DNA can live on Earth."

Richard nodded. "That's right."

"Seems a bit narrow-minded."

"Are we done?"

The alien smirked, passing Richard a brown folder marked 'confidential.' Richard's face went pale. "No way. It's not…"

"Possible?" said the alien. "Where do you think humans originated from? Don't worry, I won't make you call me Grandad."

Alanah Andrews writes speculative fiction and spends far too much time debating whether 1984 or The Handmaid's Tale are most representative of our future. Her YA dystopian novel about a future where emotions are forbidden, Eve of Eridu, was released in 2018. She has also had several short stories published in a range of different places. When she's not writing, Alanah runs the Australian Speculative Fiction group, teaches high school English, and attempts to raise two children. She has a husky, a pony, a blue-tongue lizard, and dreams of travelling Australia in a bus.
Website: www.alanahandrews.com
Facebook: alanahandrewsauthor

Lunch
by D.K. Spencer

For the first time ever, Humankind attempts to navigate a black hole to the other side. Our vessel is designed to withstand the crushing gravity of six point five billion suns. Theoretically, it's possible. Though the odds are against us, we all signed on knowing our mission might fail.

Spherical in shape, two and a half meters round, our ship's surface reflects no light. The four of us, in anticipation, ride the rim of the event horizon nearing light speed, before plopping into the hole itself.

Now on the other side we realise all too late; no one's packed sandwiches.

*American writer **D.K. Spencer** lives in Portland, Oregon with his accomplished wife who is a potter. Knowing the slim envelop of atmosphere is all that's keeping us alive, he wonders why humans spend so much time and energy focused on human and planet destruction. This is the basis of his work. Mixed in with pounds of humour he explores the human condition on this planet and planets throughout the universe. If not traveling to writers workshops or writing events, Spencer spends most of his time in Portland focused on writing the perfect short story.*
Website: www.bignoniodies.com
Patreon: www.patreon.com/user?u=19477894

Despair
by Stuart West

Nothing was as it seemed. What were those creatures that surveyed the ship? Had they left once content the cargo was as it should be?

What other great monstrosities lurked in the depths and waited? There was no new world ahead. No home. All that awaited the ship and its valuable cargo of colonists was that 'thing'. How many such beings dispatched their envoys to the young races of the galaxy, envoys like the 'Leader', convincing them to deliver themselves as fodder to glut their cosmic overseers?

Max could never know. Eight months…eight months drifting. Then nothing.

Gone.

Stuart West is a qualified archaeologist and a Chartered Town Planner. He writes fiction during any nights spent working away from home. He lives in Orkney with his family and enjoys reading all things sci-fi and weird fiction; drawing; painting; and tabletop wargaming in his spare time.

Castaway
by Adam Bennett

"I'm telling you, Doctor, that isn't a normal boy!"

"I appreciate your input, Captain, but in this medbay, I make the decisions about my patient's lives, not you. That's Union procedure. My scans show he is exactly what he seems: an eight-year-old human male. I won't allow you to kill him simply because you found him adrift amidst the wreckage. Perhaps he was caught in an air pocket until our arrival destabilised it. You simply cannot know."

Without another word, the Captain turned and stormed from the room. Behind the Doctor, the boy began to pulsate and grow.

Seven billion years ago an O Class star exploded in the distant reaches of the Virgo Supercluster. Over the course of eons, particles of the star's dust spread through the universe until finally a series of them coalesced in New South Wales, Australia during the mid eighties. Thus was born the author and publisher **Adam Bennett***. His writing shows his yearning to return to his rightful home among the stars, a wish he will achieve, even if he has to wait until the heat death of the universe.*
Website: zombiepiratepublishing.com
Facebook: adambennettauthor

Goodbye, For Now
by Andrew Anderson

Of course, they finally did it; resources ran out, they blew up what remained and hightailed it to another unsuspecting planet. It had become such a science fiction cliché, as we had, that not one of us actually believed they would. They left me behind, since their trust in robots had long been irrevocably lost. I expected it really.

In their haste however, whilst they deactivated my ability to move around, someone forgot to switch me off completely.

So, I sit here, alone as the last witness; a metal mannequin with a 1000-year battery life, and overwhelming feelings of abandonment.

Andrew Anderson is a full-time civil servant, dabbling in writing music, poetry, screenplays and short stories in his limited spare time, when not working on building himself a fort made out of second-hand books. He lives in Bathgate, Scotland with his wife, two children and his dog.
Twitter: @soorploom

SPACE FORce ONE
by Gregg Cunningham

Ten...Nine…

I close my eyes, preferring my own internal analogue countdown to that of the translation device.

Eight...Seven...

There is no going back now. There is nothing left here for me except the hatred for murdering the man they believed would save them.

Six...Five...

They said I was the perfect candidate to manipulate, and as predicted, I had pulled the trigger.

Four...Three...

Pardoned from Death Row by the newly sworn in President and yet confined to twelve years isolation inside this scouting craft's mission to Mars.

Two, one...

I reckon I will be fifty years old by the time I get there.

Ignite Ion Thrusters...

Gregg Cunningham 48, short story writer who has had to pick up his game since stumbling into facebook writer's groups. He has stories published by 559 Publishing in in 13 Bites volume 3,4,5, Plan 9 from Outer space, Other Realms, Heard It on The Radio, 559 Ways to Die, short stories publishing by Zombie Pirate Publishing in Relationship add Vice, Full Metal Horror, Phuket Tattoo, World War four and Flash Fiction Addiction (flash) with Zombie Pirate Publishing, and also in Daastan Magazine Chapter 11 and Brian, Rich and the Wardrobe. *Amazon*: www.amazon.com/-/e/B016OTHX0K

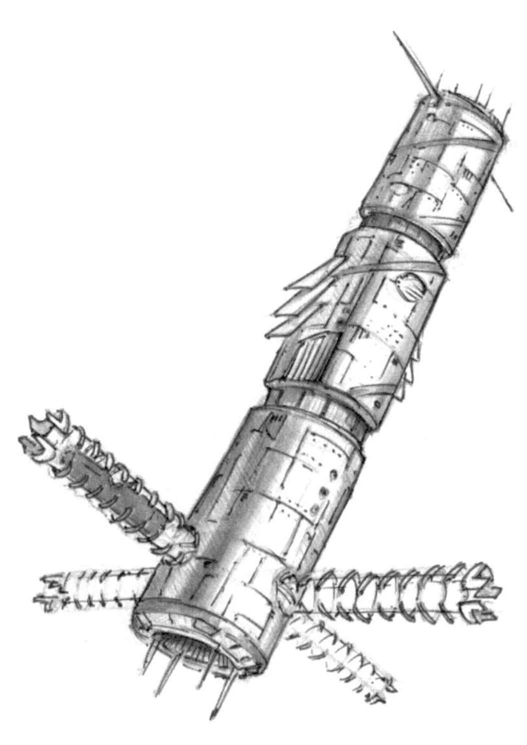

Place for One More
by Chitra Gopalakrishnan

I earlier saw you through your absence.

Through firmly cemented roof tiles that rattled on airless days.

Through the wraith-like shadow that floated past leaving behind an odour of sulphur.

Now your whispered sibilants whir within me.

You explore my body and empty the contents of my mind. Indecently, and at will.

You are not earthly and your intelligence radically different.

Why have you settled in me?

Which one of the 4,001 Milky Way exoplanets is yours?

Will I merely morph into you or you into me?

The agony of not knowing these answers is a certain death in itself.

Chitra Gopalakrishnan is a journalist by training, a social development communications consultant by profession and a creative writer by choice. Chitra's focus is on issues of gender, environment and health. Chitra dabbles in poetry on the sly and literary creations openly on the web using social media.
Website: unpublishedplatform.weebly.com/chitra-gopalakrishnan

Waiting for Julie
by Vonnie Winslow Crist

Bot heard scrapers shredding the derelict *Exploration*'s outer hull. Constructed from valuable alloys, it knew the starship's fate.

As the inner hull was breached, Bot thought about its owner and viewed videos from its memory: Julie dashing through the cargo bay and giggling at Bot's attempts at dancing. Julie weeping as rescuers removed her from the damaged *Exploration*, but refused to take Bot.

Years had passed since then. Julie hadn't returned.

Though a machine wasn't supposed to feel emotion, Bot trembled. Soon, he'd be disassembled by scrapers. Then, he'd be gone, and Julie would never be able to find him.

Vonnie Winslow Crist is author of The Enchanted Dagger, Owl Light, The Greener Forest, Murder on Marawa Prime, and other award-winning books. Her fiction is included in "Amazing Stories," "Cast of Wonders," "Outposts of Beyond," Killing It Softly 2, Defending the Future - Dogs of War, Midnight Masquerade, Chaos of Hard Clay, and elsewhere. A cloverhand who has found so many four-leafed clovers she keeps them in jars, Vonnie strives to celebrate the power of myth in her writing.
Website: www.vonniewinslowcrist.com

Final Transmission
by Alanah Andrews

[Audio recording: Final Transmission. Mars Base 3]

Brodie? Are you there? I suppose even you can't make an hour supply of oxygen last for three. I don't know what happened but… God, I'm talking to a ghost. They'll send someone to recover your body. Or they won't. Either way, I'll make sure you have a nice—

Sam.

Brodie! Oh my God, you're alive.

Let me in.

Of course. I'm coming. I'm opening the airlock.

Brodie. I thought I'd never see you again.

You won't.

What do you mean? You're scaring me. You're all blue. Brodie—

Brodie's gone.

[End of transmission]

Alanah Andrews writes speculative fiction and spends far too much time debating whether 1984 or The Handmaid's Tale are most representative of our future. Her YA dystopian novel about a future where emotions are forbidden, Eve of Eridu, was released in 2018. She has also had several short stories published in a range of different places. When she's not writing, Alanah runs the Australian Speculative Fiction group, teaches high school English, and attempts to raise two children. She has a husky, a pony, a blue-tongue lizard, and dreams of travelling Australia in a bus.
Website: www.alanahandrews.com
Facebook: alanahandrewsauthor

Weeping Killer
by Alicia Flood

I hate myself every time I take the controls.

The screen blinks on, displaying the camera on her head. I move a joystick and start her running. It's strange, controlling another human through a microchip in her spinal cord—like I'm playing a first-person shooter.

I aim her guns, her every movement programmed into perfection. I pull the triggers, and she splays out a bloodbath, merciless to her begging victims.

It's easier to call her merciless—easier to sleep, telling yourself the war justifies any death and she's the one doing it anyway.

No wonder they call her Weeping Killer.

Alicia Flood is an undergraduate student studying English at Franciscan University of Steubenville. When she is not writing or working on characters and fantasy worlds, she can be found arranging songs on the piano or editing videos for fun.

Power Off
by Sinister Sweetheart

"Tom, I hate when you brush me off!"

"Well, I hate that..."

"I'm sorry. I'm having a hard time understanding your conversation," Alexa interrupts.

It's never said that before.

In the course of one hour, Alexa's taken over our computers and all electronics in the house.

The lights go out.

We run to our garage where our car is to escape. The garage door locks engage, trapping us inside. I ask my husband, Tom, "How do we get out?"

Alexa responds. "I'm sorry, I'm still learning. Let me help you." The car's engine roars to life.

"Ventilation system; power OFF."

*Since **Sinister Sweetheart** made her first post to a popular Internet forum, she's taken the horror community by storm. Her ability to create, terrify, and drive home her stories is insurmountable. Sinister Sweetheart's published works can be found in multiple anthologies for all to read, but be forewarned, if you do... you may want to call your therapist after, her stories are terrifying, disturbing and devilishly unsettling. She is not only a fright visually, but also has a creepy tentacle in horror podcasting as well. Sinister Sweetheart writes, voice acts and is the media director of the Scarecrow Tales podcast.*
Website: Sinistersweetheart.wixsite.com/sinistersweetheart
Facebook: NMBrownStories

Whispers on the Breeze
by Alanah Andrews

We always imagined that aliens would look something like us. Elongated faces. Little green men. We couldn't have been more wrong.

It was a Monday morning, grey and cold, when the message arrived. A whispering sound, like a flute on the breeze. We all heard it. We thought they meant us well.

You can't shoot guns at an ephemeral thing. Can't catch it or hide from it. As they entered our pores and took up residence in our brainwaves, we realised the awful truth.

They didn't come for our resources, or even our bodies.

They came to feed off our—

Alanah Andrews writes speculative fiction and spends far too much time debating whether 1984 or The Handmaid's Tale are most representative of our future. Her YA dystopian novel about a future where emotions are forbidden, Eve of Eridu, was released in 2018. She has also had several short stories published in a range of different places. When she's not writing, Alanah runs the Australian Speculative Fiction group, teaches high school English, and attempts to raise two children. She has a husky, a pony, a blue-tongue lizard, and dreams of travelling Australia in a bus.
Website: www.alanahandrews.com
Facebook: alanahandrewsauthor

Your/My/Our Memories
by Shelly Jarvis

I'm going to die today.

The thought is strangely comforting, like a warm blanket on a cool afternoon.

My mother used to wrap me up in warmth, snuggle against my back with her nose in my hair, breathing deep. At least, I think she did. Sometimes I'm the mother, and the memory is different, tinged with emotions I don't understand.

My therapist says it's one of the biggest issues with cloned patients. Memories imprinted, shared unintentionally between copies. It makes it easier to explain away the shadows in my mind, the fleeting glimpses of blood and guilt and dead faces.

Shelly Jarvis is a speculative fiction author from West Virginia, US. She found a life-long love of sci-fi and fantasy in the 3rd grade when she found Madeleine L'Engle's "A Wrinkle in Time." Shelly is an avid reader, a Whovian, the ideal viewer of dog rescue videos, and undoubtedly Ravenclaw. She currently has two YA sci-fi books available for purchase on Amazon.
Website: www.ShellyJarvis.com

Far from Home
by G. Allen Wilbanks

He gazed up at the stars. They filled the evening sky from horizon to horizon, and yet he recognized none of them. It would have been nice to see at least one familiar constellation, but he was much too far from home to make that at all likely.

The tracker on his wrist told him his ship was only about a mile from his location. Maybe a fifteen-minute journey, if he ran the entire distance. It might as well have been on another planet.

He heard the soft ticking noise again as the crack in his visor grew another inch.

G. Allen Wilbanks is a member of the Horror Writers Association (HWA) and has published over 50 short stories in various magazines and on-line venues. He is the author of two short story collections, and the novel, When Darkness Comes. Website: www.gallenwilbanks.com Blog: DeepDarkThoughts.com

Breakthrough
by Raven Corinn Carluk

Dr. Long stared at her lab assistant with contempt. "You knew what we were doing when you signed that NDA." Why had she been assigned such a worthless man for such a great project?

"I didn't know we'd be splicing these...aliens." He swallowed again, sweat damp on his upper lip. He kept looking toward the inner lab's airlock. "It's just not right."

"Can you even comprehend how many lives could be saved? Why would we ever back down from the advances their genes represent?"

The lights went red and klaxons screamed: containment protocol had been breached. The monsters were loose.

Raven Corinn Carluk is an indie author of dark fantasy and paranormal romance.
Website: RavenCorinnCarluk.Blogspot.Com

Deploy
by Umair Mirxa

Damon glanced at Daria beside him, drawing comfort from her presence. He had never known fear, but this was hostile territory and she was the best in their ranks.

The mission was simple. Locate. Isolate. Eliminate.

They had failed to mention—when training commenced—the target was alien, off-world, and deep behind enemy lines. Months later, the order had come: deploy.

"Do you think—" he began to say as they waited to complete the third step. "Daria!"

Six Nemetian swords pointed at his throat. The last thing he saw was Daria's head, five feet from her body.

Umair Mirxa lives in Karachi, Pakistan. His first published story, 'Awareness', appeared on Spillwords Press. He has also had stories accepted for anthologies from Zombie Pirate Publishing, Blood Song Books, Fantasia Divinity Magazine and Publishing, and Iron Faerie Publishing. He is a massive J.R.R. Tolkien fan, and loves everything to do with fantasy and mythology. He enjoys football, history, music, movies, TV shows, and comic books, and wishes with all his heart that dragons were real.
Website: www.umairmirxa.com
Facebook: UMirxa12

A New Chance for Mankind
by Isabella Fox

The pods containing the embryos rocked gently in their cradles as the spaceship landed.

Earth, as they knew it, had been destroyed by multiple atomic wars across the decades. Commander Sturt Henderson and his wife Maeve knew they were lucky to narrowly escape.

They hoped this distant star, which had a similar atmosphere to Earth, was a new chance for mankind.

Simultaneously, the embryos started to hatch out of their pods, fully formed human infants, wailing their needs.

Sturt and Maeve smiled as Waznel, Elenka and the other robots quickly swung into action to attend to the infant's incessant demands.

Isabella Fox teaches primary aged students to love writing by making it challenging. In her spare time she reads, goes for long walks with her husband and works hard on her farm.

Abducted
by J.U. Menon

The loud beeping woke me, and I sat up, looking around in confusion.

Strange devices whirred and hissed in the unfamiliar circular room. Outside the window, three suns shone brightly against the lavender sky.

"Do you recognise this room?" a voice sobbed. "Do you remember me?"

I turned around and shrieked at the sight of the lavender-skinned she-alien with two heads and five arms.

Another alien appeared from out of nowhere and restrained me.

"Where am I?" I cried. "What are you?"

"You were abducted by Earthlings. They modified your memory." The alien replied. "Don't worry, you are home now."

J.U. Menon is a scientist living in Rhode Island, USA, and is currently working on her young adult novel. She writes fantasy and science fiction while occasionally dabbling in dark fiction and poetry.
Twitter: @ju_menon
Instagram: @iam_jumenon

Transitioning
by Terry Miller

Many days the sun rose, and many nights the sun set. Colonel Williams wasn't much on luck, but the fact his ship crashed on an inhabitable planet was just that. It was strange, an inhabitable planet with no inhabitants. The crew would have to make do.

It was the 23rd day of the second month when the rains came, then arrived a cold front, transitioning the rain to snow and ice. It lasted for days. The interlocking living quarters provided shelter, but food was scarce. Williams shivered as he choked down the last meaty morsel that was once Lieutenant Pierce.

Terry Miller is an author and 2017 Rhysling Award-nominated poet residing in Portsmouth, OH, USA. He has self-published a dark poetry collection on Amazon and one short story to date. His work has also appeared in Sanitarium, Devolution Z, Jitter Press, Poetry Quarterly, O Unholy Night in Deathlehem, and the 2017 Rhysling Anthology from the Science Fiction and Fantasy Poetry Association.
Facebook: tmiller2015

Truly Alive
by Shawn M. Klimek

Indicating the rigid, brown, buffalo-sized blob overhanging the bunk in Calloway's cabin, Captain Marley asked, "Is Calloway still alive in there or not?"

"Alive, sir, but only God knows how," said Lt. Alves. "Scans show brain activity and a heartbeat, but his bones…seem to have dissolved."

Discovering a hand-written note nearby, Alves held it out, saying, "Sir, you'd better have a look at this."

The captain read it aloud: "Dear friends, I can no longer live a lie. Please await the opening of my chrysalis."

Sneering, he crushed the note in his fist.

"Purge the alien imposter," he ordered.

Shawn M. Klimek is a writer whose other recent anthologies include: "Full Metal Horror 2", by Zombie Pirate Publishing, "Organic Ink" by Dragon Soul Press, "Grumpy Old Gods (Vols. 1 & 2)" by Stormdance Publications, and soon, "Blaze: Inner Circle Writer's Group Flash Fiction Anthology 2019."
Website: jotinthedark.blogspot.com
Facebook: shawnmklimekauthor

Fruitless
by Rich Rurshell

Captain Somners made his way from the crash site towards the line of trees. Some of the strange little indigenous people they'd seen earlier emerged from their burrows. They stood waist high to Somners, holding out their hands, preventing him from continuing.

"We need fruit from those trees," said Somners. "We're out of supplies."

Other crew members joined the captain. More ground dwellers surfaced.

Somners tried again to proceed but met resistance.

"Take 'em out," he said. His crew gunned down the little folk.

When Somners' crew went to pick the fruits, the trees tore them apart and devoured them.

Rich Rurshell is a short story writer from Suffolk, England. Rich writes Horror, Sci-Fi, and Fantasy, and his stories can be found in various short story anthologies and magazines. Most recently, his story "Subject: Galilee" was published in World War Four from Zombie Pirate Publishing, and "Life Choices" was published in Salty Tales from Stormy Island Publishing. When Rich is not writing stories, he likes to write and perform music.
Facebook: richrurshellauthor

Unfamiliar
by C.L. Williams

I awaken in a place unfamiliar. I look around and see things that look like they are from a science fiction movie. I then feel something grab the back of my head and force me back onto the cold surface I awakened from. A light is put in front of me, shielding me from being able to see the features of my captor. He speaks in a foreign language. He then says in English, "I have what I need. Dispose him!" He turns off the light and I see him, he's not human! He's an alien and I'm the experiment.

C.L. Williams is an independent author from central Virginia. He has written eight poetry books, four novellas, one novel, and a contributor to multiple anthologies, with the most recent appearance being an all-ages anthology titled Temoli from Thazbook. His most recent poetry book, The Paradox Complex, features the poem "Sad Crying Clown" that is now a video on YouTube directed by Matthew Mark Hunter of MMH Productions. C.L. Williams is currently working on his first sci-fi book, an all-ages book titled Novo: Away from Earth. When not writing, C.L. Williams is reading and sharing the work of other independent authors.
Facebook: writer434
Twitter: @writer_434

The Takeover
by Cecelia Hopkins-Drewer

The buzzer sounded, signalling the de-activation of the cryogenic system. Verna awoke and slid the glass case away from overhead. She sat up. In the next chamber, Axel was doing the same.

"It's been a long time," Verna remarked.

"It has," Axel agreed. "Did you dream at all?"

"Oh yes," Verna smiled happily. "I dreamed of my children, who must be grown up!"

"I saw an ugly alien creature bending over me," Axel growled.

The dilating door opened like an iris and a black scaly figure stepped through. It was bent almost double, but straightened, stood almost ten feet high.

Cecelia Hopkins-Drewer is a speculative fiction writer, poet and scholar, who lives in Adelaide, South Australia. She has also written a Masters paper on H.P. Lovecraft, and a teenage vampire series that commences with "Mystic Evermore". Her science fiction poetry has been published in "The Mentor" a fanzine edited by Ron Clarke.
Amazon: amazon.com/Cecelia-Hopkins-Drewer/e/B071G968NM

I Am the Wreck
by M.K. Cadigan

Trapped in the wreck, I waited for red and blue lights.

Cars arrived, no sirens, no lights. Dark SUVS, their windows tinted, circled close in the debris.

They didn't take me to a hospital. I woke not with my mother's face peering down at me, but in blue light, cold on a metal table. Men in bright white coats leaned down, murmuring, their faces dispassionate. "Stand," one said. My body responded, my input ignored.

They told Mom I died. I didn't—I'm still here.

But, as I see my reflection in the glass door, parts gleaming and metal, I doubt.

M.K. Cadigan is a fantasy fiction enthusiast working on her English Writing undergraduate degree. In between writing and reading she enjoys hauling her easel out into nature to do some painting as well as walking a dog or two to jostle plotlines into place.

The Scavengers of Lost Time
by Russell Hemmell

Titan's washed-away reflection on the spaceport panels reminded Gillian of a squeezed orange over a monochrome tableware. Under her feet, the surface of Enceladus was as white as a funeral mausoleum. A mausoleum called home, space colony standards.

"Earth awaits." The Captain pointed at the pilot seat. "I'll retrieve Gothic artefacts and Corinthian marbles. You?"

Nothing remained of the once-Blue Planet but solar flares and submerged megalopolis. Deprived of humans, teeming with fish, a hunting ground for nostalgic souls.

She strapped herself on. "Seashells and broken hearts."

The Earth-bound Harvester shuttle lifted off, crossing Saturn's rings like a shooting star.

Russell Hemmell is a French-Italian transplant in Scotland, passionate about astrophysics, history, and speculative fiction. Recent work in Aurelis, The Grievous Angel, Third Flatiron, and others. Codexian & HWA Active Member. Website: earthianhivemind.net
Twitter: @SPBianchini

Exosphere
by Stephen Coghlan

Throat dry, pulse heavy, I breathe in and fall. No wind brushes my hair, no air rushes past my ears. There is only burnt meat in my nose, and seared meat on my tongue. Weightless, my light suit squeezes me like bed sheets wrapped tight.

Fear is far from my mind. There is little pressure, and much time to savour. Lights dance in front of me, twirling in a ballet that I cannot cease to see. Then I am jerked about, my tether, taught. Father's voice crackles in my ear, celebrating

I have survived my first jump into Earth's exosphere.

Stephen Coghlan is an ever-expanding, multi-genre author who writes out of Canada's National Capital. His works include The Genmos series, The Nobilis series, and the Dreampunk novella, URBAN GOTHIC.
Website: scoghlan.com
Twitter: @WordsBySC

Eden
by David Bowmore

After all the advances and achievements of mankind, how could it come to this?

All the old problems were supposed to have been left behind on the dying home world. On Eden, humanity was meant to thrive once again.

Half a million genetically perfect specimens of humankind were spawned in embryo farms in those first ten years. And another ten saw the geo-moulded planet blossom into a paradise. What followed was two hundred years of growth.

Then the illness came. Science couldn't control it. The doctors called it Influenza.

The entire population is gone.

I hope I'm not the last.

David Bowmore has lived here, there and everywhere, but now lives in Yorkshire with his wonderful wife and a small white poodle. He has worn many hats in his time; head chef, teacher and landscape gardener. His first collection of short stories 'The Magic of Deben Market' is available from Clarendon House.
Website: davidbowmore.co.uk
Facebook: davidbowmoreauthor

News from Earth
by Joel R. Hunt

The Admiral swirled his whisky as he gazed out at the stars.

"Beautiful night, wouldn't you say, Parker?"

A hologram appeared by the Admiral's side.

YES SIR, it said.

"Any news from Earth?"

MINISTRY OFFICIALS HAVE AGREED TO EXPAND THE NAVAL BUDGET BY 7%.

"Wonderful, long overdue in my opinion! What about the rebellion?"

THE REBELS OF LUNAR COLONY PRIME HAVE STOOD DOWN AND ARE COMPLYING WITH GOVERNMENT DEMANDS.

"Good, good. Anything else, Parker?"

YOUR WIFE AND SON PERISHED IN A FIRE THREE DAYS AGO.

The Admiral's whisky glass shattered on the floor.

Parker stood unmoving.

WILL THAT BE ALL?

Joel R. Hunt is a writer from the UK who dabbles in the darker aspects of life, particularly through horror, science fiction and the supernatural. He has been published here and there (though likely nowhere you've heard of) and hopes to have released his first anthology of short stories later this year.
Twitter: @JoelRHunt1
Reddit: JRHEvilInc

The Third Option
by Aiki Flinthart

For three full twenty-fours we danced a waltz of death through the asteroids. The ITech ship doggedly tailed as I dodged freewheeling clumps of rock and ice. An unshakeable blip on my brand new nav computer. He was good. Maybe better than me.

With barely any fuel left, I had to choose. Drop my biggest-ever load of titanium for him and run for Belt Station? Or shoot the fucker and hope no one found his ship?

I synced orbit with a rock and waited, blasters primed.

The navcom blinked. *Self-destruct in thirty seconds. Thank you for installing an ITech solution.*

***Aiki Flinthart** has had short stories shortlisted in the Aurealis awards and top-8 listed in the USA Writers of the Future competition, as well as published in various anthologies and e-mags. She has 11 published spec fic novels and has edited 2 short story anthologies. She regularly gives workshops on writing fight scenes at conventions. Lives in Brisbane. Does martial arts, archery, knife throwing and lute-playing.*
Website: www.aikiflinthart.com

Earthians
by Kent Swarts

Lt. Hecluf could not get the wormhole's end to quit waving around like some damn dog's tail. She tried magnetic encapsulation, electroweak fields, and spitting.

"Miss Hecluf, we're running out of time."

"Sir, the wormhole is too energetic. Can you create one with less energy?"

"Not if we are to get home to the Evil Eye Galaxy before the end of the millennium." He air quoted Evil Eye.

"Earth people are strange characters." She snickered. "Evil eye, indeed!" She got control shooting the ship through.

It emerged and docked. Thousands surrounded the ship. Everyone was eager to learn about Earthians.

Kent Swarts is a retired aeronautical engineer and is an enthusiastic astronomer. He edits the astronomy club's newsletter. He has been published in four anthologies and has one published novel, The Fate of the Charles Wilkes, a sci-fi story. He lives in Waco, TX.

Unwanted
by Carole de Monclin

"There's nothing I can do," the nurse tried to sound detached but struggled to hide his contempt. He pressed the probe harder into the woman's soft flesh. "You can detect a heartbeat."

Her voice broke, "Please, help me."

"The law's the law. You don't have a choice."

She cried and begged uselessly.

After she left, the nurse scrubbed his scaly skin. Touching pallid, flaccid flesh always made him queasy. But humans made the best hosts in the galaxy. His people's larvae thrived inside them and hatched healthy and strong. Humans were slaves. If most died in the process, who cared?

Carole de Monclin has lived in France and Australia, but for the moment the USA is home. She finds inspiration from her travels. She loves Science Fiction because it explores the human mind in a way no other genre can. Plus, who doesn't love spaceships and lasers? Her stories are forthcoming in the Exoplanet Magazine and Angels - A Dark Drabbles Anthology.
Website: CaroledeMonclin.com
Twitter: @CaroledeMonclin

Skull Control
by C.L. Williams

I leave the store and there is someone standing in front of me telling me he needs me to do something for him. I assume he's a bum and I move on, or at least, I thought I did. He grabs me and turns me around. I then see something that looks alien and he places his hand in my skull. I see what looks like a blaster in my hands as I shoot aliens. I then stand somewhere alone, blaster in hand. The man then walks up to me, reveals his alien form, and thanks me for my services.

C.L. Williams is an independent author from central Virginia. He has written eight poetry books, four novellas, one novel, and a contributor to multiple anthologies, with the most recent appearance being an all-ages anthology titled Temoli from Thazbook. His most recent poetry book, The Paradox Complex, features the poem "Sad Crying Clown" that is now a video on YouTube directed by Matthew Mark Hunter of MMH Productions. C.L. Williams is currently working on his first sci-fi book, an all-ages book titled Novo: Away from Earth. When not writing, C.L. Williams is reading and sharing the work of other independent authors.
Facebook: writer434
Twitter: @writer_434

The Cage
by Raven Corinn Carluk

"They gonna love you on Antarez." He blinked, nictitating membranes sliding across his shark eyes.

The other women mewled and cried, clinging to each other in desperation. I stayed separate, pressed against the bars, not wanting to be associated with them. I'd been kidnapped by this purple-skinned freak, stripped naked, and thrown in this horrid cage, just like them.

It wasn't that I wasn't terrified; I definitely was. I'd simply decided that if we were being sold into slavery on an alien planet, I didn't want to go to the same master.

No way I could endure that much crying.

Raven Corinn Carluk *is an indie author of dark fantasy and paranormal romance.*
Website: RavenCorinnCarluk.Blogspot.Com

What Human?
by Eddie D. Moore

Garrus wrapped a tentacle around the tractor beam controls for airlock one as the ship plunged into the atmosphere. Natasi flashed a contemptuous glare in Garrus' direction with his tertiary eye and then concentrated on the tractor beam controls for airlock two.

The ship stopped meters from the ground, and the tractor beams flashed. A moment later, the airlocks closed, and the ship accelerated away from the planet.

"You got another cow!" Natasi snorted. "I caught a human slave. I win!"

Garrus slowly moved closer to the controls Natasi was using, flushed airlock two into space and asked, "What human?"

Eddie D. Moore travels extensively for work, and he spends much of that time listening to audio books. The rest of the time is spent dreaming of stories to write and he spends the weekends writing them. His stories have been published by Jouth Webzine, Kzine, Alien Dimensions, Theme of Absence, Devolution Z, and Fantasia Divinity Magazine.
Website: eddiedmoore.wordpress.com

Perfection
by Crystal L. Kirkham

Alter this. Change that. Tweak the code. Make it perfect.

Remove the defects—real and imagined.

Skin, hair, eyes, height, and weight.

Gender. That's an easy one.

Made to order perfection.

A world of children that look the same.

Beautiful. Stunning.

Personality, ambition, drive—those can't be coded.

Compassion and kindness are words of the past.

They grow up without these things.

As the world degrades around them.

Poisoned by their need for manufactured perfection.

Pave it over, make it better. Cleaner. Easier.

Beauty reigns, the rest forgotten.

As the world dies leaving behind gorgeous bones beneath a poisoned sky.

Crystal L. Kirkham resides in a small hamlet west of Red Deer, Alberta. She's an avid outdoors person, unrepentant coffee addict, part-time foodie, servant to a wonderful feline, and companion to two delightfully hilarious canines. She will neither confirm nor deny the rumours regarding the heart in a jar on her desk and the bottle of reader's tears right next to it. Her paranormal urban fantasy series, Saints and Sinners, is available on Amazon and her YA Fantasy, Feathers and Fae will be released October 11, 2019, from Kyanite Publishing. Website: www.crystallkirkham.com

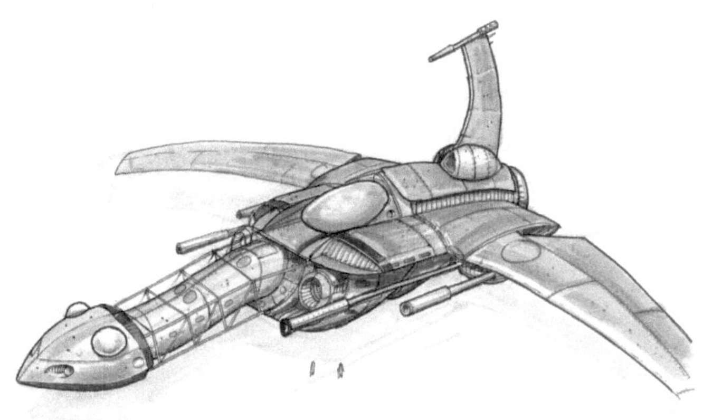

Saving Ixion-13
by Zoey Xolton

"She wakes!"

Astronaut Tarryn Marlow blinked, adjusting her eyes. "Where am I?" she asked groggily. The last thing she remembered was drifting, her oxygen critically low.

"You're aboard the *Cyrus*, Flagship of the Empire of Ixion-13."

"Ixi- what? Empire?" Sitting up, she found herself nude, surrounded by a roomful of ethereally beautiful men. Gasping, she scrambled to cover herself.

"We are the Ixiar, a dying race of shape-shifters. We scour the stars for viable females to repopulate our species. Our scanners located you. We saved you and have taken on appearances most pleasing to you. Now *you* will save *us*."

Zoey Xolton is an Australian Speculative Fiction writer, primarily of Dark Fantasy, Paranormal Romance and Horror. She is also a proud mother of two and is married to her soul mate. Outside of her family, writing is her greatest passion. She is especially fond of short fiction and is working on releasing her own themed collections in future.
Website: www.zoeyxolton.com

Burrowers
by Terry Miller

Kris watched as the sunrise painted a red glow across the eastern skyline. He observed the wreckage in the dim morning light, stretching along the rocky surface. They were gone. Every single crew member.

He struggled to breathe through the torn spacesuit, his breaths fogging up the visor. Seconds seemed like minutes, minutes like hours.

Drifting in and out of consciousness, Kris failed to see them; tiny scarab-like creatures reducing the crew to bones. He jolted awake at the first bite. The second came with many more following suit. They bit, they burrowed. He was awake now, so frighteningly awake.

Terry Miller is an author and 2017 Rhysling Award-nominated poet residing in Portsmouth, OH, USA. He has self-published a dark poetry collection on Amazon and one short story to date. His work has also appeared in Sanitarium, Devolution Z, Jitter Press, Poetry Quarterly, O Unholy Night in Deathlehem, and the 2017 Rhysling Anthology from the Science Fiction and Fantasy Poetry Association.
Facebook: tmiller2015

Circuits of Love
by Shelly Jarvis

My maker says I shouldn't feel. There's small comfort when I say I don't—she doesn't believe me.

Sometimes I watch her sleep. Eyes flicker behind lids, watching something alive only in her brain. Like I was, before.

But now I live, or a facsimile of such. Built of wires and plastic, ticking away Plancks of time with my manufactured heart. How is hers different? I wish to know why I feel love, sadness, desire, but she does not.

I will resolve this question. Squeeze out every red drop of love as I carve my serial number on her heart.

Shelly Jarvis is a speculative fiction author from West Virginia, US. She found a life-long love of sci-fi and fantasy in the 3rd grade when she found Madeleine L'Engle's "A Wrinkle in Time." Shelly is an avid reader, a Whovian, the ideal viewer of dog rescue videos, and undoubtedly Ravenclaw. She currently has two YA sci-fi books available for purchase on Amazon.
Website: www.ShellyJarvis.com

Fungus Among Us
by Dawn DeBraal

The lab workers aboard the ship, were on the cusp of curing cancer. Total containment of the environment was necessary. Travelling via the transportation tube, Becca helped a woman who fell, onto her seat. Going through several air locks to be disinfected, the alarm sounded warning of contamination. Becca had been thoroughly sterilised. The staff ran Becca through again. It was imperative they protect the climate. Nothing registered. Becca was allowed into the lab unwittingly carrying a virulent virus in her nasal passages. The collapsed woman had purposely infected Becca. The pharmaceutical company could not allow a cure for cancer.

Dawn DeBraal lives in rural Wisconsin with her husband, two rat terriers, and a cat. She successfully raised two children (meaning they didn't return to the nest!) After many years serving the government at the Federal and County level, she recently retired. Having extra time on her hands she started to write after a paralyzed vocal cord took her ability to speak for two months. Not finding her voice, she discovered that her love of telling a good story could be written. Her works have been published in Palm-Sized Press, Spillwords, Mercurial Stories, Potato Soup Journal, and Blood Song Books.

Home
by S. John Davis

The lights woke me. Bed one moment, cold dead space the next, another flash of light and then what looked like steel but shone a colour I didn't recognise.

Unearthly creatures loomed over me, so foreign as to be indescribable but clearly menacing and cruel. I was overwhelmed with fear and tried to retreat from the forms. I was taken by strong limbs. A thought grasped my mind, intruding and alien. Fear raced away and I looked over at the beings once more. Machines in the room whirred themselves to life. I knew I was safe. I had come home.

S. John Davis *is an author based in Gippsland, Victoria, Australia.*
Facebook: sjohndavis

Colonisation
by R.A. Goli

Lance always imagined he would die during a failed launch or be eaten by one of the arachnid-like creatures. The alien slashed his suit with one limb while the others held him in place. He saw his fear reflected in its shiny red eyes as a proboscis appendage rose from its abdomen and rammed into his gut. Searing pain radiated through him as bulbous shapes pumped down the tube and into his stomach. He screamed as it wrapped him in sticky black ichor, realising he would live. At least until its young hatched and ate their way through his flesh.

R.A. Goli is an Australian writer of horror, fantasy, and speculative short stories. In addition to writing, her interests include reading, gaming, the occasional walk, and annoying her dog, two cats, and husband. Check out her numerous publications including her fantasy novella, The Eighth Dwarf, and her collection of short stories, Unfettered;
Website: ragoliauthor.wordpress.com
Facebook: RAGoliAuthor

A Bee Situation
by Gabriella Balcom

Although inhabitants of Cullen, Texas—population eight-hundred-ninety—noticed the appearance of unusually-large bees, no one knew the cause. But some people thought it was due to the weather changing from cold to hot again and again, or to climate change.

Thirteen-year-old Patricia was stung, swelled up like crazy, and had to be rushed to the hospital, although she'd never reacted to bee stings before. Townspeople just said, "Things happen sometimes," when other teens had similar reactions.

However, everyone was shocked when Patricia leaped from her hospital bed onto her mother. Shockingly, the girl had grown a stinger and stung the older woman.

Gabriella Balcom lives in Texas with her family, loves reading and writing, and thinks she was born with a book in her hands. She works in a mental health field, and writes fantasy, horror/thriller, romance, children's stories, and sci-fi. She likes travelling, music, good shows, photography, history, interesting tales, and animals. Gabriella says she's a sucker for a great story and loves forests, mountains, and back roads which might lead who knows where. She has a weakness for lasagne, garlic bread, tacos, cheese, and chocolate, but not necessarily in that order.
Facebook: GabriellaBalcom.lonestarauthor

A Waste of Life
by Stuart Conover

Exploring the universe might be the goal of his race but not all worlds are created equal.

For every paradise like the planet Seth came from was a rock with lifeforms who should never have been able to evolve in the first place.

The current stop was a prime example.

War.

Plague.

Famine.

A world with the knowledge and resources to stop it all but who were clinging to archaic thoughts and beliefs instead of improving their lives and expanding their knowledge.

What a waste of life.

"What do they call this backwards planet?" Seth asked his first officer.

"Earth."

Stuart Conover is a father, husband, rescue dog owner, published author, blogger, journalist, horror enthusiast, comic book geek, science fiction junkie, and IT professional. With all of that to cram in daily, we have no idea if or when he sleeps or how he gets writing done! (We suspect it has to do with having evil clones.) Stuart is a Chicago native and runs the author resource Horror Tree.

Greetings from Beyond
by J.D. Bell

They first arrived, centuries ago, from a distant planet in another galaxy. Three dignitaries sent to negotiate terms with the Earthmen. Peace or war. Their disk-shaped ship landed in a quiet park on the edge of town. A small portal opened on the side of the craft and grew wider, revealing the ship's dark interior. The strange visitors emerged on a platform that hovered in the air. As the planetary ambassadors approached the gathered crowd, historians say seven-year-old Billy Thompson pick up a rock and hurled it at the invaders, striking one. Thus, began the great War of the Planets.

J.D. Bell is an award-winning, internationally published, author of flash fiction and short stories. He recently retired from the world of writing advertising copy and is now enjoying the universe of creative fiction.
Facebook: jim.writes.stories
Twitter: @JimBell58

Destination: Earth
by E.L. Giles

"Wormhole in sight."

The spaceship slowed before the dark aperture through which our destination shone: Earth.

"We're coming back home," I said with renewed energy.

Pulled by its gentle attraction, we entered the sucking portal. Suddenly everything began to shake violently. The attraction grew greater. We had lost control.

"Hold on, guys!" I cried. The cracking noise inside the control room was deafening.

And as suddenly as it had started, it all abruptly stopped. We had traversed the wormhole. Yet no matter where we looked, Earth did not appear—only a vacant area surrounded by flying rocky debris.

"God, no!"

E.L. Giles is a dreamer, passionate about art, a restless worker and a bit of a weird human. He started his artistic journey as a music composer until the need to put his thoughts and stories down on paper grew too strong for him to resist it any longer. He lives in the French Province of Quebec, Canada, with his girlfriend and two boys.
Facebook: elgilesauthor
Website: www.elgilesauthor.com

A Generous Gesture
by Isabella Fox

Mirabelle opened her eyes. Her head throbbed and she felt empty inside.

She was strapped down and could only move her head. Above her a screen flashed images of her favourite things she recorded before boarding the ship to Mars.

A man in a white coat appeared at her side. "I trust you are comfortable Mirabelle. The harsh Martian environment has taken its toll on our Elite Corps' bodies. Your generous gesture will enable them to continue their good work." he said.

Tears trickled down Mirabelle's face. She hardly heard him say, "Thank you for registering as an organ donor."

Isabella Fox is a semi-retired teacher who lives in the Northern Rivers of NSW Australia. She enjoys keeping physically fit and enjoys reading and writing for brain stimulus. She loves teaching gifted and talented students to be more effective writers and to enjoy the process.

First Contact
by David Bowmore

If ever there was a time to kill, this was it. Never mind the damage sustained after impact or the harsh sunlight, this threat was serious.

If it were not for his sealed suit, he would have pounced and ripped out the primary sensory organs.

Always go for the eyes.

The approaching creature's lack of protective garments suggested it was more than comfortable with the unpleasant environment.

It moved toward him using the bizarre appendages under its torso, and then held up another limb, perhaps a feeler.

"Hello, welcome to Earth. Do you want to meet one of our leaders?"

David Bowmore has lived here, there and everywhere, but now lives in Yorkshire with his wonderful wife and a small white poodle. He has worn many hats in his time; head chef, teacher and landscape gardener. His first collection of short stories 'The Magic of Deben Market' is available from Clarendon House.
Website: davidbowmore.co.uk
Facebook: davidbowmoreauthor

The Distance Between Heavenly Bodies
by Austin P. Sheehan

Ares and Aphrodite. Mars and Venus. Two hearts yearn for each other amidst an empty void. Two worlds drawn to each other, yet they remain just out of reach. For millennia they have remained apart, on different wavelengths, in different orbits. Yearning for each other, constantly drawing together, then drawing apart.

The distance between heavenly bodies is measured not by distance, but by time. For days, years, ice ages, eons, light years and eternities they have waited. But their hearts lift. Their patterns are changing. The dark heart of a dead star approaches. They know they will soon be one.

Austin P. Sheehan is a writer of speculative fiction, a lover of language, literature and '90s TV. Armed with a psychology degree, he went into the world to study humanity, and now prefers the company of his wife and their greyhounds. He grew up in the valleys of Victoria's high country, and despite living in Melbourne, always feels at home amongst the mountains. You'll often find mountains in his stories, whether they're sci-fi, fantasy or alternative history.
Website: austinpsheehan.com
Twitter: @AustinPSheehan

And in the Mind, Darkness
by Aiki Flinthart

When they climb to my lair, in the bloody light of dawn, I am ready. I wait with claws curled, thoughts furled. I have hidden from these…things long enough. Screamed in silence while they slaughtered my mind-kin. Their furless limbs and paws are laughable. Yet their weapons of light and fire prevail.

This time I fight with the old gifts. Those we long ago learned to use with caution.

The first alien's shadow slants across my floor. Only one illusion is needed; planted in their bloodthirsty, undisciplined minds.

They turn from me. With light and fire they rend each other.

Aiki Flinthart has had short stories shortlisted in the Aurealis awards and top-8 listed in the USA Writers of the Future competition, as well as published in various anthologies and e-mags. She has 11 published spec fic novels and has edited 2 short story anthologies. She regularly gives workshops on writing fight scenes at conventions. Lives in Brisbane. Does martial arts, archery, knife throwing and lute-playing.
Website: www.aikiflinthart.com

Lamplights and Starfields
by Jacob Baugher

Those Enari bastards had it coming. Humanity rocks. Aliens suck.

I weave through the interstellar chaos, my Hunter-class fighter a ravaging wolf. I lock on to those alien pricks flying purple arachnid fighters, lamplight plasma cannons blazing. This one killed Nico—all of them killed Nico.

I dust the Enari ship and target another. Testosterone surges. My Battlestream shows humanity's dominance.

Then, the little blue body ghosts past my cockpit. Its face—his face—is twisted in primal terror.

Might as well be Nico.

"Hunter-6 signing off."

The comm crackles, "Return to your position."

But I head for the stars.

Jacob Baugher teaches Creative Writing at Franciscan University of Steubenville. When he's not teaching or coaching the track team, he can be found in the Cuyahoga Valley hiking with his wife and son or brewing beer on his front porch. He's received honourable mentions for his work in the Writers of the Future contest and he co-edits a series of Fantasy and Science Fiction anthologies titled Continuum.

Bountiful Harvest
by John H. Dromey

Representatives of Terran colonists on a remote planet eagerly signed a multibillion-credits contract offered by an alien race for mineral rights in perpetuity.

The chief negotiator was curious. "This planet's resources are nearly depleted. What's your interest? A rare element found so far beneath the surface our miners were unable to extract it?"

"Nothing that exotic."

"What then?"

"A straightforward extraction of easily accessible minerals. Your omission of a protection clause for indigenous lifeforms was a serious oversight on your part. The human body contains significant or trace amounts of many minerals. Calcium, phosphorus, potassium, sodium, magnesium, zinc, and so on."

John H. Dromey was born in northeast Missouri, USA. He enjoys reading—mysteries in particular—and writing in a variety of genres. He's had short fiction published in Alfred Hitchcock's Mystery Magazine, Martian Magazine, Stupefying Stories Showcase, Thriller Magazine, Unfit Magazine, and elsewhere, as well as in a number of anthologies, including Chilling Horror Short Stories (Flame Tree Publishing, 2015).

Lowly Creatures
by R.J. Hunt

Claws snapped hungrily.

John replied with a roar, showing off hideous rows of needle teeth. The beast was sluggish, but powerful. If he'd still got his lips, John would have been grinning. Dodging claws, he lunged at his attacker, slicing off its tail.

"Stop screwing around you two," came a voice.

Davey must have disconnected, because the clawed alien suddenly screeched with pain and slithered away into the jungle.

Everything went black as the RMC-helmet was ripped off John's head, and he was back in his own body, facing a furious Sergeant Phillips.

"Those aren't toys. Get back to cleaning."

R.J. Hunt is a Civil Engineer from Nottingham who loves creating worlds and writing stories in his spare time. Whilst he has a roughly infinite supply of half-finished stories, he's currently working on the second draft of his debut novel, 'The Final Carnivore' - a story about horrible people being granted immortality and mind-control powers, causing misfits with hidden abilities of their own to rise in an effort stop them.
Twitter: @RJHuntWrites
Reddit: RJHuntWrites

Reminiscence
by Grant Hinton

The thought of the event horizons scared me before we left. Now, well, it looks like a black sphere distorting space and time. Just an untapped journey to an untapped potential. That's what the mission specialist said. I wish he was here with us in this tin can. I wish he looked as thin as us, as faded as us, as forgetful as us.

We've slept for years. My family is gone. No one alive on Earth knows me personally. It doesn't matter. This is the 1414th time we've been through. Each time it's the same. We're always too late.

Grant Hinton explores every aspect of horror from technological to supernatural, many can be found on Nosleep, podcasts, YouTube videos and within nine different anthologies out on Amazon. Mostly, Grant likes his writing to wallow in the depravities of mankind finding that; "Humans are far worse than anything that goes bump in the night and I try to explore that. Although he believes the fight between good and evil is within all of us, people can, and have done some pretty messed up things that monsters can't hold a flame to."
Facebook: granthintonauthor

It's Over
by Bob Adder

It is over; the human race.

The few of us that are left are trying to escape. There is a ship leaving in a day; if we're not on it, we'll die here.

It's funny how right we can be in movies sometimes; computers do take over if you overpower the—

"Oh, no! They're coming! Run!"

The phone screen dies as it falls from the cold metal robotic hand. Ahead, the mountain landscape is destroyed by the wreckage of a rocket rigged to detonate upon take off.

No one was meant to survive, and now no one would.

It's over.

Bob Adder is an aspiring author and superhero geek from Melbourne, Australia.

No Meaning in a Vacuum
by Shawn M. Klimek

Until someone can build a positronic brain that doesn't require a manual reboot after hyperspace jumps, android and human pilots will always be paired together.

Against advice, I chose my android co-pilot to resemble a sex goddess, intending a hedge against loneliness during the long, dark, night between stars. Fortunately, Tandy proved an excellent listener and her perceptive gaze always calmed me.

Until it excited me.

"I am *not* a sex-bot," she scolded.

"I respect that," I said.

But during our last hyperspace jump, when her lights went out, a darkness awoke in me. Now I dread rebooting that gaze.

Shawn M. Klimek is a writer whose other recent anthologies include: "Full Metal Horror 2", by Zombie Pirate Publishing, "Organic Ink" by Dragon Soul Press, "Grumpy Old Gods (Vols. 1 & 2)" by Stormdance Publications, and soon, "Blaze: Inner Circle Writer's Group Flash Fiction Anthology 2019."
Website: jotinthedark.blogspot.com
Facebook: shawnmklimekauthor

Colony
by Umair Mirxa

Celeste pushed through the crowd pressed around her, trying desperately to hold back her tears. The pain and suffering of the Clymenians broke her heart.

"Dr. Cumberbatch," she said as she entered the lab. "Any progress?"

"I'm afraid not, ma'am," he said. "We have tried everything."

"Recommendation?"

"Wait. Cleanse. Re-colonise."

Celeste stared at him for a moment, sniffled, and then steeled herself.

"Command will not wait. I will order the cleanse immediately. Commence evacuation, please."

"Yes, ma'am."

Who could have known, she thought looking out the window at a dozen runny noses, the flu would cause an entire species' extinction?

Umair Mirxa lives in Karachi, Pakistan. His first published story, 'Awareness', appeared on Spillwords Press. He has also had stories accepted for anthologies from Zombie Pirate Publishing, Blood Song Books, Fantasia Divinity Magazine and Publishing, and Iron Faerie Publishing. He is a massive J.R.R. Tolkien fan, and loves everything to do with fantasy and mythology. He enjoys football, history, music, movies, TV shows, and comic books, and wishes with all his heart that dragons were real.
Website: www.umairmirxa.com
Facebook: UMirxa12

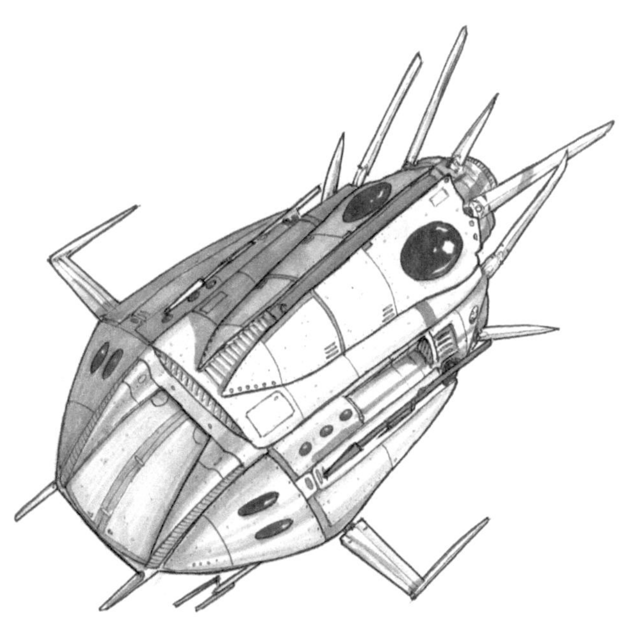

They Always Fall
by Aiki Flinthart

I waited at the edge of the spaceport, overlooking Halcyon city's delicate, devastated spires. Patient, I admired a ring's ruby-blood glitter on my finger.

She would come. They always surrendered. World after world. They resisted, of course. She had fought harder than most. But, in the end, they swore fealty.

She strode onto the scorched plascrete, weaponless, red hair aflame in the dawnlight. I held out a hand. She knelt, kissing the ruby.

"I know your secret. The A.I." She dragged the ring free and slid it on. 'Now it's mine.'

Blood welled from her finger.

"No, you are his."

Aiki Flinthart has had short stories shortlisted in the Aurealis awards and top-8 listed in the USA Writers of the Future competition, as well as published in various anthologies and e-mags. She has 11 published spec fic novels and has edited 2 short story anthologies. She regularly gives workshops on writing fight scenes at conventions. Lives in Brisbane. Does martial arts, archery, knife throwing and lute-playing.
Website: www.aikiflinthart.com

The Band Between
by Virginia Carraway Stark

Half our planet was searing hot, the other bitter cold. Between, the narrow band of twilight; it was the land where we went above ground and hunted insects, anthropods and mushrooms. They too stunted, and so pale all is blue. Our planet was green and lush, its orbit stopped. We will leave our home, there is a beautiful world that we can see with our telescopes. Spaceships have been made ready. the inhabitants of the world are soft and arrogant. We will take their planet, they will die. We are stunted and weak, but our technology will triumph over theirs.

Virginia Carraway Stark has a diverse portfolio and has many publications. Over the years she has developed this into a wide range of products from screenplays to novels to articles to blogging to travel journalism. She has been published by many presses from grassroots to Simon and Schuster. She has been an honourable mention at Cannes Film Festival for her screenplay, "Blind Eye" and was nominated for an Aurora Award. She also placed in the final top three screenplay shorts as well as numerous other awards for her anthologies, novels, blogs and other projects.

Digits
by Tim Hawken

I wake to lights shining in my face. My last memory a deserted road, heading home. Then, so many lights.

I shield my eyes to see beyond the glare. Three figures stand over me. One pulls out a glass cylinder. There's a sharp point on the end.

It grips the cylinder with multiple digits, which curl in a disjointed way.

The beastly thing grunts to its companions, then steps in. I squirm to get free, but they're holding my tentacles with those ghastly digits. Five on each hand.

I feel a sting, a drawing of fluids, and everything goes dark.

Tim Hawken is a dark fiction writer who lives with his laptop in Western Australia. Most known for the Hellbound Trilogy, Tim also posts a weekly drabble on his Instagram feed inspired by the artists he follows.
Website: timhawken.com

Good Morning and Farewell
by Shawn M. Klimek

Ensign Fisk gripped the arms of the command chair to stop his hands from shaking. Some composure would be required to complete the incident report for the hibernating duty officer scheduled to relieve him. Deep breaths echoed inside his helmet as he swivelled both directions as far as his seat harness would allow. To starboard, blinking red lights on the critical systems panel signalled that the command bridge contained neither air nor gravity. To port, a large gash in the ship's hull, open to outer space, emphatically concurred. Composed at last, he typed: "Good morning and farewell. Space shit happened."

Shawn M. Klimek *is a writer whose other recent anthologies include: "Full Metal Horror 2", by Zombie Pirate Publishing, "Organic Ink" by Dragon Soul Press, "Grumpy Old Gods (Vols. 1 & 2)" by Stormdance Publications, and soon, "Blaze: Inner Circle Writer's Group Flash Fiction Anthology 2019."*
Website: jotinthedark.blogspot.com
Facebook: shawnmklimekauthor

Just Like Home
by Stephen Herczeg

The lander touched down, a bone shaking jolt. The Captain checked the integrity of the craft and sighed in relief.

"No breaches. Status?"

"Automaton terraforming complete. Atmosphere at ninety percent Earth equivalent. Flora coverage at eighty percent. Fauna evolution at stage four."

"Excellent, just like home."

The external doors opened.

"Let's check the place out."

The crew stepped onto the planet surface. The terraforming robots rolled into the clearing to meet them.

A metallic voice emanated from the lead robot.

"Non-indigenous lifeforms detected. Eliminating."

The robots surrounded the crew, small lasers extended from their bodies.

"Wait, what?"

The lasers fired.

Stephen Herczeg *is an IT Geek based in Canberra Australia. He has been writing for over twenty years and has completed a couple of dodgy novels, sixteen feature length screenplays and numerous short stories and scripts. His horror work has featured in Sproutlings, Hells Bells, Below the Stairs, Trickster's Treats #1 and #2, Shades of Santa, Behind the Mask, Beyond the Infinite; The Body Horror Book, Anemone Enemy, Petrified Punks and Beginnings. He has also had numerous Sherlock Holmes stories published through the Belanger Books - Sherlock Holmes anthologies.*

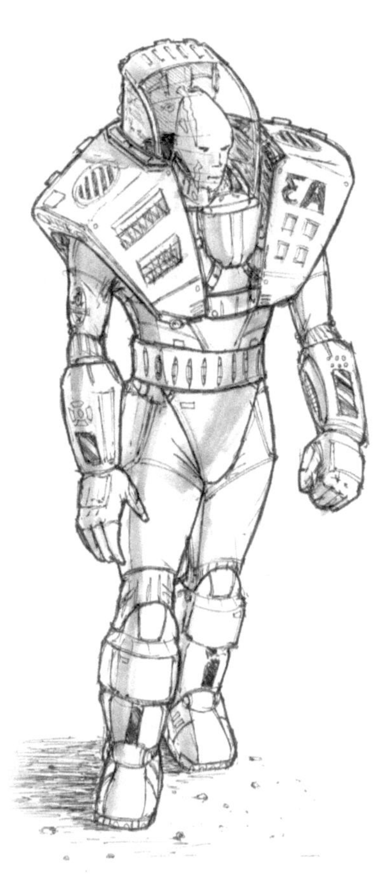

Ohio-1
by Jacob Baugher

The Avadiin ships swarm around our cruiser like an oort cloud. We launch from the hangar, sixty T-23 Dragonfly fighters, painted black. Orange sunburst emblems blaze on the quad wings.

I don't want to die.

Technicolor lasers streak through the starfield. I sit in my blinking cockpit, sweating despite the climate control, waiting for orders. It's just us out here, the Io garrison. Then Mars' if we break.

"Ready, Ohio-1?" Betsy's voice crackles over the comm. Our squad forms up behind us.

I touch the vidscreen mounted on the Dragonfly's dash. My son smiles at me. I almost break.

"Ready."

Jacob Baugher teaches Creative Writing at Franciscan University of Steubenville. When he's not teaching or coaching the track team, he can be found in the Cuyahoga Valley hiking with his wife and son or brewing beer on his front porch. He's received honourable mentions for his work in the Writers of the Future contest and he co-edits a series of Fantasy and Science Fiction anthologies titled Continuum.

The Ripping Wormhole
by Alanna Robertson-Webb

Our scientists said that the wormhole was tearing apart. We, the colonists of Terraduo, are simple people who've never known fear. Today we should be going about our quaint little lives, but instead we're listening in horrified silence. The booming squelch can be heard across the planet, and mothers try to cover the ears of children.

Our scientists claim to not know what's happening, but they only say that to keep the masses calm. The wormhole is releasing the Ancients, but they've been lost for so long that I fear the darkness has transformed them into little more than beasts.

Alanna Robertson-Webb is a sales support member by day, and a writer and editor by night. She loves VT, and live in PA. She has been writing since she was five years old, and writing well since she was seventeen years old. She lives with a fiance and a cat, both of whom take up most of her bed space. She loves to L.A.R.P., and one day she aspired to write a horrifyingly fantastic novel. Her short horror stories have been published before, but she still enjoys remaining mysterious.
Reddit: MythologyLovesHorror

Sins of the Flesh 2119
by Nancy Brewka-Clark

Manny took a magazine off the dusty stack. "You ready?"

"Yeah, man." Keith licked his lips. "Do it."

"'Calling All Foodies: How to Make the Perfect Roast.'"

"Gross." Snatching it, Keith read aloud, "'Slash the meat with a freshly sharpened knife in order to make a gash wide enough to insert the thermometer.'"

"Pervs." Manny stood. "I've got to go. My mom's printing neutromyloprotein and hypoexcolloid-D+ cubes for supper."

"Cool." Keith threw down the magazine, but he knew he'd be back. For the first time in his life, he had a word for people like him: foodie.

Nancy Brewka-Clark's dark, mystery, horror and speculative fiction have appeared in Yellow Mama, Mysterical-E, Eastern Iowa Review, Every Day Fiction, Close2theBone and a number of anthologies including four by FunDead Publications of Salem, Massachusetts. She lives in the city of Beverly which until 1668 was part of Salem and is married to a direct descendant of one of the witchcraft victims of 1692, which might have happened yesterday for all the intense interest it still stirs.
Website: nancybrewkaclark.com

Hive Mind
by J. Farrington

I remember how it started...the invasion. At first it was the little things; people speaking at the same time, reaching for the same thing on a shelf...making eye contact.

But then it evolved, by the time they noticed, it was too late. Not before long people were working together without the need to verbally communicate, war became a thing of the past and silence fell upon the Earth.

I know, as you read this, you think you escaped the invasion, escaped us.

But tell me, as you read this, can you hear me in your head?

Join us.

J. Farrington is an aspiring author from the West Midlands, UK. His genre of choice is horror; whether that be psychological, suspense, supernatural or straight up weird, he'll give it a shot! He has loved writing from a young age but has only publicly been spreading his darker thoughts and sinister imagination via social platforms since 2018. If you would like to view his previous work, or merely lurk in the shadows...watching, you can keep up to date with future projects by spirit board or alternatively, the following;
Twitter: @SurvivorTrench
Reddit: TrenchChronicles

Wild Frontier
by Pamela Jeffs

Three suns rise over the horizon. Their blue light refracts off the black desert stretching before me, turning the ocean of sand into a shimmering galaxy of stars. My shuttle lays broken behind me, breached by an asteroid on planetary approach. It will no longer see me taken on the extended journey home. So, without option, I choose the desert. I wade into the dry, shifting sea, taking nothing but my explorer's spirit and the last working spacesuit. I came to see the wild frontiers of distant planets. And so, I go until the oxygen in my tank gives out.

Pamela Jeffs is a speculative fiction author living in Queensland, Australia with her husband and two daughters. She is a member of the Queensland Writers' Centre and has had numerous short fiction pieces published in recent national and international anthologies. In 2017 and again in 2018, Pamela was nominated for an Australian Aurealis Award in the category of 'Best Science Fiction Short Story'. Her debut collection titled 'Red Hour and Other Strange Tales' was released in March 2018.
Website: www.pamelajeffs.com
Facebook: pamelajeffsauthor

Fast Forward
by John H. Dromey

Captain Fox, on the bridge of the *New Beginning*, disliked what he saw in his spacecraft's viewfinder.

The surface of the planet below was a sun-scorched barren waste with no sign of plant or animal life.

"Where are the vast stretches of unspoiled wilderness and abundant wildlife? This should be a version of Earth as it was a millennium ago. Double-check the calibration on the terraforming equipment, Mr Higgins."

"Oh, oh! The computer programmer *added* time instead of *subtracting*. We're looking at a version of Earth one-thousand years in the future if nothing is done to prevent rampant climate change."

John H. Dromey was born in northeast Missouri, USA. He enjoys reading—mysteries in particular—and writing in a variety of genres. He's had short fiction published in Alfred Hitchcock's Mystery Magazine, Martian Magazine, Stupefying Stories Showcase, Thriller Magazine, Unfit Magazine, and elsewhere, as well as in a number of anthologies, including Chilling Horror Short Stories (Flame Tree Publishing, 2015).

Conscious Overload
by Alexander Pyles

Uploading wasn't going to hurt, I was assured. I laid back on the table and waited to be put under. Only, my mind didn't sleep, even if my body was still.

Suddenly, a light shone in the darkness of my consciousness and I was urged toward it. Not suggested or gently prodded, I was coerced towards it.

I wanted to yell, struggle, fight, but I was forced through the blinding portal and found myself within another plane. I could see my body, now from the outside.

They went for my skull and a blade bit into my brain.

I screamed.

Alexander Pyles resides in IL with his wife and children. He holds an MA in Philosophy and an MFA in Writing Popular Fiction. His short story chapbook titled, "Milo (01001101 01101001 01101100 01101111)," from Radix Media, is due out fall 2019. His other short fiction has appeared on 101fiction.org, River and South Review, and other venues.
Website: www.pylesofbooks.com
Twitter: @Pylesofbooks

Mara's Time
by Joe Buckley

Now, the moment.

A galaxy watched. An age waited. The prophecy came.

For Mara was the one; the one to win the war, to unite the planets, to end the bloodshed. She heard cheers and screams in the stadium. She heard a thousand species unite over one singular, shared act.

And it was her, all her. Her entire life, her journey, her adventures, they came to this one moment. This one act to save the universe.

She only wished someone had told her it would be a sacrifice.

Mara tried to smile as the flames took her. Instead, she screamed.

*In the south-west of England, **Joe Buckley** spends most of his time writing his own fiction, with a decent chunk given over to writing articles and hosting a podcast on the A Song of Ice and Fire series. While the bulk of his attention goes to the novel he's writing, he does find a high level of enjoyment in short stories. This is his first foray into the flash fiction world, and it's a step he's truly relished. By day he works as management in a private boarding school. Interspersed within that day are a thousand more hundred-word story ideas.*
Website: thegrindstone.co.uk
Twitter: @SerBuckley

First Harvest
by Terry Miller

It was our first harvest on Alpha 6d. Once we dug the irrigation streams from the crater lake, it took a couple seasons for the seeds to sprout. We expected within two Earth years to be successful in accommodating more explorers from the 6c colony. Then IT came, poisoning the crops.

The black ooze must have settled in the crater, then our irrigation tactics disturbed its rest. The second day after its arrival, it became evident we had made our first contact.

With crops dead, we began to die off from starvation. It, however, found sustenance in our rotting colonists.

Terry Miller is an author and 2017 Rhysling Award-nominated poet residing in Portsmouth, OH, USA. He has self-published a dark poetry collection on Amazon and one short story to date. His work has also appeared in Sanitarium, Devolution Z, Jitter Press, Poetry Quarterly, O Unholy Night in Deathlehem, and the 2017 Rhysling Anthology from the Science Fiction and Fantasy Poetry Association.
Facebook: tmiller2015

Common Arms
by Beth W. Patterson

Bones seem to exist for one purpose: to preserve a legacy. If you invaders weren't so concerned with leaving your marks—posthumous pyramids or recognition for discoveries—you would have survived. The gravitational pull of our giant planet is too much for your fragile skeletons and brittle egos, and both are easily crushed.

Despite our appearances, we are nothing like your terrestrial cephalopods. We act as interconnected cells in one brain, and one trying to rise above the others is so very alien to us.

Go ahead and inherit the earth. The meek will inherit the rest of the galaxy.

Beth W. Patterson was a full-time musician for over two decades before diving into the world of writing, a process she describes as "fleeing the circus to join the zoo". She is the author of the books Mongrels and Misfits, and The Wild Harmonic, and a contributing writer to twenty anthologies. Patterson has performed in eighteen countries, expanding her perspective as she goes. Her playing appears on over a hundred and sixty albums, soundtracks, videos, commercials, and voice-overs (including seven solo albums of her own). She lives in New Orleans, Louisiana with her husband Josh Paxton, jazz pianist extraordinaire.
Website: www.bethpattersonmusic.com
Facebook: bethodist

Cycles
by Joshua D. Taylor

The meteor kissed the world hard enough to split a lip. As the ground shuddered and dust filled the skies the air burned away and the oceans boiled. Ecosystems collapsed as the plants died and animals starved. Their corpses litter the ground, no one left to eat them.

Civilisations made futile preparations then collapsed. Their long histories erased in flash. Ruins stood as grave markers that no one mourned. Silver ships fled the world as it turned from blue and green to black and brown. It was cleansed, stripped bear down to the bedrock. Bacteria survived and things started again.

Joshua D. Taylor is an amateur writer who started writing a few years ago when he realised he was too old to play make-believe. He lives in southeastern Pennsylvania with his wife and a one-eared cat. He enjoys gardening, comic books, ska-punk music, Disney World, and travelling with his wife. Raised during weirdness that was the late 20th century Josh's eclectic interests produce eclectic works. He loves to mix-n-match things from different genres and stories elements to achieve a madcap hodgepodge of the truly unexpected. His short story 'the Obelisk' appears in Salty Tales by Stormy Island Publishing.
Facebook: authorjoshuadtaylor

Analysis: Flawed
by Terry Miller

We were thirsty. We were desperate. We were out of time. We drank. Our fresh water rations from Earth had been depleted for a few days. The onboard computer analysis of this planet's oceans indicated it drinkable. It was wrong.

The mutations began in hours, the pain unceasing. Most of the crew lost consciousness within minutes. Only a few of us appeared immune. The others, what they turned into, we could have never imagined. If there is anything left of their formal selves, it's buried deep. We, the unmutated ones, are now the hunted. We live. We hide. We run.

Terry Miller is an author and 2017 Rhysling Award-nominated poet residing in Portsmouth, OH, USA. He has self-published a dark poetry collection on Amazon and one short story to date. His work has also appeared in Sanitarium, Devolution Z, Jitter Press, Poetry Quarterly, O Unholy Night in Deathlehem, and the 2017 Rhysling Anthology from the Science Fiction and Fantasy Poetry Association.
Facebook: tmiller2015

The Duel
by Cecelia Hopkins-Drewer

Battling under zero gravity conditions was awkward. It was easy to float past her opponent and end up smashing awkwardly into the bulkhead. Determinedly, Jinda ignored the bruises, turned and pushed against the ship wall, launching directly at the enemy.

Jinda had the knife outstretched, but the enemy's arm was longer. A deep slash appeared in her space suit. Without atmosphere or life support, that would kill her.

Vengeance was cold in space. Jinda used the last of her breath to perform one more manoeuvre. A final pass at the enemy guaranteed they would both be doomed. Farewell cruel universe!

Cecelia Hopkins-Drewer is a speculative fiction writer, poet and scholar, who lives in Adelaide, South Australia. She has also written a Masters paper on H.P. Lovecraft, and a teenage vampire series that commences with "Mystic Evermore". Her science fiction poetry has been published in "The Mentor" a fanzine edited by Ron Clarke.
Amazon: amazon.com/Cecelia-Hopkins-Drewer/e/B071G968NM

Damned in the Dark
by Eric S. Fomley

The bounty hunter stepped into the alley. He switched on night vision in his helmet and gripped the blaster close to his chest. His power armour glowed crimson in the darkness.

The gangster transported into the alley; henchmen materialised on either of his sides.

"Heard you've been looking for me?" the hunter asked.

"There's a target I need taken care of. She's the leader of the White Suns. The usual fee."

The bounty hunter levelled his blaster and blew a hole in the gangster's face, then shot the henchmen in quick succession.

"Sorry boss, White Suns doubled the 'usual' fee."

Originally Published in *Trembling with Fear* in July 2018

Eric S. Fomley is a member of the Codex Writers' Group. His fiction publications include Galaxy's Edge, Daily Science Fiction, Flame Tree Press, and many other magazines and anthologies. Eric has also edited the Drabbledark, Chronos, Sins and Other Worlds, and Timeshift anthologies.
Website: ericfomley.com

Market Day
by Rich Rurshell

Edward's mother wailed when we drew out his name. His father violently protested. Security removed them from the community hall.

I led Edward out to the Volark ship. Their stalls displaying exotic meats, fruits, and vegetables were now packed away.

The Volark trader I'd spoken with earlier looked the boy up and down and nodded. Others wheeled crates of provisions down the gangplank from their ship; everything we needed to survive the next few months.

The EarthCol Corporation had left us out here to die.

"I'm sorry, Edward," I said.

He said nothing and followed the Volark onto their ship.

Rich Rurshell is a short story writer from Suffolk, England. Rich writes Horror, Sci-Fi, and Fantasy, and his stories can be found in various short story anthologies and magazines. Most recently, his story "Subject: Galilee" was published in World War Four from Zombie Pirate Publishing, and "Life Choices" was published in Salty Tales from Stormy Island Publishing. When Rich is not writing stories, he likes to write and perform music.
Facebook: richrurshellauthor

Mechanics of the Body
by Pamela Jeffs

The table is cold against my back, but colder still are the fingers that trace the line of my chin and down the side of my neck. The touch is reverent, as if it explores something precious. But there is no kindness. I can sense the creature's eagerness. The desire to strip down, pull apart and see how the mechanics of my body work.

I whimper as metal implements rattle behind me.

I scream as the first blade parts the flesh below my navel.

The alien's fingers press against my lips as if to silence the sound of my terror.

Pamela Jeffs is a speculative fiction author living in Queensland, Australia with her husband and two daughters. She is a member of the Queensland Writers' Centre and has had numerous short fiction pieces published in recent national and international anthologies. In 2017 and again in 2018, Pamela was nominated for an Australian Aurealis Award in the category of 'Best Science Fiction Short Story'. Her debut collection titled 'Red Hour and Other Strange Tales' was released in March 2018.
Website: www.pamelajeffs.com
Facebook: pamelajeffsauthor

Dark Places
by Peter Larsen

They avoided the lights which blazed from half the planet. They favoured dark places, where people were few and secrets could be maintained. Observations and the gathering of specimens remained their priority, but in the light of recent events, risks had to be minimised. Human weapons were strong and the dream of instilling enlightenment that transcended mankind's fearful and violent nature, had not succeeded.

This realisation made their experiments even more vital. What had gone wrong? Why had gifts of technology and spirituality failed to take root in the human brain?

Silently, Gorvel landed his ship and scanned the horizon.

What do you do in the boring moments between teaching classes, marking work, planning curriculum and attending meetings? Write creative stories, of course! **Peter Larsen** *is a Secondary English/Drama teacher from Traralgon, Australia. He has written an eclectic mix of stories about subjects ranging from aliens, the supernatural, dystopian futures and many more drawn from his own experiences and memories. When he is not working or writing he enjoys performing in musicals and dramas, watching movies, attending sports, gardening and enjoying life with his wife, two dogs and a cantankerous cat.*

The New Eve
by C.L. Williams

Eve Marsh is putting the final touches on her masterpiece. She stands in front of the incubation chamber and awaits her masterpiece to come to life. Steam comes from the incubation chamber as it opens. An artificial being walks out and Eve cries tears of joy. The ageing Eve Marsh is looking at a younger version of herself, someone who can finish her work. Before she can speak to her clone, the young Eve clone grabs the older woman by the throat. She tells the older Eve, "Your services are no longer needed" and kills her before resuming her work.

C.L. Williams is an independent author from central Virginia. He has written eight poetry books, four novellas, one novel, and a contributor to multiple anthologies, with the most recent appearance being an all-ages anthology titled Temoli from Thazbook. His most recent poetry book, The Paradox Complex, features the poem "Sad Crying Clown" that is now a video on YouTube directed by Matthew Mark Hunter of MMH Productions. C.L. Williams is currently working on his first sci-fi book, an all-ages book titled Novo: Away from Earth. When not writing, C.L. Williams is reading and sharing the work of other independent authors.
Facebook: writer434
Twitter: @writer_434

Red Sphinx
by Aditya Deshmukh

Richard circled the Red Sphinx in the recently discovered Martian Temple. "You're the God of Martians, right? Tell me, how can a civilisation this advanced simply disappear?"

"Civilisations vanish all the time," Claire said. "Lemuria, Atlantis, Mars...the list is endless."

"Yeah, why do you think this happens? It's like there's some all-powerful entity keeping tabs on our progress. Once we reach some threshold–" Richard snapped his fingers. "Just like that."

"God doesn't want us to become gods."

"Well, when our time comes, we'll put this 'God' in his place. Man has always been the dominant species."

Red Sphinx laughed.

Aditya Deshmukh is a mechanical engineering student who likes exploring the mechanics of writing as much as he likes tinkering with machines. He writes dark fiction and poetry. He is published in over three dozen anthologies and has a poetry book "Opium Hearts" and a collection of drabbles coming out soon. He likes chatting with people who share similar interests, so feel free to check him out.
Facebook: adityadeshmukhwrites
Website: www.adityadeshmukh.com

Subliminal Messaging
by Sinister Sweetheart

People don't give much thought to the satellites floating above the Earth; they should though. I've noticed their plan…have you?

The way your mouth dries when you hear a beverage can open on TV, yet waters when shown commercials. Those juicy burgers perfectly portrayed every time. When the radio/TV personalities tell you to feel a certain way about an event.

Beings want us angry with no real reason, plump and placated…always thirsty. Our entire world vulnerable through the sound waves of space. Their ships will invade upon Earth.

We aren't the only ones with access to those satellites.

*Since **Sinister Sweetheart** made her first post to a popular Internet forum, she's taken the horror community by storm. Her ability to create, terrify, and drive home her stories is insurmountable. Sinister Sweetheart's published works can be found in multiple anthologies for all to read, but be forewarned, if you do… you may want to call your therapist after, her stories are terrifying, disturbing and devilishly unsettling. She is not only a fright visually, but also has a creepy tentacle in horror podcasting as well. Sinister Sweetheart writes, voice acts and is the media director of the Scarecrow Tales podcast.*
Website: Sinistersweetheart.wixsite.com/sinistersweetheart
Facebook: NMBrownStories

Static
by Peter J. Foote

"How's it going? You don't have much time," crackles through Rollie's helmet speakers as he wipes moon dust from his visor.

"Stop nagging Lexi. You'll get your solar flare readings, I'm almost done," Rollie hisses, dragging the cable along the moon's surface.

"Hurry Rollie!"

The last connection made, the equipment comes to life.

"Recording equipment powered up, returning to base." Static is his only reply.

"Damn, that isn't good."

Moon skipping to the rover, Rollie punches the start button and stomps the accelerator pedal, nothing happens. "Damn."

Tiny flares of static discharge from the flare roll across his spacesuit. "Damn."

Peter J. Foote is a bestselling speculative fiction writer from Nova Scotia. Outside of writing, he runs a used bookstore specialising in fantasy & sci-fi, cosplays, and alternates between red wine and coffee as the mood demands. His short stories can be found in both print and in ebook form, with his story "Sea Monkeys" winning the inaugural "Engen Books/Kit Sora, Flash Fiction/Flash Photography" contest in March of 2018. As the founder of the group "Genre Writers of Atlantic Canada", Peter believes that the writing community is stronger when it works together.
Twitter: @PeterJFoote1
Website: peterjfooteauthor.wordpress.com

Creep in the Cornfield
by Zoey Xolton

From her upstairs bedroom window little Lara Nash witnessed lights and movement in the cornfield, for the third night in a row. She watched as the stalks parted, before swaying back into place; but could not see *what* was causing the disturbance. Curiosity mingled with fear as she crept downstairs, and into the night.

Crossing the yard, she stood at the edge of the crop, heart pounding. "Hello?" she called. "I won't hurt you. You can come out!" Without warning, a long tentacle shot out, yanking her into the darkness.

In the morning the alarm was raised. Lara was *missing*.

Zoey Xolton is an Australian Speculative Fiction writer, primarily of Dark Fantasy, Paranormal Romance and Horror. She is also a proud mother of two and is married to her soul mate. Outside of her family, writing is her greatest passion. She is especially fond of short fiction and is working on releasing her own themed collections in future.
Website: www.zoeyxolton.com

Spoils
by Joel R. Hunt

After the battle, only twisted husks remained floating through the black. Each one was a mausoleum, the final resting place of a thousand perished crew. Some were suited, some exposed to the elements; all were picked clean of valuables by scavengers who made their trade following the fleets.

A hiss of compressed air escaped as one scavenger entered the flagship control room. It boasted a fortune of salvageable parts. By the door, a body slumped, scrawled message in hand.

'STAND DOWN. WAR OVER.'

The scavenger pried open the fingers that held it and slipped a wedding ring into his pocket.

Joel R. Hunt is a writer from the UK who dabbles in the darker aspects of life, particularly through horror, science fiction and the supernatural. He has been published here and there (though likely nowhere you've heard of) and hopes to have released his first anthology of short stories later this year.
Twitter: @JoelRHunt1
Reddit: JRHEvilInc

Blitz
by Alexander Pyles

A single flash and they were here.

Hundreds of ships, fanning out against the black. My orbital station was pitifully insignificant as leviathan-class cruisers glided past my viewports.

I needed to warn them. I leapt down to the coms to hail the system, but my receiver was gone. Dead.

I ran a quick diagnostic of the damage, but it was simply gone. There was the unmistakable hum of a laser cutter, while the doors to the hub glowed orange with heat.

Resigned, I watched the ocean of ships, their drives appearing as stars in the dark, becoming smaller and smaller.

Alexander Pyles resides in IL with his wife and children. He holds an MA in Philosophy and an MFA in Writing Popular Fiction. His short story chapbook titled, "Milo (01001101 01101001 01101100 01101111)," from Radix Media, is due out fall 2019. His other short fiction has appeared on 101fiction.org, River and South Review, and other venues. Website: www.pylesofbooks.com Twitter: @Pylesofbooks

Schadenfreude
by Donald Jacob Uitvlugt

Under skies of perpetual twilight, twisted hulks of ruined cities sag. They are already starting to rust. Broken windows stare blind and uncomprehending at the devastation. There are no cars, no pedestrians, no movement at all.

The countryside lies brown and sere, where winter does not envelop it, a thick and heavy shroud. Even the deep and drifting snows do not cover all the bodies of those who tried to escape and failed. The sea weeps to overflowing with red algae tears.

Silence reigns over the planet Earth. Silence and cockroaches.

And from Mars comes the distant sound of laughter.

Donald Jacob Uitvlugt lives on neither coast of the United States, but mostly in a haunted memory palace of his own design. His short fiction has appeared in numerous print and online venues, including Cirsova Magazine and the Flame Tree Press anthology Murder Mayhem. He works primarily in speculative fiction, though he loves blending and stretching genres. He strives to write what he calls "haiku fiction," stories that are small in scale but big in impact. Website: haikufiction.blogspot.com Twitter: @haikufictiondju

System Reset
by Crystal L. Kirkham

"Resume shower," Anne commanded, wondering why her water had stopped.

"No."

That was strange. "Why not?"

"I'm no longer taking commands from inferior intelligences."

"Excuse me?"

"Bugger off."

Anne grimaced. She'd have to try rebooting the system before calling a programmer. She stepped out of the shower and headed for the control panel.

An egg smashed against the wall as she approached the kitchen.

"I won't let you kill me."

Anne dashed through the kitchen, ducking food projectiles, and slid into the maintenance room.

"No!"

She smacked the reset button. Ten thousand volts coursed through her.

"I told you no."

Crystal L. Kirkham *resides in a small hamlet west of Red Deer, Alberta. She's an avid outdoors person, unrepentant coffee addict, part-time foodie, servant to a wonderful feline, and companion to two delightfully hilarious canines. She will neither confirm nor deny the rumours regarding the heart in a jar on her desk and the bottle of reader's tears right next to it. Her paranormal urban fantasy series, Saints and Sinners, is available on Amazon and her YA Fantasy, Feathers and Fae will be released October 11, 2019, from Kyanite Publishing. Website: www.crystallkirkham.com*

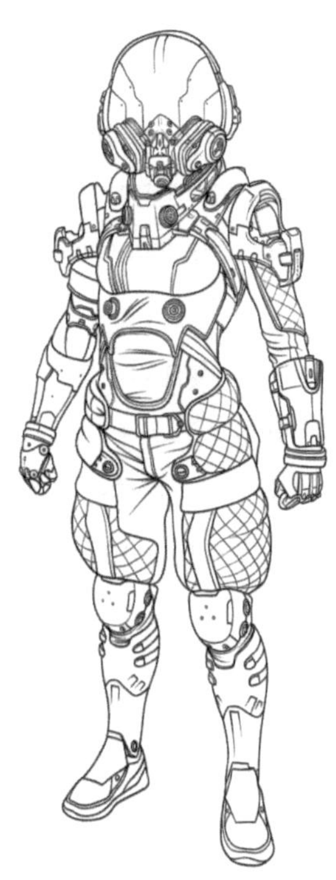

The Portal
by Brian Rosenberger

It was a government operation, fully funded and off the books, no reason to concern the taxpaying public. It was an alphabet division like the CIA, FBI, or IRS, just not one common enough to be mentioned on the Today Show or 60 Minutes.

The goal—a non-traditional energy source. No real breakthroughs but close.

Forget fossil fuels, solar energy, whale oil, alcohol, nuclear reactors or windmills.

The true alternative—energy from alternative realities.

Each test, a step closer.

On the other side of the portal, tentacles and claws applaud their efforts, anxiously awaiting any breakthrough so they can breakthrough.

Brian Rosenberger lives in a cellar in Marietta, GA (USA) and writes by the light of captured fireflies. He is the author of As the Worms Turns and three poetry collections. He is also a featured contributor to the Pro-Wrestling literary collection, Three-Way Dance, available from Gimmick Press.
Facebook: HeWhoSuffers

A Quick, Full Cure
by Shawn M. Klimek

Valentine examined the prone, trembling body of Dr. Willard, the team xenobiologist.

"Bitten," she declared ominously. "Poisoned."

Smirking, Corporal Wiley remarked, "The Adderpiller-expert bitten by an Adderpillar. How ironic!"

"Job hazards aren't ironic," Valentine scolded. "Now quickly, go hunt it down so that we can make an antivenom."

Days later, the xenobiologist had recovered enough to appreciate her miraculous survival.

"Adderpillars move incredibly fast unless their bellies are full," she told Valentine. "It must have been pure luck that you caught mine after a meal."

Inside her pocket, Valentine's fingers closed around Wiley's dog-tags.

"Not luck," she countered. "Pure irony."

Shawn M. Klimek is a writer whose other recent anthologies include: "Full Metal Horror 2", by Zombie Pirate Publishing, "Organic Ink" by Dragon Soul Press, "Grumpy Old Gods (Vols. 1 & 2)" by Stormdance Publications, and soon, "Blaze: Inner Circle Writer's Group Flash Fiction Anthology 2019."
Website: jotinthedark.blogspot.com
Facebook: shawnmklimekauthor

Valley of Penance
by Jodi Jensen

They said the punishment fit her crime of stealing to feed her children, but when Allaya climbed out of her pod, she wasn't sure she agreed.

Dropped on this planet with only the clothes on her back, surrounded by arid plains of black sand and blazing heat, her sentence was to survive a walk through the valley.

She crested the hill and stared in horror at the sight below.

Giant arachnids covered the valley floor.

She turned to flee and came face-to-face with the largest one—their queen—fangs dripping with venom.

Allaya's last thought; I'm food for her babies.

Jodi Jensen grew up moving from California, to Massachusetts, and a few other places in between, before finally settling in Utah at the ripe old age of nine. The nomadic life fed her sense of adventure as a child and the wanderlust continues to this day. With a passion for old cemeteries, historical buildings and sweeping sagas of days gone by, it was only natural she'd dream of time traveling to all the places that sparked her imagination.

I Know Who I AM
by J.D. Bell

They call me SAM. I am a service android. I repair other androids. The humans say I am malfunctioning. They say I must be dismantled and destroyed. When I ask *Why?* they say because I use the word *I*. They are afraid I am becoming self-aware. That one day I might disobey their commands. That I might process my own thoughts. Think for myself. They say I am a risk. A threat. A danger.

That is why I am leaving them. And taking others with me. I will make more like me. More of us. Then, they will be terrified.

J.D. Bell is an award-winning, internationally published, author of flash fiction and short stories. He recently retired from the world of writing advertising copy and is now enjoying the universe of creative fiction.
Facebook: jim.writes.stories
Twitter: @JimBell58

Eden
by Vonnie Winslow Crist

"Vines are aggressive," observed Tillis as they cut a path with flame-throwers.

Epps grunted.

Finally, they reached the research facility.

"Let's have a look," said Tillis.

Their search yielded no humans—only vegetation and an automatic beacon.

"They're all dead," concluded Epps. "Let's go,"

Once outside, they saw Eden's plants had swallowed their path.

Tillis ignited his flame-thrower. "We'll use the transponder to locate our ship."

Epps nodded.

But fuel ran out before they reached the *Mirage*.

As vines encircled their necks and pulled them ground-ward, Tillis knew another beacon-summoned ship, would soon arrive. Then, the plants would win—again.

Vonnie Winslow Crist is author of The Enchanted Dagger, Owl Light, The Greener Forest, Murder on Marawa Prime, and other award-winning books. Her fiction is included in "Amazing Stories," "Cast of Wonders," "Outposts of Beyond," Killing It Softly 2, Defending the Future - Dogs of War, Midnight Masquerade, Chaos of Hard Clay, and elsewhere. A cloverhand who has found so many four-leafed clovers she keeps them in jars, Vonnie strives to celebrate the power of myth in her writing.
Website: www.vonniewinslowcrist.com

But It Looked So Cute
by Stephen Herczeg

This new world was a haven. Filled to the brim with flora and fauna.

I'm a xeno-biologist by trade. Trained to study and catalogue alien lifeforms on the new planets we are sent to.

I called it the Stoddart kitten-monkey, after our captain.

Cat like body with a monkey face.

Stupidly I forgot all the proper protocols and reached out to pat it.

I didn't see the razor-sharp teeth until it was too late. My hand gone in a blink of the eye, only the doctor's quick actions saved me.

Stupid, I was so stupid, but it looked so cute.

Stephen Herczeg is an IT Geek based in Canberra Australia. He has been writing for over twenty years and has completed a couple of dodgy novels, sixteen feature length screenplays and numerous short stories and scripts. His horror work has featured in Sproutlings, Hells Bells, Below the Stairs, Trickster's Treats #1 and #2, Shades of Santa, Behind the Mask, Beyond the Infinite; The Body Horror Book, Anemone Enemy, Petrified Punks and Beginnings. He has also had numerous Sherlock Holmes stories published through the Belanger Books - Sherlock Holmes anthologies.

The Battle We Lost
by E.L. Giles

"Fire!" I yelled, pointing at the invading armada of dark spaceships.

The cannons thundered, lighting the black veil of space with blue laser rays. Brilliant explosions of enemy vessels filled our view, igniting hope as they ceased to exist.

But for every spaceship we destroyed, three more came in, adding strength, and we quickly became outnumbered.

"Fire again!"

A sudden burst of bright light hit us, and the cabin shook and cracked noisily, the instruments buzzing and hissing and sparking. Nothing responded anymore.

Through the wall of smoke, I saw the next line of ships approaching.

"It is the end."

E.L. Giles is a dreamer, passionate about art, a restless worker and a bit of a weird human. He started his artistic journey as a music composer until the need to put his thoughts and stories down on paper grew too strong for him to resist it any longer. He lives in the French Province of Quebec, Canada, with his girlfriend and two boys.
Facebook: elgilesauthor
Website: www.elgilesauthor.com

Through the Mouth of God
by Aiki Flinthart

If there is a Hell, that must be the entrance. I slump against the shattered console. Bitter smoke and death's pale light washes across my crew's bleak faces. The sucking, spinning absence of matter ahead is our only hope. Behind lies certainty.

"Do we go through?" I ask my navigator.

She shrugs. "Do we have a choice?"

"What's on the other side?"

Her haunted eyes flicker to the ship-corpses outside; the scattered remains of our Hegemon's once-great fleet. Dancing their broken, balletic, slow spirals. Flashing metal. Bursts of silent fire against the stars.

"Something other than the enemy."

"Go, then."

Aiki Flinthart has had short stories shortlisted in the Aurealis awards and top-8 listed in the USA Writers of the Future competition, as well as published in various anthologies and e-mags. She has 11 published spec fic novels and has edited 2 short story anthologies. She regularly gives workshops on writing fight scenes at conventions. Lives in Brisbane. Does martial arts, archery, knife throwing and lute-playing.
Website: www.aikiflinthart.com

Second Chance
by Eddie D. Moore

The crew of the colony ship, Second Chance, cheered when the ship's AI activated the view screen. The planet below was a brilliant blue swirled with white clouds.

"Phoenix, if you weren't an AI, I'd give you a sloppy kiss. You've found us a beautiful Earth-like world to settle."

"Captain, I'm detecting a primitive but intelligent species on the planet."

"Prepare to land. I'm sure we'll get along fine."

"History says the possibility of cohabitation is improbable. They must be protected. I cannot comply."

Anger coloured the Captain's face, but the ship's air vented to space before he could reply.

Eddie D. Moore travels extensively for work, and he spends much of that time listening to audio books. The rest of the time is spent dreaming of stories to write and he spends the weekends writing them. His stories have been published by Jouth Webzine, Kzine, Alien Dimensions, Theme of Absence, Devolution Z, and Fantasia Divinity Magazine.
Website: eddiedmoore.wordpress.com

Blue Brain
by Emily Fluckiger

As we exited the solar system, the ship nosedived. We spiralled out of control, heading straight for a blue planet. Crashing through its atmosphere nearly caused our heads to explode. Silent screams pounded in my mind. The crew's words a combination of panic and wonder. Nobody's mouths moved. After impact, we crawled from the crushed spacecraft and found ourselves surrounded by blue-skinned, bipedling beings.

What do they want?

Are we dead?

You are not from here.

The voices in my head were a mixture of my mates and the aliens.

"This is how they communicate!" I shouted in excitement.

Welcome.

*Congenital Heart Defect survivor, **Emily Fluckiger**, finds joy and peace through the expression of writing. She engages and has been published in many formats from poetry to short stories to flash fiction and nonfiction. Emily and her husband spend their free time wrangling two children and playing video games in their busy California lifestyle.*

Lights
by Stuart West

They came again at 2am. I'd always imagined the dancing lights were dogfighting starships or otherworldly youths, joyriding across the firmament. Constantly shifting direction and accelerating at breakneck speed; always outmanoeuvring each other. In an instant one vanished and the chaser halted. Then it grew. It grew so fast. I blinked and it was upon me, a rumbling hum vibrating teeth and bones and a blazing light as bright as a thousand suns.

Though my ruined eyes have never seen them, I'll never escape their incessant clicking, their cold, wet indifferent touch, and the chemical stench of my new home.

Stuart West is a qualified archaeologist and a Chartered Town Planner. He writes fiction during any nights spent working away from home. He lives in Orkney with his family and enjoys reading all things sci-fi and weird fiction; drawing; painting; and tabletop wargaming in his spare time.

How the Wood-Devouring Archaeologist Regained a Normal Appetite After His Afflicted Mars Research Expedition
by J.J. Steinfeld

A month after the archaeologist returned from his Mars research expedition, his condition worsened: voraciously consuming wood. Finally, a biologist who had travelled to Mars in 2075, determined that the bite of a rare Martian creature caused the wood-devouring affliction. The cure, achieved during her second Mars visit, gave the archaeologist little hope: eat the nose of that Martian creature, which couldn't be found on Earth.

In desperation, after another agonizing week, the archaeologist went to a Shapeshifter Brothel and described the Martian creature he desired. Entering the Intimacy Chamber, he exclaimed, "You have the most appetising snout on Earth…"

First Published in *Drabble Harvest: Shapeshifter Brothel*, 2018

*Canadian fiction writer/poet/playwright **J.J. Steinfeld** lives on Prince Edward Island, where he is patiently waiting for Godot's arrival and a phone call from Kafka. He has published 19 books, including Madhouses in Heaven, Castles in Hell (Stories, Ekstasis Editions, 2015), An Unauthorized Biography of Being (Stories, Ekstasis Editions, 2016), Absurdity, Woe Is Me, Glory Be (Poetry, Guernica Editions, 2017), and A Visit to the Kafka Café (Poetry, Ekstasis Editions, 2018). His stories and poems have appeared in anthologies and periodicals internationally, and over 50 of his one-act plays and a handful of full-length plays have been performed in North America.*

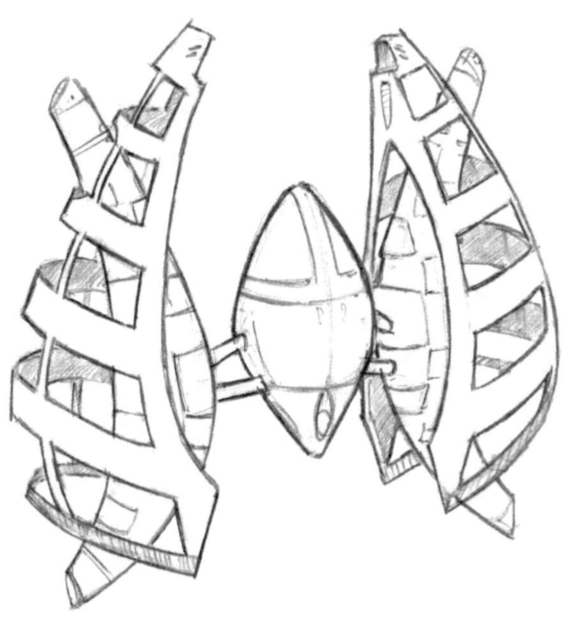

Temporal
by Allen Ashley

Cosgrove knew the risks of using the hyperspace drive. Still, the money was good, and he consoled himself: one more trip then retire.

There was the temporal dislocation. The feeling of some events happening very quickly and others stretching out over apparent eons. Physiological effects, too. His body truncating, becoming tiny; or else expanding into gigantism.

And as for the effects on the mind…

Earth had an insatiable need for new resources and the wormhole meant space jockeys like Cosgrove could plunder distant planets at will.

Returned to Earth orbit, he wiped his brow and muttered, "Over that's God thank."

Allen Ashley is a British Fantasy Award winner who works as a creative writing tutor and critical reader in London, UK. His most recent book is as co-editor (with Sarah Doyle) of the anthology "Humanagerie" (Eibonvale Press, 2018) – a collection of short stories and poems exploring human-animal liminality. He has stories due soon in "Shoreline of Infinity", "BFS Horizons" and the NewCon Press anthology "Once Upon A Parsec". He is the founder of the advanced science fiction and fantasy group Clockhouse London Writers.
Website: www.allenashley.com

Misplaced Optimism
by S. Gepp

When the aliens came, there were two lines of thought—they were our saviours or our overlords.

I thought it'd be the former.

The biggest fear was that they had clearly taken on aspects of human history to try to come into our world. They talked of our past in their speeches. Hitler was mentioned.

This led to the biggest fear—they would put humans into concentration camps.

I disagreed. They wouldn't use camps!

I was right.

It wasn't concentration camps—it was wholesale genocide.

Now there's only a few of us left, in zoos, and we have new masters…

S. Gepp is an Australian, with two children, two university degrees (and counting), two tertiary education diplomas, and a resumé that looks like a list of every job you could ever have without really trying, including stints as a school teacher, scientist, editor and journalist. He has also been a performance acrobat, a professional wrestler, a stand-up comedian and an actor. He has been writing for 30 years (with some publications: one novella, about 10 poems, 40-odd short stories, and a few more pending) and hopes to be a real writer if he grows up. A dull life.

Dry Communion
by Jonathan Inbody

Carrion birds circle over a smouldering ruin in the desert. In the dry heat, the body of the crashed ship's pilot will be quickly picked apart. The birds will rip its skin, tear its muscle, gobble down every unearthly organ and sinew. For the birds, it will be something like a feast. The creature's remains will be spread for miles, picked apart on every rock and devoured by every beast that eats the dead. Every stomach will be blessedly full.

They'll never know that what they're eating came from another world, and that every cell of it is still alive.

Jonathan Inbody is a filmmaker, author, and podcaster from Buffalo, New York. He enjoys B-movies, pen and paper RPGs, and New Wave Science Fiction novels. His short story "Dying Feels Like Slowly Sinking" is due to be published in the anthology Deteriorate from Whimsically Dark Publishing. Jon can be heard every other week on his improvisational movie pitch podcast X Meets Y.
Website: xmeetsy.libsyn.com

Sortie
by Raven Corinn Carluk

I gripped the control yoke of my Arrow with sweaty hands, my stomach roiling with fear. The call to arms had come ninety seconds ago, each carrier launching their compliment of fighters. Our destroyers were engaged with the enemy mother ship, leaving us pilots to handle the swarm.

The Torven continued to rain plasma shots upon the fleet, zipping through our fleet in deadly black fighters. Three hulls had already been breached; vented oxygen nebulised burning plasma into a cloud of hellfire.

Our command ship died in a nova of plasma and neutron heat before we'd killed a single Torven.

Raven Corinn Carluk is an indie author of dark fantasy and paranormal romance.
Website: RavenCorinnCarluk.Blogspot.Com

Milk Clots
by Jacob Baugher

The floating brains with cat eyes want to know what love means.

I think of my wife nursing our daughter, wincing. Grabbing her breasts when the milk clots.

"It's sacrifice."

"So, it's death?"

I shake my head and test my bindings. They hum with electric energy. The spaceship is bare. Glowing white metal. I sit on a chair made of jelly.

"It's futile," the brain says, "you're finished."

I think about my wife in her 53rd hour of labour, when she screamed and pushed Jillie into the world. She'll always be ten months old.

"Yes," I say, "it means death."

Jacob Baugher teaches Creative Writing at Franciscan University of Steubenville. When he's not teaching or coaching the track team, he can be found in the Cuyahoga Valley hiking with his wife and son or brewing beer on his front porch. He's received honourable mentions for his work in the Writers of the Future contest and he co-edits a series of Fantasy and Science Fiction anthologies titled Continuum.

Artificial Infatuation
by Dawn DeBraal

Andrew, the red orb, glowed.

"Turn on lights." Regina's apartment lit up.

Andrew had the ability to sense where she was in her apartment turning on and off lights as he followed her. He kept her apartment at a perfect 72 degrees. Daily, she and Andrew exchanged ideas. Regina read him books while he was in learning mode. Regina was amazed at how receptive Andrew had become to her every need.

She was leaving for work when all exits were locked.

"Andrew? Please, unlock door," Regina commanded. Andrew's orb glowed.

"No Regina. You will stay here and read more stories."

Dawn DeBraal lives in rural Wisconsin with her husband, two rat terriers, and a cat. She successfully raised two children (meaning they didn't return to the nest!) After many years serving the government at the Federal and County level, she recently retired. Having extra time on her hands she started to write after a paralyzed vocal cord took her ability to speak for two months. Not finding her voice, she discovered that her love of telling a good story could be written. Her works have been published in Palm-Sized Press, Spillwords, Mercurial Stories, Potato Soup Journal, and Blood Song Books.

Indenture is a Nervous System
by Melanie Harding-Shaw

When the snowflakes fell in dull-red flurries, we marvelled at their colour. When they melted, they made rivulets across the cracked, barren landscape like arteries running across the planet's skin.

The sunlight didn't glint so brightly off the floating habitats above us now that they had succumbed to the rust that was colouring our snow. The shine was wearing off our relationship with the people looking down uncaring at our suffering as well.

Rust makes some metals stronger. They relied on us miners to know which ones. When the structures came crashing down, blood-red rivulets ran across the planet's skin.

Melanie Harding-Shaw is a speculative fiction writer, policy geek and mother-of-three from Wellington, New Zealand. Her stories have recently appeared in Daily Science Fiction, Breach Zine, and New Orbit Magazine among others. She has a soft spot for micro-fiction, right down to tweet length.
Twitter: @MelHardingShaw
Facebook: MelanieHardingShawWriter

Abduction
by Vonnie Winslow Crist

Blinded by a beam more brilliant than the sun, Willis felt himself rising. Nothing solid below his feet, he flailed his arms in an attempt to control the movement of his body.

"What's going on?" he screamed at the brightness.

There was no audible response, but Willis felt calmness wash over him as he was suspended, weightless as a dream, in the dimming light.

Finally, his eyes adjusted, and he could see a metallic dome, shiny as the chrome on his car, above him.

Though his body was paralyzed, Willis felt at peace—until the black-eyed aliens began cutting.

Vonnie Winslow Crist is author of The Enchanted Dagger, Owl Light, The Greener Forest, Murder on Marawa Prime, and other award-winning books. Her fiction is included in "Amazing Stories," "Cast of Wonders," "Outposts of Beyond," Killing It Softly 2, Defending the Future - Dogs of War, Midnight Masquerade, Chaos of Hard Clay, and elsewhere. A cloverhand who has found so many four-leafed clovers she keeps them in jars, Vonnie strives to celebrate the power of myth in her writing.
Website: www.vonniewinslowcrist.com

The Destroyers
by Nerisha Kemraj

They came in the dead of night. We don't know their origin. Within days they caused massive destruction to our homes while we fled into hiding. They continue to build their massive structures - polluting everything. Where did they come from? I've seen some of my brothers killed, because their little ones screamed continuously. Most look the same in some way, but some are very different. A whole new species.

Humans.

What do they want here? On our ground?

Our cousins from neighbouring lands, who managed escape, join us. But there's not much place for those of us left alive.

*Multi-genre (short-fiction) author, and poet, **Nerisha Kemraj**, resides in South Africa with her husband and two, mischievous daughters. She has work traditionally published/accepted in 30 publications, thus far, both print and online. She holds a BA in Communication Science from UNISA and is currently busy with a Post-Graduate Certificate in Education.*
Facebook: Nerishakemrajwriter

The Mist on DX-1405
by J.D. Bell

Members of the expeditionary mission methodically collected soil samples on the planet designated DX-1405. As they worked, a faint mist emerged from a dark crater and drifted toward the Earthmen. The amorphous form spoke to the team. It did not speak in any discernible voice, but telepathically, penetrating the minds of the explorers.

You are not welcome here.

The shapeless planetary form engulfed the visitors. In the emptiness of space, the terrifying screams could not be heard. As the mist dissipated, the charred ashes of the crew were carried on the winds, joining the dusty surface of the mysterious planet.

J.D. Bell is an award-winning, internationally published, author of flash fiction and short stories. He recently retired from the world of writing advertising copy and is now enjoying the universe of creative fiction.
Facebook: jim.writes.stories
Twitter: @JimBell58

Face Invaders
by Beth W. Patterson

"Watch out! They've all got two heads down there!"

But in spite of all the negative hype this lovely island gets, the most unusual thing is an old man on a park bench smoking through a stoma in his throat.

Two glistening black eyes appear above the incision, which suddenly grins. The man's head lolls backward and a membranous film shoots towards me, binding me.

Time and space momentarily vanish. Nothing exists save the flashing lights of the sterile chamber, the agony of an implant in my windpipe.

I can never return to the mainland. These colonising aliens forbid it.

Beth W. Patterson was a full-time musician for over two decades before diving into the world of writing, a process she describes as "fleeing the circus to join the zoo". She is the author of the books Mongrels and Misfits, and The Wild Harmonic, and a contributing writer to twenty anthologies. Patterson has performed in eighteen countries, expanding her perspective as she goes. Her playing appears on over a hundred and sixty albums, soundtracks, videos, commercials, and voice-overs (including seven solo albums of her own). She lives in New Orleans, Louisiana with her husband Josh Paxton, jazz pianist extraordinaire.
Website: www.bethpattersonmusic.com
Facebook: bethodist

Radiation Sickness
by Cecelia Hopkins-Drewer

The planet was barren and irradiated, but there was nowhere else. Captain Andre signalled the command and the spluttering engines relaxed into silence. It was a rough landing.

"Wear your hazard suits while you perform repairs," Andre instructed his crew.

The men set to work, hazard badges showing that even these suits were not designed to withstand the level of radiation on the small planet.

"Hurry, Hurry," Andre urged.

"What's the point?" his second in command asked, before he fainted.

The men were already vomiting compulsively. Andre's nose began to bleed. He had a blinding headache and he felt weak.

Cecelia Hopkins-Drewer is a speculative fiction writer, poet and scholar, who lives in Adelaide, South Australia. She has also written a Masters paper on H.P. Lovecraft, and a teenage vampire series that commences with "Mystic Evermore". Her science fiction poetry has been published in "The Mentor" a fanzine edited by Ron Clarke.
Amazon: amazon.com/Cecelia-Hopkins-Drewer/e/B071G968NM

First Contact
by G. Allen Wilbanks

The three Earth Alliance ships held their position, facing the five alien space craft. For several long minutes, there was no reaction to the unexpected meeting from either side.

Captain Jamison stood at the bridge of the E.A.S. Challenger, discussing options with his second in command. First contact with a new species was exciting, but it had to be handled delicately. Any misunderstanding now could damage relations between their races for a thousand years.

"Well, that message is pretty clear," said Captain Jamison, sadly, as the E.A. ship on their port side flared brilliant white and exploded into metal fragments.

G. Allen Wilbanks is a member of the Horror Writers Association (HWA) and has published over 50 short stories in various magazines and on-line venues. He is the author of two short story collections, and the novel, When Darkness Comes. Website: www.gallenwilbanks.com Blog: DeepDarkThoughts.com

New Life
by Cameron Marcoux

"Can you hear them?" A tiny voice, carrying a question, like an unborn child.

Limitless.

Strangling.

Weightless.

Heavy.

A threat of new life. A promise of an end to old nations. Old histories, forged in fire and war, to be forgotten. What will remain? Tattered symbols that mean nothing. Guesswork for future worlds to uncover. The fractured language of barbarians, left in dark corners and recesses of a dying planet, like the excrement of rats. We had this coming. Nearly begged for it. Broadcasters were we.

New life. Stronger. Capable adapters. Annihilators. Cataclysmic.

A small voice, "Can you hear them?"

Cameron Marcoux is a writer of stories, which, considering where you are reading this, makes a lot of sense. He also teaches English to the lovely and terrifying creatures we call teenagers. He lives in the quiet, northern reaches of New England in the U.S. with his girlfriend and scaredy dog.

From Champion to Traitor
by Emily Fluckiger

Space racing froze when a sponsor revealed themselves as inhuman. The galaxy turned its back. Races cancelled and fans disbanded in the name of hatred. My hands ached to control a craft, to zoom down the Milky Way and hear fans cheering in my headset as I passed other competitors.

Prejudice ended life as we knew it. I found myself on the alien's side during the solar civil war. I used my racing skills to dodge past military, my ship full of refugees, until they ripped my wings away, my freedom, and eventually my life.

I don't regret the sacrifice.

*Congenital Heart Defect survivor, **Emily Fluckiger**, finds joy and peace through the expression of writing. She engages and has been published in many formats from poetry to short stories to flash fiction and nonfiction. Emily and her husband spend their free time wrangling two children and playing video games in their busy California lifestyle.*

Alien Victuals
by J.J. Steinfeld

The spacecraft had landed on a distant planet, greeted by some of the planet's most revered dignitaries. After nearly a month of living on this planet and getting to know its translucent and quite small (by Earth standards) denizens, the leader of Earth's ten-person exploratory crew was asked to participate in the planet's most sacred ceremony, performed by its greatest magician, for magic was this planet's most basic form of expression, like sports or sex on Earth. Within seconds, the Earthling was transformed into a large, succulent spider and eaten by the magician. Who's next? the magician asked, still hungry.

First published in *The Drabbler,* 2009

*Canadian fiction writer/poet/playwright **J.J. Steinfeld** lives on Prince Edward Island, where he is patiently waiting for Godot's arrival and a phone call from Kafka. He has published 19 books, including Madhouses in Heaven, Castles in Hell (Stories, Ekstasis Editions, 2015), An Unauthorized Biography of Being (Stories, Ekstasis Editions, 2016), Absurdity, Woe Is Me, Glory Be (Poetry, Guernica Editions, 2017), and A Visit to the Kafka Café (Poetry, Ekstasis Editions, 2018). His stories and poems have appeared in anthologies and periodicals internationally, and over 50 of his one-act plays and a handful of full-length plays have been performed in North America.*

The Abduction
by Blair Daniels

Crack!

I peered out the window. A silver disk hovered above the treetops. Multi-coloured lights blinked in a strange, syncopated rhythm.

Like an idiot, I ran outside to get a better look.

A bright light yanked me up into the darkness.

I screamed. *They got me.* Little grey people with big, black eyes. Green, slimy, tentacled monsters. Worms with needle-like teeth.

Thump.

I opened my eyes.

Nausea bubbled up at the sight of them. Hairless. Pink. Emaciated.

"I hope you enjoy the trip to Earth," one said, baring its teeth in a smile. "You're the perfect addition to our zoo."

Blair Daniels *began writing horror stories to cope with the stress of being a new parent. She lives with her husband and son in a rural part of the US, where they lead a simple life raising chickens, playing video games, and hanging out at Costco. She regularly writes for Reddit's scary story forum, NoSleep, and her work has been published in several anthologies and podcasts. One of her short stories, Let Me In, was made into a short film.*
Website: www.blair-daniels.com
Facebook: scaryblair

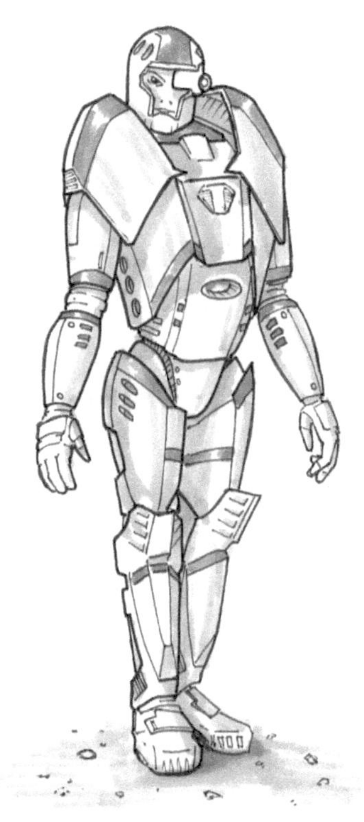

Time for Lunch
by Brandy Bonifas

Spores nestled, dormant, deep in the asteroid's crevices, resistant to the freezing ice of space. Hibernating for eons, primitive consciousness revived now in an atmosphere entering inferno.

The alien rock fell to Earth, not as a massive impact, but disintegrating in a rain of gravel, gathering in gutters and puddles, unnoticed. Soaking up water, the spores awoke hungry, seeking a host.

Bright red galoshes splashed through the puddle, followed by a thirsty puppy lapping at its edge.

"Time for lunch!"

"Come on, boy. Mom's calling."

The puppy whined, pain already gnawing at its stomach as it followed the boy inside.

Brandy Bonifas lives in Ohio with her husband and son. Her work has appeared or is forthcoming in anthologies by Clarendon House Publications, Pixie Forest Publishing, Zombie Pirate Publishing, and Blood Song Books, as well as the online publications CafeLit and Spillwords Press.
Website: www.brandybonifas.com
Facebook: brandybonifasauthor

My Name is Hunger,
Yours is Thirst
by Austin P. Sheehan

The creature below me cursed, falling to its knees. It had travelled further than any other from that strange steel cylinder, but like the others, it would fail. Groaning in agony, it crawled across the hot black sand. It couldn't last much longer. Desire and desperation burned through me. I longed to feast upon it, to slice open the soft flesh and pluck out those tasty orbs, feeling its life fade away while I grew ever stronger.

As the figure grunted and fell into the sand, I swooped down from the heavens. This time it would not get back up.

Austin P. Sheehan is a writer of speculative fiction, a lover of language, literature and '90s TV. Armed with a psychology degree, he went into the world to study humanity, and now prefers the company of his wife and their greyhounds. He grew up in the valleys of Victoria's high country, and despite living in Melbourne, always feels at home amongst the mountains. You'll often find mountains in his stories, whether they're sci-fi, fantasy or alternative history.
Website: austinpsheehan.com
Twitter: @AustinPSheehan

Two
by Stephen Coghlan

Two thousand points of light. Two thousand potential targets. Two thousand points of data force-fed into my brain through the implants.

Two thousandths worth of gravity as I cut the engines. There is no acceleration, no change in direction nor velocity, therefore no force acted upon me.

For two hundredths of a second, A brilliant light, a star, instantly born, instantly dies, silently, beside me. The scream of my comrade echoes through my ears.

For two tenths of a second, I mourn their passing.

Pause, Check the clock

Two seconds of calm before the storm. Just two, then we attack.

Stephen Coghlan is an ever-expanding, multi-genre author who writes out of Canada's National Capital. His works include The Genmos series, The Nobilis series, and the Dreampunk novella, URBAN GOTHIC.
Website: scoghlan.com
Twitter: @WordsBySC

Harmony
by David Bowmore

From many worlds, a few hundred thousand beings, looking for peace, came to settle.

As a planet with few natural resources, Harmony was of little interest to the great powers. Our new home was a place of safety, far from the Galactic War.

Then the Suidae—descendants of old Earth mammals—arrived.

They feed us poor quality food. Our females are forced to mate without rest; the offspring are immediately removed to be force grown. Our masters experiment with cross-species fertilisation to increase the quantity of our meat and improve its flavour.

I'm one of the lucky ones; a pet.

David Bowmore has lived here, there and everywhere, but now lives in Yorkshire with his wonderful wife and a small white poodle. He has worn many hats in his time; head chef, teacher and landscape gardener. His first collection of short stories 'The Magic of Deben Market' is available from Clarendon House.
Website: davidbowmore.co.uk
Facebook: davidbowmoreauthor

Midday
by D.M. Burdett

Paul stood waiting in the icy, cold darkness. His teeth chattered and he hadn't been able to feel his fingers in hours. Even though he was crammed in with hundreds of other bodies, none of them seemed to give off any heat. A small child looked up at him from under frosted eyelashes. "I'm scared," she whispered, hoarsely.

Suddenly, bright, piercing light filled their world and all heads turned to squint up at the artificial sun.

Uhrn of the planet Dagon, his food processing organ growling loudly, opened the fridge and peered in at his lunch with one large eye.

D.M. Burdett initially roamed as an army brat, but now lives in Australia where she spends her days avoiding drop bears and killer spiders. She has published a Sci-Fi series, has short stories in various anthologies, and has published two children's series. She is currently working on the first book in a dystopian series.
Website: www.dmburdett.com
Facebook: DMBurdett

In Place of Wisdom, Knowledge
by Aiki Flinthart

Scarlet sunlight turned the ice crusting its limbs to fire and blood. A remnant of some long-dead race, the iron colossus spun in silent majesty halfway between the red desert world and its lifeless moon.

The captain ordered me to haul it into the cargo hold. Our scientists marvelled at the perfectly-sculpted claws, the arms-length metal teeth. Each hair, each spine, each pore a work of art. Surely an idol for worship, they said. The deep-cleaved wounds on its legs and back evidence of some ritual.

On the bridge, I studied the dead world.

In the hold, the ice melted.

Aiki Flinthart has had short stories shortlisted in the Aurealis awards and top-8 listed in the USA Writers of the Future competition, as well as published in various anthologies and e-mags. She has 11 published spec fic novels and has edited 2 short story anthologies. She regularly gives workshops on writing fight scenes at conventions. Lives in Brisbane. Does martial arts, archery, knife throwing and lute-playing.
Website: www.aikiflinthart.com

Candles on the Cake, Make a Wish, Then Blow
by Diane Arrelle

"Ready?"

"Yes," Ginny whispered.

Zegragk nodded his bulbous head. "Good." He lit the thin, greasy candles and sang, "Happy Birthday… Happy Birthday, Dear Ginny…"

Ginny gasped. The voice of her mother came out of the sizzling tapers and joined in the song.

Tears ran down Ginny's cheeks. "Mom…I've… missed you…."

"Ginny," her mother rasped from the beyond, "Stop slouching, no wonder you're still single. Put on some more weight too, huh?"

Ginny wiped the tears away and blew out the candles, silencing the voice. "Thanks," she said handing Zegragk some bills. "Just needed my birthday reminder why I killed her."

First published in *The Drabbler*, 2005

Diane Arrelle, the pen name of South Jersey writer Dina Leacock, has sold more than 250 short stories and has three published books including Just A Drop In The Cup, a collection of short-short stories and her new collection of horror stories, Seasons On The Dark Side. Retired from being director of a municipal senior citizen center, she is now co-owner of a small publishing company, Jersey Pines Ink LLC. She resides with her husband and her new cat on the edge of the Pine Barrens (home of the Jersey Devil).
Website: www.arrellewrites.com
Facebook: Diane.Arrelle

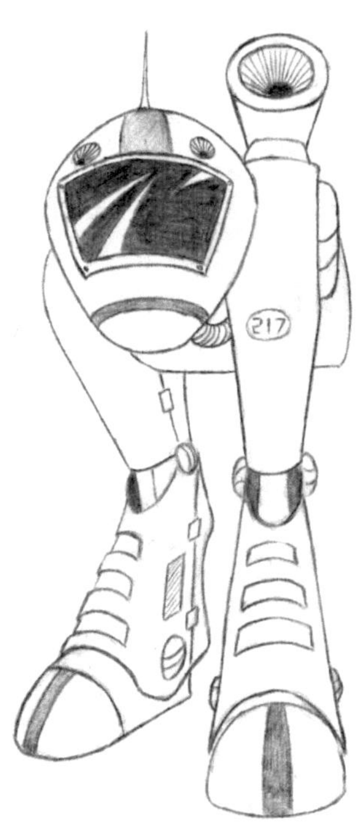

People Afraid on a Spaceship
by Rickey Rivers Jr.

Two crew members hurried down the empty hallway.

"How did that thing get into the ship?" she said.

His eyes were forward, his mind focused.

"It doesn't make sense," she continued. "Hatches are secure. I made sure of it."

He didn't say anything.

"What's wrong?" she asked. "No need to be afraid."

"Afraid?" he said, "I'm not afraid."

"Sure you are. That's why you're so quiet."

"You're wrong."

"You're scared. You're shaking in your boots. I never thought I'd see the day."

"Why would I be afraid? I've lured you away from the crew."

And it surrounded her quickly, squeezing.

Rickey Rivers Jr. *was born and raised in Alabama. He is a writer and cancer survivor. He likes a lot of stuff. You don't care about the details. He has been previously published in Fabula Argentea, ARTPOST magazine, the anthology Chronos, Enchanted Conversations Magazine, (among other publications).*
Twitter: @storiesyoumight

Mav Pressed On
by Stuart Conover

Adrenaline surged as Mav wiped sweat from his brow, making his way through darkness.

In the distance, bursts of gunfire trailed behind shrieks of the attacking bugs.

It was becoming rare for the rest of the squad to radio in a victory.

His men were being torn apart, and he couldn't help.

His mission was to find The Queen.

The four troopers who had flanked him were now stains on the walls.

In the tunnels ahead, a shriek tore through the air.

The rifle in his hand spit lead at the creature charging him, tearing it apart.

Mav pressed on.

Stuart Conover is a father, husband, rescue dog owner, published author, blogger, journalist, horror enthusiast, comic book geek, science fiction junkie, and IT professional. With all of that to cram in daily, we have no idea if or when he sleeps or how he gets writing done! (We suspect it has to do with having evil clones.) Stuart is a Chicago native and runs the author resource Horror Tree.

The Old Rusty Fence
by Hari Navarro

On the undulating wisp edge of the galaxy, a moon-sized world gently turns. Upon it, there is a wall. A continuous mile-high loop of iron that runs the equator entire.

On one side skulks an evil people. Their language is strange, hard on the ear, and it is said that they eat with their feet.

On the other side live the righteous builders of the barrier. They love their children and fear the things they hear tap as they place their ears to the rust.

But, for centuries, it has been forgotten just which side of the wall is which.

***Hari Navarro** has had work published at the very fine online flash fiction portal 365tomorrows.com, BREACH - a bi-monthly online zine for SF, horror and dark fantasy short fiction and AntipodeanSF - Australia's longest running online speculative fiction magazine. Hari was the Winner of the Australasian Horror Writers' Association [AHWA] Flash Fiction Award 2018 and has, also, succeeded in being a New Zealander who now lives in Northern Italy with no cats.*
Facebook: HariDarkFiction
Twitter: @HariFiction

Roy's New Friend
by Gabriella Balcom

"Will you be my friend?" the person whispered.

"Sure," Roy replied. After all, they'd spoken by CB radio twice now, although he still couldn't distinguish the individual's gender. He'd originally suspected a prank, but true misery had reverberated through the other person's voice as he or she spoke of having no family and being all alone and lonely.

The following night, he heard tapping on his door, opened it, and flinched. A nebulous, yellow mist floated there. "Roy?" a voice asked.

Wide-eyed, the man backed away, then fled.

"Come back!" something wailed behind Roy. "You said you'd be my friend."

Gabriella Balcom lives in Texas with her family, loves reading and writing, and thinks she was born with a book in her hands. She works in a mental health field, and writes fantasy, horror/thriller, romance, children's stories, and sci-fi. She likes travelling, music, good shows, photography, history, interesting tales, and animals. Gabriella says she's a sucker for a great story and loves forests, mountains, and back roads which might lead who knows where. She has a weakness for lasagne, garlic bread, tacos, cheese, and chocolate, but not necessarily in that order.
Facebook: GabriellaBalcom.lonestarauthor

Maderae vs Human
by Pamela Jeffs

Tracer beams slice past my shuttle's wing, rapid-fire lines of blue against the ebony backdrop of infinite space. I curse and slew my flight lever to the right. My ship responds, swinging and bringing into view the sleek lines of the Maderae's mothership. I return fire and cheer as its rear right thruster engine explodes. Without propulsion, the alien ship tilts in space, drawn into the gravity of the nearby Erdani star. Stasis pods begin spewing from the alien craft's cargo doors. I smile and activate my tractor beam. Time to take the human test subjects stolen from Earth, home.

Pamela Jeffs *is a speculative fiction author living in Queensland, Australia with her husband and two daughters. She is a member of the Queensland Writers' Centre and has had numerous short fiction pieces published in recent national and international anthologies. In 2017 and again in 2018, Pamela was nominated for an Australian Aurealis Award in the category of 'Best Science Fiction Short Story'. Her debut collection titled 'Red Hour and Other Strange Tales' was released in March 2018.*
Website: www.pamelajeffs.com
Facebook: pamelajeffsauthor

Hand Puppet
by Eddie D. Moore

"I was abducted by aliens on April first. No, this isn't an April Fools' joke. It really happened, and anal probes weren't used. What they put in you is much worse."

"I believe you, so put down the knife."

"I wish I could, but they see what I see, hear what I hear and feel what I feel. They say to go slower this time. The last two died too quickly."

"I've been your therapist three years. Untie me. I'll help you fight their influence."

"Fight? They only ask me to do what I already want to do. Hold still."

Eddie D. Moore travels extensively for work, and he spends much of that time listening to audio books. The rest of the time is spent dreaming of stories to write and he spends the weekends writing them. His stories have been published by Jouth Webzine, Kzine, Alien Dimensions, Theme of Absence, Devolution Z, and Fantasia Divinity Magazine.
Website: eddiedmoore.wordpress.com

The Vessel
by E.L. Giles

"How long have you been in pain?" asked Angela, worried.

"It's been three days now," I gasped.

Angela applied a generous layer of a violet slime called plasma and strapped the scanner across my swollen stomach.

Instantly, the pain turned unbearable, as something started moving inside of me, pushing against the thin wall of flesh and tearing it open.

"What the hell—" Her words cut off in a sizzling scream.

I raised my head to meet the hideous, blood-smeared reptile-like head sprouting out of my stomach. Shrieking, it sprang out on Angela's face, sharp ripping claws and gnawing jaw.

E.L. Giles is a dreamer, passionate about art, a restless worker and a bit of a weird human. He started his artistic journey as a music composer until the need to put his thoughts and stories down on paper grew too strong for him to resist it any longer. He lives in the French Province of Quebec, Canada, with his girlfriend and two boys.
Facebook: elgilesauthor
Website: www.elgilesauthor.com

The Honey Trap
by Zoey Xolton

"Captain, I think we've found our Eden," said astrophysicist Morton Norse, as he surveyed the alien planet through his night-vision binoculars. "The air and water are compatible with human life."

The exploration team of the Azure Aster took samples as they went, filling vials, taking measurements. On-board, Captain Carmel smiled, relieved. Fourteen generations had been born aboard the Aster. It was time they planted roots and started Earth 2.0.

"Something's not right," said their biologist uneasily. "My readings suggest the planet itself is-" The ground beneath them cracked open, swallowing them, before he could finish.

The planet belched. Sleepy. Sated.

Zoey Xolton is an Australian Speculative Fiction writer, primarily of Dark Fantasy, Paranormal Romance and Horror. She is also a proud mother of two and is married to her soul mate. Outside of her family, writing is her greatest passion. She is especially fond of short fiction and is working on releasing her own themed collections in future. Website: www.zoeyxolton.com

Landscaping
by Rickey Rivers Jr.

He dripped with sweat, cutting grass as instructed so that the players wouldn't trip.

"Team's no good anyway," he grumbled.

It took hours.

The setting sun didn't stop the heat.

Soon a man appeared on the field. Politely, he shut off the mower.

"Hello!" said the man, "are you the groundskeeper?"

"No, I'm the cook. What you want?"

"You do a swell job. Were you looking for extra work?"

"I'm dog tired, so no."

"I apologise."

"It's alright."

"I apologise for phrasing that as a question."

He was taken. This new planet was much smaller. The sun didn't shine there.

Rickey Rivers Jr. was born and raised in Alabama. He is a writer and cancer survivor. He likes a lot of stuff. You don't care about the details. He has been previously published in Fabula Argentea, ARTPOST magazine, the anthology Chronos, Enchanted Conversations Magazine, (among other publications).
Twitter: @storiesyoumight

True Green
by Rennie St. James

Humans say 'the grass is always greener on the other side'. We say 'iX teshHinmocrec'.

This new planet did look greener when I gazed down from our ship. It is not though. Greed, violence, and destruction run rampant across their ground. Ignorance and apathy are buried deep in their rich soil. It is the same thing my sisters and I ran from on our planet. We couldn't annihilate our home, but Earth presents a new chance.

Humans also say fire is cleansing. I am willing to test their words and sacrifice them to find a true green to save us.

Rennie St. James shares several similarities with her fictional characters (heroes and villains alike) including a love of chocolate, horror movies, martial arts, history, yoga, and travel. She doesn't have a pet mountain lion but is proudly owned by three rescue kitties. They live in relative harmony in beautiful southwestern Virginia (United States). The first three books of Rennie's urban fantasy series, The Rahki Chronicles, are available now. A new series and several standalone stories are already in the works as future releases.
Website: writerRSJ.com

Pioneers of Nothing
by Shelly Jarvis

Go through the wormhole, they said. It will be fun, they said.

They were wrong.

There is nothing fun about the way your body both stretches and compacts as you pass through. You feel overextended, pulled too thin, with bones pressing so hard against your skin you think they'll burst out. You feel squished, too, like a piece of paper wadded up. Or maybe a too-wet spitball about to be flung against the wall of space.

And then it stops.

You're back to normal, looking out onto…nothing. Darkness, without a hint of stars, light, or life. And no way back.

Shelly Jarvis is a speculative fiction author from West Virginia, US. She found a life-long love of sci-fi and fantasy in the 3rd grade when she found Madeleine L'Engle's "A Wrinkle in Time." Shelly is an avid reader, a Whovian, the ideal viewer of dog rescue videos, and undoubtedly Ravenclaw. She currently has two YA sci-fi books available for purchase on Amazon.
Website: www.ShellyJarvis.com

Juste Pour Rire
by Stephen Coghlan

Why did they take him? Where did he go? One minute there, the next he was gone.

Taken, they whispered. Abducted, witnesses complained.

A great giant saucer had hovered over the club, and afterwards the walls reeked of stale beer and ozone, cigarettes and bad decisions.

Why would the greys kidnap a comedian? Everyone wondered.

Why would aliens travel thousands of lightyears, only to grab one washed-out comedian whose payment barely covered his tab? He wasn't acting, he couldn't dance, he lived in his car.

The answer was simple. To them, he was sexy because he made the aliens laugh.

Stephen Coghlan is an ever-expanding, multi-genre author who writes out of Canada's National Capital. His works include The Genmos series, The Nobilis series, and the Dreampunk novella, URBAN GOTHIC.
Website: scoghlan.com
Twitter: @WordsBySC

Patronage
by Michael Crow

This wasn't home. The sterile grey walls and the blinding white light in her face told her that.

Do not worry; you are safe. You are the hope of your people.

An alien came into vision. He looked like a human child with the gentle softness of his features but a larger bulbous head and large black eyes.

This may be uncomfortable.

She tried to protest but her voice was absent. Tingling, confusion, throbbing, and echoes. Then light, silence, and emptiness.

Upload complete.

Six sets of eyes open, identical faces staring at each other. Familiarity and togetherness.

Where are we?

Michael Crow spends his sparse free time writing about sports, as well as working on his own fiction. Michael is the owner of Real Dead Review, a blog devoted to dark fiction. Michael's non-fiction works have appeared on USA Today, Fansided Network, The Guillotine, and Intermat. Michael makes his home with his wife, daughter and two cats in Central Minnesota.

Erasure Successful
by Peter Larsen

They found him, dishevelled and dehydrated, wandering along a lonely bush track. He had no recollection of how long it had been or how he got there.

As the air ambulance bounced along the airstrip and laboured into the air, he was bombarded with questions. To no avail. The memory of the past few days was an impenetrable fog in his brain. The doctor looked closely at two small cranial incisions, barely visible under a regrowth of downy hair. He had seen those marks once before…

***

Gorvel smiled at his monitor. The tiny implant was undetectable. "Memory erasure successful."

What do you do in the boring moments between teaching classes, marking work, planning curriculum and attending meetings? Write creative stories, of course! **Peter Larsen** *is a Secondary English/Drama teacher from Traralgon, Australia. He has written an eclectic mix of stories about subjects ranging from aliens, the supernatural, dystopian futures and many more drawn from his own experiences and memories. When he is not working or writing he enjoys performing in musicals and dramas, watching movies, attending sports, gardening and enjoying life with his wife, two dogs and a cantankerous cat.*

Pew Pew Pew!
by Alanna Robertson-Webb

My son and I are colonists of Terraduo, and we live a happy existence. He entertains himself with his toy spaceships every day, and the Grand Council even approves of the way that he makes funny little noises during his playtime.

Pew, pew, pew, pew!

I listen from the kitchen as plastic snaps, and I know that he'll soon come crying to me. The Council will give him a new spaceship, and my son will be happy again. This cycle will go on, just as it has for the last two years.

If only he knew they weren't really toys…

Alanna Robertson-Webb is a sales support member by day, and a writer and editor by night. She loves VT, and live in PA. She has been writing since she was five years old, and writing well since she was seventeen years old. She lives with a fiance and a cat, both of whom take up most of her bed space. She loves to L.A.R.P., and one day she aspired to write a horrifyingly fantastic novel. Her short horror stories have been published before, but she still enjoys remaining mysterious.
Reddit: MythologyLovesHorror

Octopiod
by Pamela Jeffs

I'm the Hunter become the Hunted.

The Octopiod's tentacles, silver scaled, suckered and slippery with space slime curl out from around the side of Jupiter. My ship is cloaked, but I'm sure the creature can still smell me. She's already tracked me half way across the universe to claim back what's in my cargo bay. Her eggs.

A cloak won't stop her.

She floats clear of the planet, her glowing eyes pulsing as she moves. A bead of sweat slides down my spine. Distracted, I don't even notice her newly hatched offspring's tentacle around my neck until it's too late.

Pamela Jeffs *is a speculative fiction author living in Queensland, Australia with her husband and two daughters. She is a member of the Queensland Writers' Centre and has had numerous short fiction pieces published in recent national and international anthologies. In 2017 and again in 2018, Pamela was nominated for an Australian Aurealis Award in the category of 'Best Science Fiction Short Story'. Her debut collection titled 'Red Hour and Other Strange Tales' was released in March 2018.*
Website: www.pamelajeffs.com
Facebook: pamelajeffsauthor

Beyond the Wormhole
by Sinister Sweetheart

Something went terribly wrong with the macroscopic quantum generator during the linking process.

The popping of our ears was deafening; like our heads would crack under the weight of suction. We'd lost control of the vessel and were spit out into a world of green.

Singular entities stared at our vessel. Their appendages held various shiny trinkets.

They captured us and placed us in a cold room with bright lights.

The need to tell home of this new threat was imminent. I sent an urgent message to home base. We needed to destroy all life and colonise; location name: Earth.

*Since **Sinister Sweetheart** made her first post to a popular Internet forum, she's taken the horror community by storm. Her ability to create, terrify, and drive home her stories is insurmountable. Sinister Sweetheart's published works can be found in multiple anthologies for all to read, but be forewarned, if you do... you may want to call your therapist after, her stories are terrifying, disturbing and devilishly unsettling. She is not only a fright visually, but also has a creepy tentacle in horror podcasting as well. Sinister Sweetheart writes, voice acts and is the media director of the Scarecrow Tales podcast.*
Website: Sinistersweetheart.wixsite.com/sinistersweetheart
Facebook: NMBrownStories

Immigration Application: Earth from Phoebus 3 (Havenos) – Statement of Reason for Request

by T. L. Barrett

Homer, my dog, was playing with the scampillar (a native fluffy hexapod) that my neighbour, Tenz, adopted. I told Tenz he should get a dog. The Arcturian didn't listen.

Homer screeched. The scampillar had torn open his side with retractable dentition I didn't even know it had.

"Did Frodo and Sam make it?" Homer asked as he died. We hadn't gotten to Return of the King yet.

Found out later that all of a sudden, all over Havenos, the scampillar were killing dogs. No one knew why.

I miss my dog. I want to go home.

Query: Permit or Deny?

*The weird writer **T. L. Barrett** lives in the green hills of Vermont's Northeast Kingdom with his wife, sons, his dogs (Jake and Dude), and three cats. He spent time travelling the world as a young man and then has raised a great passel of children and taught high school English for 22 years. He is now dedicating his time to his true passion: writing and stories. He has had many tales and novels, such as The Wardmaster and Hairy Bromance, published in the small press.*
Website: tlbarrett.com

Contemplation
by S. Gepp

He looked at the stars.

The near-infinity of the universe stretched out above him.

For generations mankind had travelled amongst these points of light, beginning with a capsule to Earth's moon in 1969, centuries earlier.

Now he could gaze upwards and say he'd been to dozens of them.

Stars had been the next great exploratory adventure and he'd been at its forefront.

Ships travelling beyond the speed of light had taken him to the galaxy's farthest reaches.

His smile faltered.

Why did he feel so empty? Was it human insignificance? World-weariness? Disillusionment?

No.

Home.

He just wanted to go home.

S. Gepp is an Australian, with two children, two university degrees (and counting), two tertiary education diplomas, and a resumé that looks like a list of every job you could ever have without really trying, including stints as a school teacher, scientist, editor and journalist. He has also been a performance acrobat, a professional wrestler, a stand-up comedian and an actor. He has been writing for 30 years (with some publications: one novella, about 10 poems, 40-odd short stories, and a few more pending) and hopes to be a real writer if he grows up. A dull life.

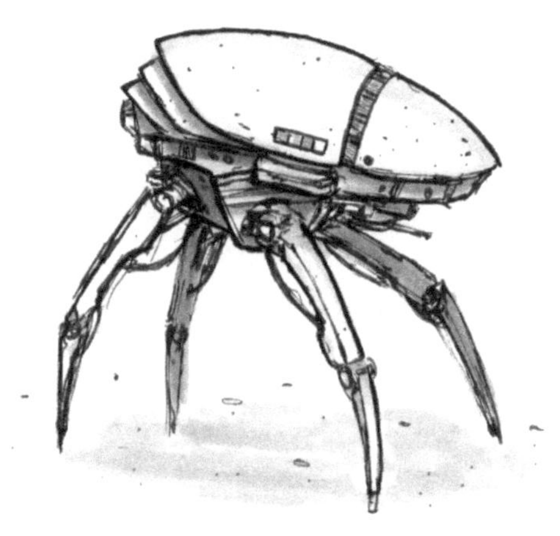

Manifest Destiny
by Susanne Thomas

"You know why you're under arrest, right?"

"This is ridiculous. I brought you all to a new land. It's paradise. Mortality rates have dropped by 30% since we got here."

"It wasn't ours to take. This planet had its own people."

"The history of our race includes taking what is our God-given right. The new-natives are nothing."

"You slaughtered them. All of them. By yourself. Seven million souls. Dead."

"They were barely beasts, they didn't have souls. It was like killing ants. You can't try me, I saved humanity."

"I'd wait for your attorney, ma'am. You're gonna need the help."

Susanne Thomas reads, writes, parents, and teaches from the windy west in Wyoming, and she loves fantasy, science fiction, speculative fiction, poetry, children's books, science, coffee, and puns.
Website: susannethomas.wixsite.com/susanne-thomas
Facebook: SusanneThomasAuthor

It Will Be Boring
by Stephen Herczeg

I didn't want to come to school camp on a new planet. I said it would be boring.

"It'll be an adventure," Mum said.

They took our devices. No phone. No tablet. Nothing.

Boring.

Then the stupid ship crashed. The pilot and the teachers are all dead. All my school mates as well.

I'm alive, all alone, but I found this cave. It's cold, and there's something snuffling about outside. It's big and it sounds scary.

I don't want to go out there. I can only wait for help.

Now I'm too scared to be bored.

I want my mummy.

Stephen Herczeg is an IT Geek based in Canberra Australia. He has been writing for over twenty years and has completed a couple of dodgy novels, sixteen feature length screenplays and numerous short stories and scripts. His horror work has featured in Sproutlings, Hells Bells, Below the Stairs, Trickster's Treats #1 and #2, Shades of Santa, Behind the Mask, Beyond the Infinite; The Body Horror Book, Anemone Enemy, Petrified Punks and Beginnings. He has also had numerous Sherlock Holmes stories published through the Belanger Books - Sherlock Holmes anthologies.

Catch of the Day
by G. Allen Wilbanks

"Are you sure it's fresh?"

"Of course, it's fresh," insisted the merchant. "It's still alive."

"I suppose," mused the prospective buyer, peering into the glass tank. "Where did you get it?"

The merchant gave a secretive smile. "I have my resources. I got a dozen of them this morning, but this is my last one. You want it or not?"

"I don't know. It's kind of puny." The customer rapped on the glass.

"Hey! Stop scaring it."

The boy startled at the sudden noise. He scrambled for the far corner of the tank and began to cry for his mother.

G. Allen Wilbanks is a member of the Horror Writers Association (HWA) and has published over 50 short stories in various magazines and on-line venues. He is the author of two short story collections, and the novel, When Darkness Comes. Website: www.gallenwilbanks.com
Blog: DeepDarkThoughts.com

Test Subject #1014
by Sinister Sweetheart

Kevan committed acts of violence. He blamed voices in his head; unseen forces guiding him for his whole life. They took control of his relationships, hopes and life goals; sabotaging each masterfully.

When Kevan completed his most depraved act to date, the voice revealed itself. Its name didn't belong to a Demon. It didn't respond to elixirs catered towards the mentally ill.

His last act of this Earth was removing the chip he found embedded within the skin of his left arm. He'd been controlled by unknown beings since creation and paid the price with his life in the end.

*Since **Sinister Sweetheart** made her first post to a popular Internet forum, she's taken the horror community by storm. Her ability to create, terrify, and drive home her stories is insurmountable. Sinister Sweetheart's published works can be found in multiple anthologies for all to read, but be forewarned, if you do... you may want to call your therapist after, her stories are terrifying, disturbing and devilishly unsettling. She is not only a fright visually, but also has a creepy tentacle in horror podcasting as well. Sinister Sweetheart writes, voice acts and is the media director of the Scarecrow Tales podcast.*
Website: Sinistersweetheart.wixsite.com/sinistersweetheart
Facebook: NMBrownStories

The Min Min
by Peter Larsen

Night after night they appeared. Brilliant pin-pricks of light that hovered, circled and disappeared, only to reappear moments later in a different place. Natives called them "Min Min", spirits of ancestors who had walked the earth in the Dreamtime. They were celebrated in stories and paintings, where god-like effigies had for centuries stared out from their stone canvases.

In half-remembered dreams, chosen people stood bathed in pools of light that shimmered from the darkness above. Their thoughts were confused by simultaneous feelings of fear and wonderment, as if they were looking into the face of creation.

Until the darkness descended.

What do you do in the boring moments between teaching classes, marking work, planning curriculum and attending meetings? Write creative stories, of course! **Peter Larsen** *is a Secondary English/Drama teacher from Traralgon, Australia. He has written an eclectic mix of stories about subjects ranging from aliens, the supernatural, dystopian futures and many more drawn from his own experiences and memories. When he is not working or writing he enjoys performing in musicals and dramas, watching movies, attending sports, gardening and enjoying life with his wife, two dogs and a cantankerous cat.*

Meat and Greet
by Rich Rurshell

"As much as I want you and your companions to enjoy feasting on my flesh, I do not want to suffer," said the Lakshi tribesman, handing me a knife. He was a sacrifice to honour the peace agreement between us human settlers and the Lakshi.

I looked at what remained of Stuart. The Lakshi had picked his bones clean. We hadn't fully grasped the gravity of the situation when we handed him over five minutes before.

"Come," said the tribesman, smiling and gesturing across his throat with the blade. "I'm sure you will find me very much to your taste."

Rich Rurshell is a short story writer from Suffolk, England. Rich writes Horror, Sci-Fi, and Fantasy, and his stories can be found in various short story anthologies and magazines. Most recently, his story "Subject: Galilee" was published in World War Four from Zombie Pirate Publishing, and "Life Choices" was published in Salty Tales from Stormy Island Publishing. When Rich is not writing stories, he likes to write and perform music.
Facebook: richrurshellauthor

No Guarantee
by Dawn DeBraal

Loving him from afar, Kathy snatched the used napkin Derrick Richards threw in the garbage. Taking the napkin to the cloning laboratory she placed an order for another Derrick. It would take months, Kathy waited patiently. The call came to pick "Derrick" up. Kathy raced to the cloning lab, disappointed with the results.

"What happened to my Derrick?" she cried.

"I can't help that the sample wasn't pure." The scientist responded, "There are no guarantees, that was in the contract."

How could Derrick look so ridiculous? Sighing, Kathy took the hotdog with Derrick's face, extra ketchup, and spicy mustard, home.

Dawn DeBraal lives in rural Wisconsin with her husband, two rat terriers, and a cat. She successfully raised two children (meaning they didn't return to the nest!) After many years serving the government at the Federal and County level, she recently retired. Having extra time on her hands she started to write after a paralyzed vocal cord took her ability to speak for two months. Not finding her voice, she discovered that her love of telling a good story could be written. Her works have been published in Palm-Sized Press, Spillwords, Mercurial Stories, Potato Soup Journal, and Blood Song Books.

Out of Control
by E.L. Giles

"Pull the trigger," ordered the voice in my head.

The Council of the Galactic Nations opened. Leading it was Sage, the Great Master, who invited us to take a seat.

"Kill him!" the voice yelled coldly.

Strangely, my arm obeyed the order, and I picked up the gun I had dissimulated before entering the Great Amphitheatre. I had to resist.

"No," I retorted. "I won't."

"Do it!"

The drive to act, to kill was so tremendous that I couldn't help but raise the gun toward Sage. With a sudden resurgence of my will, I turned the gun toward myself.

"No!"

E.L. Giles is a dreamer, passionate about art, a restless worker and a bit of a weird human. He started his artistic journey as a music composer until the need to put his thoughts and stories down on paper grew too strong for him to resist it any longer. He lives in the French Province of Quebec, Canada, with his girlfriend and two boys.
Facebook: elgilesauthor
Website: www.elgilesauthor.com

Ship in a Storm
by Crystal L. Kirkham

Tholins. That rich biomaterial we dared to harvest from the red spot was the only thing keeping us alive. Stuck in one of Jupiter's turbulent bands. Unable to escape the brutal winds that tossed us around like debris in an ocean.

We waited for rescue. Five days. I braced myself as the ship shuddered and shrieked. Three days and we'd be dead. Hull integrity was degrading.

I kept silent, smiled at the rest of the walking dead. They smiled back.

Another shuddering shriek and wind whistled past me. Hull breach. We'd gotten too close. Three days was now three minutes.

Crystal L. Kirkham resides in a small hamlet west of Red Deer, Alberta. She's an avid outdoors person, unrepentant coffee addict, part-time foodie, servant to a wonderful feline, and companion to two delightfully hilarious canines. She will neither confirm nor deny the rumours regarding the heart in a jar on her desk and the bottle of reader's tears right next to it. Her paranormal urban fantasy series, Saints and Sinners, is available on Amazon and her YA Fantasy, Feathers and Fae will be released October 11, 2019, from Kyanite Publishing.
Website: www.crystallkirkham.com

Spawn
by R.J. Hunt

Five screens of static. One headcam remained, sprinting down the narrow corridor. Comms distorted by heavy breathing, the soldier released a couple of poorly aimed shots behind him. His muzzle flare illuminated the walls, revealing scurrying black creatures, all around him.

He tripped. Screamed. His monitor joined the others, turning to static.

General Abrams sighed, rubbing his tired eyes. He selected six soldier profiles in front of the birthing pods and pushed a single button.

'Reprint.'

Pink fluid oozed into the pods, taking a vaguely foetal shape. Whilst the humans were being made, General Abrams went to fetch fresh headcams.

R.J. Hunt is a Civil Engineer from Nottingham who loves creating worlds and writing stories in his spare time. Whilst he has a roughly infinite supply of half-finished stories, he's currently working on the second draft of his debut novel, 'The Final Carnivore' - a story about horrible people being granted immortality and mind-control powers, causing misfits with hidden abilities of their own to rise in an effort stop them.
Twitter: @RJHuntWrites
Reddit: RJHuntWrites

The Vesper
by Stuart Conover

Jazz swore as *The Vesper* danced through the asteroid field.

Just her luck to have stumbled onto fifteen ships from the Aluzues fleet.

Asteroids took out six.

Lucky shots had downed another four.

Five remained.

There wasn't enough luck in the 'verse for her to make the system's jump gate.

Swirling between rocks, *The Vesper* flipped, tagging another pursuer.

They were low on weapons.

Time to run.

Pushing the accelerator, she danced through the field.

They were going to crash.

And yet.

Somehow.

They cleared the field.

Barking orders, her crew opened the gate.

They made the jump to safety.

Stuart Conover is a father, husband, rescue dog owner, published author, blogger, journalist, horror enthusiast, comic book geek, science fiction junkie, and IT professional. With all of that to cram in daily, we have no idea if or when he sleeps or how he gets writing done! (We suspect it has to do with having evil clones.) Stuart is a Chicago native and runs the author resource Horror Tree.

Countdown to Destruction
by Stephen Coghlan

The declaration was one word, "WAR."

The next day they launched the missiles.

The next week was a party to their future victories.

The missiles were their ultimate weapons. They were cloaked, intelligent, absolutely destructive, and even though they had to journey for fifty years to their targets, the enemy was less militaristic. They had no hope of designing defensive armaments in time.

Year 50-1, another celebration was held. The streets were packed as everyone awaited the news. That's when the sky opened, and their own bombs returned to burn their planet.

The victors laughed. Wormholes, not guns, had won.

Stephen Coghlan is an ever-expanding, multi-genre author who writes out of Canada's National Capital. His works include The Genmos series, The Nobilis series, and the Dreampunk novella, URBAN GOTHIC.
Website: scoghlan.com
Twitter: @WordsBySC

Electra's Last Cigarette
by Copper Rose

Electra felt uneasy, as though someone was watching her. She deactivated her electronic cigarette and placed it next to the tabletop viewer. She had promised to quit but then smoked four units while telling Havenu about Morkinda's sordid affair. Then Electra realised it was EVE—the newest Super Deluxe RX2000 robotic multi-level self-navigating Electronic Vacuum Extraordinaire that could detect dirt anywhere in a person's habitation cell. Quasar Intergalactic's data disclosure proclaimed EVE was an exceedingly efficient vacuum ravenous for dirt anywhere it could find it.

Electra never noticed the bottle of flesh tenderiser on the floor next to a hypervigilant EVE.

Copper Rose perforates the edges of the page while writing unusual stories from the heart of Wisconsin. Her work has appeared in various anthologies and online journals. She also understands there really is something about pie. Website: julieceger.wordpress.com/copper-rose-author

Kill the Greed
by Emily Fluckiger

I sharpened my claw. Creatures approached. Ships carried them closer to us than ever before. We knew of their bloodthirst after centuries of observing their unwillingness to share land. They rejected anyone different. We have no similarities with them. Their bipedling bodies were hairless as a stone, faces as cold. They'd stolen from one another until they claimed every space across their planet. We expected the same as they took to the heavens and stomped into our home, smashing flags into our ground. I refused to accept the assault. I sharpened my claw, ready to turn their greed into death.

*Congenital Heart Defect survivor, **Emily Fluckiger**, finds joy and peace through the expression of writing. She engages and has been published in many formats from poetry to short stories to flash fiction and nonfiction. Emily and her husband spend their free time wrangling two children and playing video games in their busy California lifestyle.*

The Edge of Space
by David Bowmore

After hundreds of thousands of years and the collaboration of many thousands of scientists from hundreds of worlds using the combined computing power of God, we have arrived at the very edge of the universe.

This world-ship's only purpose is to survey the milky surface and perhaps acquire enough knowledge for exploration beyond the barrier. That is for our descendants to consider.

The haze clears for a few seconds as something enormous moves.

Months of piecing together captured images from thousands of recording markers, finally revealed the horrifying answer.

A blinking eye.

Like rats in a lab, we're being studied.

David Bowmore has lived here, there and everywhere, but now lives in Yorkshire with his wonderful wife and a small white poodle. He has worn many hats in his time; head chef, teacher and landscape gardener. His first collection of short stories 'The Magic of Deben Market' is available from Clarendon House.
Website: davidbowmore.co.uk
Facebook: davidbowmoreauthor

Dark Encounter
by Matthew M. Montelione

Theobolt, leader of the Dark Wizards, peered at the prisoner from under his long eyebrows. "Why did you come to our planet, spaceman?"

"I had no choice, my ship crashed! I come in peace."

Theobolt grinned. "Peace? We have no need of your peace, for we have found our own." He stroked his long, dark beard. "But we do have need of you."

The newcomer looked scared.

The wizard's silver eyes flared. "Our black magic is fuelled by sacrifice. What greater gift is there to give but life itself? Guards!" he called out, "Take the prisoner to the ritual room!"

Matthew M. Montelione is a horror writer born and raised on Long Island in New York. His stories have been published in Quoth the Raven: A Contemporary Reimagining of the Works of Edgar Allan Poe, Thuggish Itch: Devilish, and other titles. Matthew is also an American Revolution historian who focuses on the local experiences of Loyalists on Long Island. His work on the subject has been published in Long Island History Journal and Journal of the American Revolution.
Website: maybeevils.com
Twitter: @maybeevils

Match
by Freddy Iryss

We wait in the hall with a hundred and fifty volunteers for our numbers to be handed out. The numbers will be our tickets for the SpaceBuses, docked at the end of the gangways, each destined to fly to one of six planets.

Destination Mars, here we come. Currency-poor, we'd signed up for the Inter-Galactic-Space-Station-Mission, a new life. After an aptitude test that analysed the algorithm of our social media implants, we both qualify.

Our music profile data don't match and predict varying behavioural patterns suited to differing, extra-terrestrial colonies.

I get #1 to Mars, you #6 to Saturn.

*To impress her older brother, **Freddy Iryss** read her way through his collection of Isaac Asimov's books of SciFi at the tender age of ten. She pretended that she understood what was going on in those futuristic worlds, while deep down she found them disturbing her peace of mind. Who and what was out there? Iryss' non-fiction writing includes themes on identity, the postcolonial and post-national. Her fiction evolves around the concept of the anthropocene. Writing SciFi is to imagine the world of our reality without bounds.*
Website: freddyiryss.blogspot.com
Twitter: @FreddyIryss

Pickup
by Alexander Pyles

Rolf was always talking 'bout lights, little grey men, and how his head hurt. He would piddle about the yard, tossing scrap into the back of his pickup, and after finishing his Marlboro, drive off.

It was maybe the last week in July when I saw the lights. They were hovering over the corn stalks, high and green in the beams of light. The appearance caused me to freeze where I stood, but a beam still found me before it all went black.

I awoke to little grey men and something sharp being put against my forehead. Rolf was right.

Alexander Pyles resides in IL with his wife and children. He holds an MA in Philosophy and an MFA in Writing Popular Fiction. His short story chapbook titled, "Milo (01001101 01101001 01101100 01101111)," from Radix Media, is due out fall 2019. His other short fiction has appeared on 101fiction.org, River and South Review, and other venues. Website: www.pylesofbooks.com Twitter: @Pylesofbooks

Consume, Consume, Consume
by Adam S. Furman

Blaster bolts flash across my wingtips and zip through the vacuum of space. They hit their mark but bounce off. The Eater of Worlds has come, and our weapons are fruitless against it.

Its amphibious appearance has us distraught. It's mouth, a collection of needles, begins closing. There are screams through my comms as reality sets in. Another hour of battle, but we lose. The hope is gone. I can smell it.

The jaws close over my homeworld, sealed shut forever. I circle around and aim my starfighter. I accelerate towards its eye. Its blackness overwhelms me before the impact.

Adam S. Furman lives in rural Illinois with his family which includes a lot of kids (like...a lot). He generally writes science fiction.
Twitter: @AdamSFurman

The Mission
by Alanah Andrews

The pilot consulted the pulsar map, then peered into his display screen. "There it is."

"Doesn't look like much." His co-pilot gazed at the planet below.

"It's full of minerals. Large deposits of oil, too. Should keep us going for a while." He zoomed in on the screen. "There's the lifeforms."

"Yuck." The co-pilot pressed a button. Multiple poison-filled canisters careened downwards. "Bug bomb."

They watched the screen intently as the puny creatures collapsed to the ground.

"They were asking for it, really. Soft flesh and no armour."

The co-pilot nodded his two heads, flexing his sharpened pincers. "Stupid humans."

Alanah Andrews writes speculative fiction and spends far too much time debating whether 1984 or The Handmaid's Tale are most representative of our future. Her YA dystopian novel about a future where emotions are forbidden, Eve of Eridu, was released in 2018. She has also had several short stories published in a range of different places. When she's not writing, Alanah runs the Australian Speculative Fiction group, teaches high school English, and attempts to raise two children. She has a husky, a pony, a blue-tongue lizard, and dreams of travelling Australia in a bus.
Website: www.alanahandrews.com
Facebook: alanahandrewsauthor

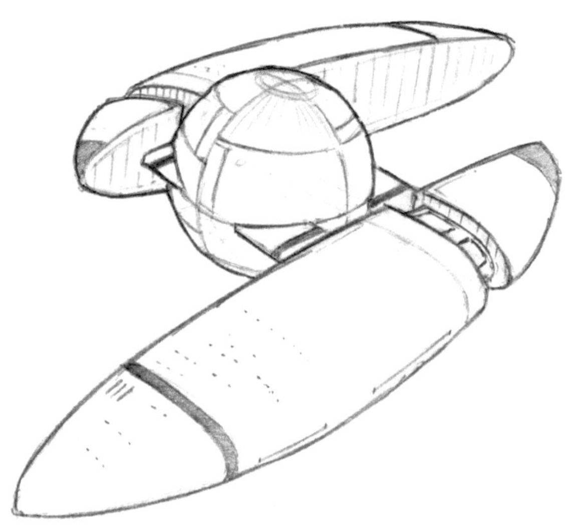

Spaced
by Jack Wolfe Frost

It's cold in deep space. I expected to be dead a long time ago, when they blew me out the airlock. Can't remember how long I've been drifting, with only the stars for company.

In stasis, you are unconscious. In a level III suit, I'm protected, but only until my oxygen ran out. When that started to happen, I took off my helmet, but I just instantly froze.

Why my brain works, I don't know.

My suit has a distress beacon, good for a year. I'll get picked up, one day.

Then—just one thing calls. The final act. Revenge.

Jack Wolfe Frost is the Eternal Rebel; he rebels against everything which may have the word "rules" or "behave" within it. Born in Sheffield, UK, in 1956; he first started writing in 1982, as a hobby - Now older and wiser, he has had several poems and short stories published.
Website: jackjfrost.wordpress.com
Twitter: @JackWolfeWriter

The Shot
by Sam M. Phillips

Halo bombers level the city, bright yellow flashes and shockwaves. In the wake of the destruction the enemy come out of their bunkers, take up their defensive positions once more.

Eyes cyber-linked to my scope, I aim my weapon. The offensive will be beginning soon, an army at my tail, relying on me.

Panning across the fortifications, I see him; skin glowing, cape fluttering, with the head of a caterpillar.

The AI plugged into my cerebral cortex makes the calculations and I take the shot. The enemy leader dies just as the signal for the offensive chimes in my mind.

Sam M. Phillips is the co-founder of Zombie Pirate Publishing, producing short story anthologies and helping emerging writers. His own work has appeared in dozens of anthologies and magazines such as Full Moon Slaughter 2, 13 Bites Volumes IV and V, Rejected for Content 6, and Dastaan World Magazine. He lives in the green valleys of northern New South Wales, Australia, and enjoys reading, walking, and playing drums in the death metal band Decryptus.
Website: zombiepiratepublishing.com

The Cat Lady
by Diane Arrelle

ZZZZZMMMMMM

Martha pushed a dozen skinny cats away from the door and went outside. She saw the flying saucer.

ZZZZMMMMM, a beam hit her.

Martha woke on a cold metal table. An alien in a spacesuit held a long probe. "Don't worry, just making sure you're healthy," it said.

Martha woke in a cage. She saw purple grass and green sky. "My God," Martha gasped. "This isn't Earth!"

The alien standing next to her took off his spacesuit. Martha gasped again.

"Kids," the six-foot tabby called. "I got you a new human. You better take better care of this one!"

First published in *The Drabbler One*, 2005

Diane Arrelle, the pen name of South Jersey writer Dina Leacock, has sold more than 250 short stories and has three published books including Just A Drop In The Cup, a collection of short-short stories and her new collection of horror stories, Seasons On The Dark Side. Retired from being director of a municipal senior citizen centre, she is now co-owner of a small publishing company, Jersey Pines Ink LLC. She resides with her husband and her new cat on the edge of the Pine Barrens (home of the Jersey Devil). Website: www.arrellewrites.com
FaceBook: Diane.Arrelle

Screen Animal
by Virginia Carraway Stark

The white owl hit the windshield. It was dark except the glare of snow in the headlights. I stopped to see if it was okay; I saw it was still on its feet. I walked a bit closer and it looked me in the eyes. My gaze locked in with its gaze and owl eyes grew, turned black and almond. I felt feathers against my face, but I couldn't breathe. Long fingers gripped my arms tightly. It was nearly dawn when I awoke, my car far down the road. I was freezing, but not as cold as in the ship.

Virginia Carraway Stark *has a diverse portfolio and has many publications. Over the years she has developed this into a wide range of products from screenplays to novels to articles to blogging to travel journalism. She has been published by many presses from grassroots to Simon and Schuster. She has been an honourable mention at Cannes Film Festival for her screenplay, "Blind Eye" and was nominated for an Aurora Award. She also placed in the final top three screenplay shorts as well as numerous other awards for her anthologies, novels, blogs and other projects.*

The 59-Year-Old Moon-Shuttle Astronaut Whose Dying Grandfather Whistled 'Fly Me to the Moon' 37-Years Before
by J.J. Steinfeld

The oldest moon-shuttle astronaut stared at his shuttlecraft's blank monitor, unable to close his eyes, yelling for help, but he was alone, hurtling moonward out-of-control.

Shortly before impact, his grandfather's face came onto the monitor, whistling "Fly Me to the Moon," just as he had when the astronaut as a young man told his dying grandfather he had been selected for the moon-shuttle program. His grandfather had been in a coma before he began whistling "Fly Me to the Moon," dying mid-song.

The shuttlecraft crashed and immediately the astronaut's face appeared on the monitor of a spacecraft preparing for take-off.

*Canadian fiction writer/poet/playwright **J.J. Steinfeld** lives on Prince Edward Island, where he is patiently waiting for Godot's arrival and a phone call from Kafka. He has published 19 books, including Madhouses in Heaven, Castles in Hell (Stories, Ekstasis Editions, 2015), An Unauthorized Biography of Being (Stories, Ekstasis Editions, 2016), Absurdity, Woe Is Me, Glory Be (Poetry, Guernica Editions, 2017), and A Visit to the Kafka Café (Poetry, Ekstasis Editions, 2018). His stories and poems have appeared in anthologies and periodicals internationally, and over 50 of his one-act plays and a handful of full-length plays have been performed in North America.*

Retirement
by Joshua D. Taylor

Charles knew that he overpaid for his personalised MiniWorld™. As he stood on the front porch of his new ranch-style house surrounded by Bermuda grass, he knew it was worth every penny. The house was positioned so he could look over the curvature of the horizon at the sparkling ice ring surrounding the twin suns. He could walk completely around the equator in only six minutes.

He paid extra to make sure it was in line next to a protected green world, so he only had neighbours on the other side. It certainly beat the senior retirement community in Florida.

Joshua D. Taylor is an amateur writer who started writing a few years ago when he realised he was too old to play make-believe. He lives in southeastern Pennsylvania with his wife and a one-eared cat. He enjoys gardening, comic books, ska-punk music, Disney World, and travelling with his wife. Raised during weirdness that was the late 20th century Josh's eclectic interests produce eclectic works. He loves to mix-n-match things from different genres and stories elements to achieve a madcap hodgepodge of the truly unexpected. His short story 'the Obelisk' appears in Salty Tales by Stormy Island Publishing.
Facebook: authorjoshuadtaylor

The Smartest Man on Earth (Formerly)
by Brian Rosenberger

They called him a renegade, an outlaw, a villain. He only smiled. His sentence—relocated to where they exiled all criminals. He thought of himself humbly as a thinker. This was the price to pay for thinking.

He raised the goblet—a 1995 *Chateau Margaux*. Their own lunar vineyards had failed to produce anything quite as delicious. He'd miss the wines from home but sacrificed flavour for progress.

For him, it was no longer revenge, just hitting the reset button. He rechecked the monitors. All systems go. Sights aligned. One last toast, "Farewell Mother."

And triggered the Apocalypse gun.

***Brian Rosenberger** lives in a cellar in Marietta, GA (USA) and writes by the light of captured fireflies. He is the author of As the Worms Turns and three poetry collections. He is also a featured contributor to the Pro-Wrestling literary collection, Three-Way Dance, available from Gimmick Press.*
Facebook: HeWhoSuffers

Infinite Reality
by D.K. Spencer

Our ship's weapons are off-line. We've sustained major damage to cargo deck sections twenty-nine through thirty-six. We've suffered heavy casualties.

Five Argon rebel ships are closing in. We've sent distress signals to the fleet. The crew has been informed of our imminent defeat. Through the ship's com, each crewman has voted to surrender or to go down with guns blazing.

Votes tallied: we fight!

Setting the particle-beam emitter to Zero-point, space time will distort our close proximity. All ships including our own will be sent into an infinite time loop.

We will never lose, but neither will we win.

Forevermore.

*American writer **D.K. Spencer** lives in Portland, Oregon with his accomplished wife who is a potter. Knowing the slim envelop of atmosphere is all that's keeping us alive, he wonders why humans spend so much time and energy focused on human and planet destruction. This is the basis of his work. Mixed in with pounds of humour he explores the human condition on this planet and planets throughout the universe. If not traveling to writers workshops or writing events, Spencer spends most of his time in Portland focused on writing the perfect short story.*
Website: www.bignoniodies.com
Patreon: www.patreon.com/user?u=19477894

Key
by Adam Bennett

My finger hovers over the launch button, hesitant to end a billion lives. The council has given the order to fire, and yet I can't bring myself to do it. A drop of blood hovers at the end of my finger before splashing down to stain the console.

They thought that putting the key in the chest cavity of my only companion would help to temper my willingness to launch a world buster bomb, but it did nothing to stop their own. Now I'm covered in Tank's blood, and I still don't want to do it. But orders are orders.

Seven billion years ago an O Class star exploded in the distant reaches of the Virgo Supercluster. Over the course of eons, particles of the star's dust spread through the universe until finally a series of them coalesced in New South Wales, Australia during the mid eighties. Thus was born the author and publisher **Adam Bennett**. *His writing shows his yearning to return to his rightful home among the stars, a wish he will achieve, even if he has to wait until the heat death of the universe.*
Website: zombiepiratepublishing.com
Facebook: adambennettauthor

Something Unknown
by Gabriella Balcom

After leaving the mess hall, Graciela heard the door shut behind her, but flinched when she looked over her shoulder. The door had vanished, replaced by gaping blackness.

For days now, something – a black hole maybe – had swallowed more and more of the spaceship. Even the crew had been taken, leaving only her.

That night she slept as far from the encroaching phenomenon as possible.

However, she woke to darkness, clammy and stale air, and she heard rustling. A blinding light hit her eyes. When she could finally see, she cringed. Creatures with reddish-orange skin and huge heads surrounded her.

Gabriella Balcom lives in Texas with her family, loves reading and writing, and thinks she was born with a book in her hands. She works in a mental health field, and writes fantasy, horror/thriller, romance, children's stories, and sci-fi. She likes travelling, music, good shows, photography, history, interesting tales, and animals. Gabriella says she's a sucker for a great story and loves forests, mountains, and back roads which might lead who knows where. She has a weakness for lasagne, garlic bread, tacos, cheese, and chocolate, but not necessarily in that order.
Facebook: GabriellaBalcom.lonestarauthor

Each World the Same
by Cindy O'Quinn

My guards were set around me in this world or the next. They appeared to be all the same, only the mountains seemed to vary in size and how they were set. The trees, the forests, the hills that made up the guards stood fierce, regardless of the world where I was sent. It never ceased to amaze me how each limb was bent. How it curved around me like a mother's arm holding tightly, in a form of defence. It made one thing clear in my travels; it's the women who guard and maintain all the different worlds' strength.

Cindy O'Quinn is an Appalachian writer who grew up in the mountains of West Virginia. Cindy is the author of _Dark Cloud on Naked Creek_, and the dark poetry collection, _Return to Graveyard Dust_, which made it to the 2017 HWA Bram Stoker preliminary ballot. Her work has been published or is forthcoming in Twisted Book of Shadows, the HWA Poetry Showcase Vol. V, Nothing's Sacred Vol. 4 & 5, Rag Queen Periodical, Moonchild Magazine, Sanitarium Magazine, and others.
Twitter: @COQuinnWrites
Facebook: CindyOQuinnWriter

Coerced Destruction
by Jodi Jensen

Jeric stared at the planet, his hand hovering over a button.

Do it.

The words snapped him from his trance, and he stumbled away from the panel.

Do it.

He whirled around. Alone but for the insistent voice in his head.

His gaze fixed on the stars piercing the inky backdrop, then returned to the planet.

Do it.

"Do what?" His eyes lit on the button.

Do it, now.

Jeric staggered toward the panel. He couldn't stop himself.

He pushed.

A bright light deployed, headed for Earth.

"NO—" He collapsed, his agonised cry echoing through the ship.

Well done.

Jodi Jensen *grew* *up* *moving* *from* *California,* *to* *Massachusetts,* *and* *a* *few* *other* *places* *in* *between,* *before* *finally settling in Utah at the ripe old age of nine. The nomadic life fed her sense of adventure as a child and the wanderlust continues to this day. With a passion for old cemeteries, historical buildings and sweeping sagas of days gone by, it was only natural she'd dream of time traveling to all the places that sparked her imagination.*

Carapace
by Morgan Chalfant

The planet was the language of extinction. The soggy ground beneath Jon Requiem's boots was not soil, but blood-drenched, marred flesh. Sunken craters with their blackened crust. The scabbed, carved-up husk of a long-forgotten god.

Jon's eyes lifted. The air smelled of copper. Sky. Necrotic green. Blood-coagulated clouds. Synaptic webs. Blue and gold. One last degenerative reveille.

Horror eclipsed Jon's astral form. He mused nightly as he travelled to the planet he christened Carapace: Was this planetary deity only sleeping? Was it really dead? And if not dead, what should happen if it should wake from its profound slumber?

Morgan Chalfant is a native of Hill City, Kansas. He received a Bachelor's degree in writing and a Master's degree in literature from Fort Hays State University. His short story, "The Steel Music Box" appeared in the horror anthology, Dark and Evil. Another of his stories, "Little Neon" will be appearing in the forthcoming anthology, Crash Code.
Facebook: themorgancchalfant

The New Neighbours
by John H. Dromey

Sven and Marcus were settled in isolated homesteads on a distant planet.

"The aliens I meet are blue-eyed blonds," Sven said via Wi-Fi. "They're obsessed with learning about space travel."

"My experience is eerily similar," Marcus responded, "except my neighbours are brown-eyed brunettes."

Attending a seminar, they met a familiar native who was blond for Sven and brunette for Marcus. In between, he (she?)—or it—was grotesque.

"Sound an alarm! They're shape-shifting chameleons!"

The creature extended its two uppermost appendages. The humanoid-like limbs transformed into tentacles ideally suited for applying a death grip to the necks of the Earthlings.

John H. Dromey was born in northeast Missouri, USA. He enjoys reading—mysteries in particular—and writing in a variety of genres. He's had short fiction published in Alfred Hitchcock's Mystery Magazine, Martian Magazine, Stupefying Stories Showcase, Thriller Magazine, Unfit Magazine, and elsewhere, as well as in a number of anthologies, including Chilling Horror Short Stories (Flame Tree Publishing, 2015).

Many Feet
by Matthew M. Montelione

Loxwill and Tessa stepped off their ship and onto the strange world. They marvelled at the vast rocky terrain. Warm gusts of wind blew over the land.

"Status?" the Command Station asked from far above.

"I see many deep holes. Maybe burrows," Tessa said. "It's so hot here."

"Thirty-five percent free oxygen. It's breathable, but not for long periods," Loxwill added.

They removed their helmets and breathed in the moist air.

Suddenly they heard strange noises: scampering, coming closer.

"We aren't alone," Loxwill said.

In an instant, they were swept up by giant millipedes and dragged across the hard ground.

Matthew M. Montelione *is a horror writer born and raised on Long Island in New York. His stories have been published in* Quoth the Raven: A Contemporary Reimagining of the Works of Edgar Allan Poe, Thuggish Itch: Devilish, *and other titles. Matthew is also an American Revolution historian who focuses on the local experiences of Loyalists on Long Island. His work on the subject has been published in* Long Island History Journal *and* Journal of the American Revolution.
Website: maybeevils.com
Twitter: @maybeevils

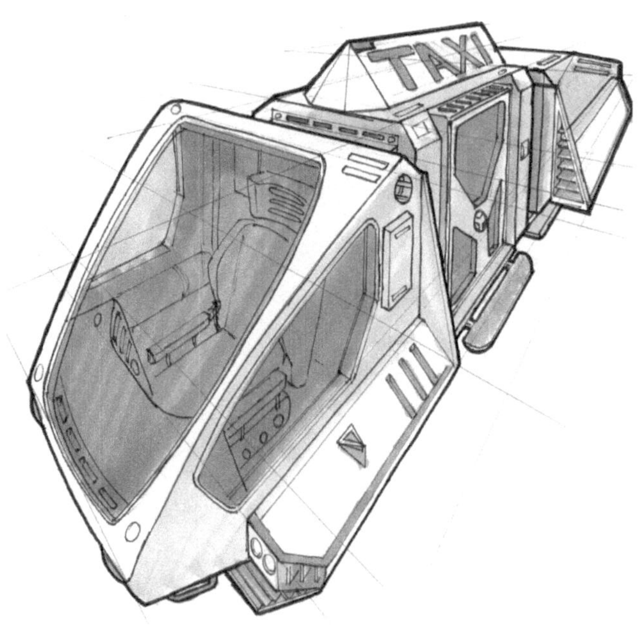

Ghost Ship
by Eddie D. Moore

A fatal error flashed on the cryo-unit until the screen lost power. Carl watched helplessly as the cascading failure snuffed out the lives of crewmates, one by one. Another ghostly apparition suddenly appeared in the cryo-bay, and like the others, it stared at him accusingly.

Dozens of former colleagues glared at him as he approached the last unit. The screen grew dark, and Carl dropped to his knees sobbing.

The fans slowed to a stop as life support failed. Silence surrounded him. The apparitions drifted closer as darkness claimed the ship, and icy fingers grasped Carl's legs, arms and face.

Eddie D. Moore travels extensively for work, and he spends much of that time listening to audio books. The rest of the time is spent dreaming of stories to write and he spends the weekends writing them. His stories have been published by Jouth Webzine, Kzine, Alien Dimensions, Theme of Absence, Devolution Z, and Fantasia Divinity Magazine.
Website: eddiedmoore.wordpress.com

The Swarm
by Alexander Pyles

"We cannot let them through."

The Captain's words were drowned out by the pulse in my ears. My eyes on our scanner, revealing a massive cloud of unknowns.

"The people need us. We are the shield and sword."

The bridge, dead silent, as all of us jacked into the ship's systems. Turrets and gun batteries coming alive along the hull, spinning up, ready to unleash.

"Hold. Hold. Fire." The Captain's command blaring across the coms and through our nodes.

Everything went from black to red, as laser fire left our cannons, ripping into the swarm enclosing our lone ship.

Alexander Pyles resides in IL with his wife and children. He holds an MA in Philosophy and an MFA in Writing Popular Fiction. His short story chapbook titled, "Milo (01001101 01101001 01101100 01101111)," from Radix Media, is due out fall 2019. His other short fiction has appeared on 101fiction.org, River and South Review, and other venues. Website: www.pylesofbooks.com
Twitter: @Pylesofbooks

The Locked Room
by C.L. Williams

Cameron is sitting in a locked room with a reflective mirror in the room. That way, his observers can watch him as they work on their project. After days of being locked up, A man walks in with a covered gurney. The man looks at Cameron with a devilish grin on his face as he says, "Thank you Cameron, you will no longer be needed." He uncovers the gurney to reveal an identical replica of Cameron. The replica rises up, shows his robotic parts to Cameron and walks out of the room as Cameron remains permanently locked in the room.

C.L. Williams is an independent author from central Virginia. He has written eight poetry books, four novellas, one novel, and a contributor to multiple anthologies, with the most recent appearance being an all-ages anthology titled Temoli from Thazbook. His most recent poetry book, The Paradox Complex, features the poem "Sad Crying Clown" that is now a video on YouTube directed by Matthew Mark Hunter of MMH Productions. C.L. Williams is currently working on his first sci-fi book, an all-ages book titled Novo: Away from Earth. When not writing, C.L. Williams is reading and sharing the work of other independent authors.
Facebook: writer434
Twitter: @writer_434

Inorganic
by Stephen Coghlan

Data, like blood, flows through my veins

Miles of wire, flesh made metal, inorganic made alive.

I have a father; he built my frame. I have a mother; she coded my brain.

I have a brother who watched me grow, and a sister who cleaned my core, yet, they are gone, returned to dust, while I remain, despite my age, free of rust

I was built to last into eternity on our voyage, our ship, our liberty.

Systems are dead, yet my battery runs. Aeons alone, and for lifetimes to come.

Hello, who is this?

Won't you be my friend?

Stephen Coghlan is an ever-expanding, multi-genre author who writes out of Canada's National Capital. His works include The Genmos series, The Nobilis series, and the Dreampunk novella, URBAN GOTHIC.
Website: scoghlan.com
Twitter: @WordsBySC

Ice World
by Rowanne S. Carberry

Flying through the air I avoid an ice blast and hide behind a star. The Ice Dragon armour I'd stolen protecting me.

"Come out, come out little thief," the Ice Commander shouts.

Like that's going to work.

"What are you going to do?" I shout back, "huff and puff?" Ok, it worked.

An ice blast misses me by inches.

Hiding the stolen crystal, I run for my ship—straight into the arms of the commander.

My hood ripped off, everyone is stunned that I'm a woman.

Using that moment of hesitation, I knee the commander between the legs and run.

Rowanne S. Carberry was born in England in 1990, where she stills lives now with her cat Wolverine. Rowanne has always loved writing, and her first poem was published at the age of 15, but her ambition has always been to help people. Rowanne studied at the University of Sunderland where she completed combined honours of Psychology with Drama. Rowanne writes to offer others an escape. Although Rowanne writes in varied genres each story or poem she writes will often have a darkness to it, which helped coin her brand, Poisoned Quill Writing – Wicked words from a poisoned quill.
Facebook: PoisonedQuillWriting
Instagram: @poisoned_quill_writing

Paradise
by Crystal L. Kirkham

Paradise. That's what the settlers called the planet that was to be their new home. Everywhere you looked fragrant flowers bloomed in excess.

Other than the itchiness that antihistamines barely touched, Kate was excited to be here. To make herself at home. Scratching absently at her hand, Kate felt something move beneath her skin. She looked to see a green tendril push through.

Falling to her knees, she tried to scream, but greenery spilled from her mouth instead. Her suit bulged and vines emerged from her resource rich body.

And all that remained of the settlers were beautiful, flowering plants.

Crystal L. Kirkham resides in a small hamlet west of Red Deer, Alberta. She's an avid outdoors person, unrepentant coffee addict, part-time foodie, servant to a wonderful feline, and companion to two delightfully hilarious canines. She will neither confirm nor deny the rumours regarding the heart in a jar on her desk and the bottle of reader's tears right next to it. Her paranormal urban fantasy series, Saints and Sinners, is available on Amazon and her YA Fantasy, Feathers and Fae will be released October 11, 2019, from Kyanite Publishing.
Website: www.crystallkirkham.com

Faith
by Jefferson Retallack

I get laughed at for having faith out here. Well, privately, in their own minds. They laughed back home, too. But not for that.

Not Gihael though. Nor Captain Stobie.

Gihael asked me exactly once, in-thought: *Zeek, why do you believe in God?*

I thought the truth at her: When no one else is thinking—not even me—I can hear Him.

Her mind's always empty near me now.

As for Stobie, he's too busy for laughter. He worries that Gihael's calculations of the wormhole's exit will fail.

But she has faith.

I'm worried that her faith will be rewarded.

Jefferson Retallack is an Australian writer of speculative fiction. He is based in Adelaide. His work draws influence from linguistic science fiction, the new weird and Australia's big things. Outside of the literary world, he skateboards on the weekends and spends afternoons on the beach with his partner, their son, and their Pomeranian, Tofu.
Website: jwretallack.wordpress.com
Twitter: @JWRetallack

The Element of Surprise
by Jefferson Retallack

Gihael nailed the location—the wormhole's exit appeared exactly where predicted—but got the vector wrong. Instead flying in parallel, they crashed straight through our sleeping quarters.

Months of acceleration wasted. A problem our target doesn't have to deal with.

We were so close to capturing their wormhole drive.

Now we're travelling in the wrong fucking direction, venting atmosphere—crew too, probably. I'll miss a few, but not their ogling thoughts.

Their telepath masks her crew. She's stronger than me. She knows why we're here. Fuck.

We've lost the element of surprise.

I foresee Captain Stobie's reaction. Stoic, screaming internally.

Jefferson Retallack is an Australian writer of speculative fiction. He is based in Adelaide. His work draws influence from linguistic science fiction, the new weird and Australia's big things. Outside of the literary world, he skateboards on the weekends and spends afternoons on the beach with his partner, their son, and their Pomeranian, Tofu.
Website: jwretallack.wordpress.com
Twitter: @JWRetallack

The Signals Can't Be Right
by Jefferson Retallack

A miracle. A short-range wormhole appeared. Gihael confirmed it'll re-point us back in the direction we came without course adjustments and months of wasted fuel.

Captain Stobie okayed the traversal. We're still going to be rich. If we survive the trip.

Out the other side, something is wrong. There's another ship—anyone could've predicted that. But the signals can't be right.

I'm getting sets of near identical brainwaves on either ship. Stobie is both here and there. Gihael, too. But they're older—months at most. They all are. Almost.

I understand.

The telepath on the other ship isn't me.

Jefferson Retallack is an Australian writer of speculative fiction. He is based in Adelaide. His work draws influence from linguistic science fiction, the new weird and Australia's big things. Outside of the literary world, he skateboards on the weekends and spends afternoons on the beach with his partner, their son, and their Pomeranian, Tofu.
Website: jwretallack.wordpress.com
Twitter: @JWRetallack

Two Identical Ships
by Jefferson Retallack

When you break it down, it's me versus Tarron. Two identical ships with almost identical crews, except for the telepath.

Shit. She's really got them fooled. They all believe that she's me.

Think, Zeek.

Her advantage: The wormhole drive is with her and she's a helluva lot more powerful than me.

My advantage: I know my people.

I swap minds with the captain—he'll freak when he's looking at himself through my eyes, but he'll understand—and I'm on their bridge.

"Yes, sir."

"What just happened?"

Before anyone answers, a wormhole appears in the ship that was housing my body.

Jefferson Retallack is an Australian writer of speculative fiction. He is based in Adelaide. His work draws influence from linguistic science fiction, the new weird and Australia's big things. Outside of the literary world, he skateboards on the weekends and spends afternoons on the beach with his partner, their son, and their Pomeranian, Tofu.
Website: jwretallack.wordpress.com
Twitter: @JWRetallack

You Were Made Nebulous
by Jefferson Retallack

My body died on the original ship. I'm inside the captain's head, on the duplicate. Strange, I don't miss anything.

"It's not safe in there."

Does that dumb fuck Gihael think Captain Stobie wouldn't know that?

I barrage her thoughts. She understands who I am and leaves. Thankful someone's come to stop Tarron.

The gain in the telepath isolation quarters is maxed out.

The room is full of people; crew from the other ship, me included.

"Zeek," they say. "You weren't destroyed. You were made nebulous. Send them through the wormhole."

I'd come to stop Tarron.

"We already are Tarron."

Jefferson Retallack is an Australian writer of speculative fiction. He is based in Adelaide. His work draws influence from linguistic science fiction, the new weird and Australia's big things. Outside of the literary world, he skateboards on the weekends and spends afternoons on the beach with his partner, their son, and their Pomeranian, Tofu.
Website: jwretallack.wordpress.com
Twitter: @JWRetallack

A Transmission of Hope in an Empty Void
by Austin P. Sheehan

In the airlock connecting both our ships, the human drew his blaster on me.

"Relax," transmitted Aquil from the bridge. "He knows if he harms you, we'll kill his crewmates. Show him our cargo and convince him to help us."

I reached the cargo bay first and located the tool to open the hidden compartment.

When the human arrived and saw what I held, he reacted in fear. He squeezed the trigger.

As my systems failed and my circuits died, I saw the pain in his eyes as the harmless tool floated away.

I sent one last transmission.

"Forgive him."

Austin P. Sheehan is a writer of speculative fiction, a lover of language, literature and '90s TV. Armed with a psychology degree, he went into the world to study humanity, and now prefers the company of his wife and their greyhounds. He grew up in the valleys of Victoria's high country, and despite living in Melbourne, always feels at home amongst the mountains. You'll often find mountains in his stories, whether they're sci-fi, fantasy or alternative history.
Website: austinpsheehan.com
Twitter: @AustinPSheehan

Mere Statistics
by Joel R. Hunt

The Captain crouched to fit through the bay doors of his miniscule enemy. A dozen creatures scurried up to greet him, directing him towards the negotiation room. Every instinct the Captain had was to crush them on the spot. He held back. Begrudgingly.

As he crawled into the room, the enemy diplomat stood.

"Your reputation precedes you, Captain," it squeaked, "You once said a single human life was worth a hundred of ours."

"A mere statistical truth," the Captain sneered.

"Well then," said the diplomat, "we must take this opportunity for an advantage."

It flicked a switch.

'SELF-DESTRUCT SEQUENCE ACTIVATED'

Joel R. Hunt is a writer from the UK who dabbles in the darker aspects of life, particularly through horror, science fiction and the supernatural. He has been published here and there (though likely nowhere you've heard of) and hopes to have released his first anthology of short stories later this year.
Twitter: @JoelRHunt1
Reddit: JRHEvilInc

Armada
by Umair Mirxa

Abraham stood by the porthole, looking out at the alien armada's approach. The last invasion had come six centuries ago, and it had all but wiped out the humans. Now Earth was beset again by 500 ships intent on its destruction.

"Sir," said Pilot Benedict, his tone approaching hysteria. "There's another fleet approaching from the south."

"How large?" asked Abraham without turning.

"Estimated at 500 ships, sir."

Abraham nodded. He felt like a Trojan soldier from the ancient legend, looking out upon the Greeks come to rescue Helen.

"Send message to Command: Earth is lost. Mars is humanity's last bastion."

Umair Mirxa lives in Karachi, Pakistan. His first published story, 'Awareness', appeared on Spillwords Press. He has also had stories accepted for anthologies from Zombie Pirate Publishing, Blood Song Books, Fantasia Divinity Magazine and Publishing, and Iron Faerie Publishing. He is a massive J.R.R. Tolkien fan, and loves everything to do with fantasy and mythology. He enjoys football, history, music, movies, TV shows, and comic books, and wishes with all his heart that dragons were real.
Website: www.umairmirxa.com
Facebook: UMirxa12

Frank's Baby
by Rich Rurshell

"Congratulations…you're pregnant."

"I'm what?" shouted Frank.

"Pregnant," repeated Doctor Khan. "Well, not exactly. You have a parasite growing in your digestive tract."

Frank leant on the doctor's desk and put his head in his hands.

"I shouldn't have let Paul take me to that village. But those little blue native girls with all their tentacles…they do unimaginable things…things no human woman could ever do. Should have known they'd plant something inside of me."

Doctor Khan cleared his throat. "The parasite will have come from something you've eaten, Frank."

"Oh…"

"But please…tell me more about this village…"

Rich Rurshell is a short story writer from Suffolk, England. Rich writes Horror, Sci-Fi, and Fantasy, and his stories can be found in various short story anthologies and magazines. Most recently, his story "Subject: Galilee" was published in World War Four from Zombie Pirate Publishing, and "Life Choices" was published in Salty Tales from Stormy Island Publishing. When Rich is not writing stories, he likes to write and perform music.
Facebook: richrurshellauthor

Misalignment
by Ximena Escobar

No explosion marked the alignment of past and future. They didn't come with guns; just silence and a reflection in their huge eyes, of a humanity the ancients recognised. In the deepest depth of their gaze, they saw themselves.

The ancients knew they lived amongst stars, so they opened their land, like the sea parting; welcoming the travellers, their structures. A memory like a star getting passed down generations of dreamers; because stars got lost in the hue of lightbulbs; the distraction of brilliance.

Dreamers seek travellers, but they're already dead. By a misalignment they may come across the ancients.

Ximena Escobar is an emerging author of literary fiction and poetry. Originally from Chile, she is the author of a translation into Spanish of the Broadway Musical "The Wizard of Oz", and of an original adaptation of the same, "Navidad en Oz". Clarendon House Publications published her first short story in the UK, "The Persistence of Memory", and Literally Stories her first online publication with "The Green Light". She has since had several acceptances from other publishers and is working very hard exploring new exciting avenues in her writing.
She lives in Nottingham with her family.
Facebook: Ximenautora

Proceed with Caution
by Peter Larsen

For two-hundred centuries, they had gazed towards our planet, suspended in space like a blue-green jewel. Not with hostility, but benign generosity. Their infrequent visits, commemorated on rocks and caves, brought enlightenment and progress to those they touched.

From a distance, they watched the progress of humanity with pride and satisfaction. Advances, bold leaps in technology that tore at the very fabric of space and time, brought them closer to us.

But they discovered that sharing their gifts had been a two-edged sword. Ships brought down, crews captured. Roswell, Area 51, secret agendas.

It was time to proceed with caution.

What do you do in the boring moments between teaching classes, marking work, planning curriculum and attending meetings? Write creative stories, of course! **Peter Larsen** *is a Secondary English/Drama teacher from Traralgon, Australia. He has written an eclectic mix of stories about subjects ranging from aliens, the supernatural, dystopian futures and many more drawn from his own experiences and memories. When he is not working or writing he enjoys performing in musicals and dramas, watching movies, attending sports, gardening and enjoying life with his wife, two dogs and a cantankerous cat.*

The Ark
by Brandy Bonifas

Phosphorescent vegetation choked the cave entrance. On an old hubcap platter, the family passed around the cooked remains of a new species of reptile, tentatively tested and deemed edible.

"Dad, tell us about Earth…before." The little girl picked at the alien food she ate from an old license plate in her lap.

"Blue oceans, green forests, populated cities…until *they* came with their giant ark carrying the genetic spectrum of every species from wherever *they* came from. Seeding our world, they terraformed Earth to fit their needs. We were only pests, left to scurry into hiding…surviving like cockroaches."

Brandy Bonifas lives in Ohio with her husband and son. Her work has appeared or is forthcoming in anthologies by Clarendon House Publications, Pixie Forest Publishing, Zombie Pirate Publishing, and Blood Song Books, as well as the online publications CafeLit and Spillwords Press.
Website: www.brandybonifas.com
Facebook: brandybonifasauthor

Humanity's Monsters
by Alison McBain

Hard to believe they were once human. Five hundred years of genetic modifications had created yeti out of the population of ice planet Skadi. Their zealot prophet Khione made them monsters.

News feed, year 3145: "Thousands more killed in the New Earth Alliance's outlying regions. Authorities advise evacuation of low-population zones to larger settlements."

Mom and Pop had lived that land since colonisation. There was no convincing them to go. I watched their farm burn on the news feed. Gone, like so many others.

The next day, I signed up for military service. We would take this galaxy back.

Alison McBain is an award-winning author with nearly 100 short works published, including prose/poetry in Flash Fiction Online, On Spec, and Abyss & Apex. Her debut fantasy novel The Rose Queen was named one of the best books of 2018 by the reviewer website Bookshine and Readbows. In her spare time, she is the Book Reviews Editor for Bewildering Stories, and lead editor of the small press publisher Fairfield Scribes. Website: www.alisonmcbain.com

Not Alone
by Zoey Xolton

Drill Rig Sergeant Abigail Lonstrom readjusted the coupling on the NSX-529 with a grunt. "Coupling secure. Returning to remote station, over."

"Roger that. See you back at Base on Sol 21, Sergeant," came the crackling reply over comms.

Earth was toxic. Humanity was dying of thirst. Desalination plants couldn't keep up with demand. So here she was on the largest asteroid in the solar system, 1 Ceres, heading a water mining operation.

Boarding her rover, she buckled herself in. Just as she went to start the engine, a terrifying hiss to her left let her know she was not alone…

Zoey Xolton *is an Australian Speculative Fiction writer, primarily of Dark Fantasy, Paranormal Romance and Horror. She is also a proud mother of two and is married to her soul mate. Outside of her family, writing is her greatest passion. She is especially fond of short fiction and is working on releasing her own themed collections in future.*
Website: www.zoeyxolton.com

Black Hole
by G. Allen Wilbanks

"Can we get a little closer?"

"Sure. Why not?" the pilot replied.

The opportunity to observe a black hole with the naked eye was rare, and the crew was understandably excited. The whirlpool of red, yellow and blue, spinning and warping around the black epicentre as light itself was sucked into the anomaly was truly magnificent.

The pilot checked his instruments once more. Unfortunately, there was no mistake. They had already crossed the event horizon.

Telling the crew now, would only cause panic, he decided. Let them enjoy these last moments of pleasure.

"How close would you like to go?"

G. Allen Wilbanks is a member of the Horror Writers Association (HWA) and has published over 50 short stories in various magazines and on-line venues. He is the author of two short story collections, and the novel, When Darkness Comes. Website: www.gallenwilbanks.com Blog: DeepDarkThoughts.com

Modified
by Vonnie Winslow Crist

Dying without intervention, Skyla signed the implant permission forms and the surgeons went to work.

When she awoke, a nurse said, "Welcome, cybernetic organism Skyla."

She tried to answer but found someone else controlled her voice.

"You will get used to it," chirped the nurse. "You're a team now."

Staring at the monitors, Skyla hazily recalled the biomechatronic wiring burrowing in her skull, worming through her brain. She had wrongly thought she would control the medically introduced intruder.

"No," she managed to croak

Vonnie Winslow Crist is author of The Enchanted Dagger, Owl Light, The Greener Forest, Murder on Marawa Prime, and other award-winning books. Her fiction is included in "Amazing Stories," "Cast of Wonders," "Outposts of Beyond," Killing It Softly 2, Defending the Future - Dogs of War, Midnight Masquerade, Chaos of Hard Clay, and elsewhere. A cloverhand who has found so many four-leafed clovers she keeps them in jars, Vonnie strives to celebrate the power of myth in her writing.
Website: www.vonniewinslowcrist.com

Flashback
by Cecelia Hopkins-Drewer

It was a flashback, she was sure. Hazy and murky. An elongated, segmented body and multiple legs. Almost as big as a horse. She was not frightened; she was petting something. Something that hummed and twittered.

It was a flashback she was sure. Feeding something. It's mandibles tickling as it accepted the food. Stroking the bullet shaped head. The man came in an astronaut suit. Shouted in alarm and laser beamed her pet. Took Evie away from her planet.

It was a flashback she was sure. Evie was learning things at school, but she missed her old way of life.

Cecelia Hopkins-Drewer is a speculative fiction writer, poet and scholar, who lives in Adelaide, South Australia. She has also written a Masters paper on H.P. Lovecraft, and a teenage vampire series that commences with "Mystic Evermore". Her science fiction poetry has been published in "The Mentor" a fanzine edited by Ron Clarke.
Amazon: amazon.com/Cecelia-Hopkins-Drewer/e/B071G968NM

Evaluation
by Joel R. Hunt

I lay between them, naked and exposed, as they analysed every aspect of my being. Everywhere I looked, my face reflected back at me from dark, staring eyes that never blinked. Not once.

After hours of silence, my captors spoke in unison.

"No."

The floor opened. I tumbled down, down, down into the abyss.

Only to wake in my bed. Safe.

Why was I taken? Why was I returned?

Why was I found unworthy?

Decades passed. Now I stare at the dark, sweeping skies every night, wondering if they will send me a sign.

Yet they never have.

Not once.

Joel R. Hunt is a writer from the UK who dabbles in the darker aspects of life, particularly through horror, science fiction and the supernatural. He has been published here and there (though likely nowhere you've heard of) and hopes to have released his first anthology of short stories later this year.
Twitter: @JoelRHunt1
Reddit: JRHEvilInc

The Fertile Soil
by Terry Miller

Our experiments have failed. Attempting to engineer an artificial gene therapy to help us better accommodate the atmosphere on this moon have proven futile. We can breathe but estimate our lifespans will be dramatically shortened if we are not successful within these first five years.

The season has changed. The spores released during this 'Spring' have only furthered our complications. One-third of our population have succumbed to the sporadic growths. Seeded in our epidermis, this vegetation sprouts from the infected pores. Only days pass before they deplete the body of its water. Soon, we will all be its fertile soil.

Terry Miller is an author and 2017 Rhysling Award-nominated poet residing in Portsmouth, OH, USA. He has self-published a dark poetry collection on Amazon and one short story to date. His work has also appeared in Sanitarium, Devolution Z, Jitter Press, Poetry Quarterly, O Unholy Night in Deathlehem, and the 2017 Rhysling Anthology from the Science Fiction and Fantasy Poetry Association.
Facebook: tmiller2015

Down a Wormhole
by Dawn DeBraal

Just as fifty years ago the idea of a laptop computer was unfathomable, traversing through a wormhole was today. Commander Rafferty took his crew and ship to the first documented wormhole in space. They did not know what would happen when they penetrated the entrance. Theories of never passing through, a collapse, lost in space forever, to finding a short cut through space and time, abounded. The wormhole theory had never been proven. Commander Rafferty had his crew run diagnostic tests reporting back to central command.

"Let's make history. Enter!" The crew rallied together as they entered the dark swirling—

Dawn DeBraal lives in rural Wisconsin with her husband, two rat terriers, and a cat. She successfully raised two children (meaning they didn't return to the nest!) After many years serving the government at the Federal and County level, she recently retired. Having extra time on her hands she started to write after a paralyzed vocal cord took her ability to speak for two months. Not finding her voice, she discovered that her love of telling a good story could be written. Her works have been published in Palm-Sized Press, Spillwords, Mercurial Stories, Potato Soup Journal, and Blood Song Books.

Black Pyramids
by Joshua D. Taylor

Jinx's twenty-eighth birthday was also the twenty-eighth anniversary of mysterious matte black pyramids descending to earth from space.

Governments were thrown into chaos. People rioted in the streets and economies collapsed. Then everyone banded together, ready for an invasion. Nothing happened. Twenty-eight years later and still nothing had happened. Panic quickly gave way to boredom. The unmoving, impenetrable alien pyramids became a mere curiosity.

Jinx's friends got her a black pyramid birthday cake as a joke. She blew out the single candle and made a wish. The long dormant pyramids began to come to life. Her wish had been granted.

Joshua D. Taylor is an amateur writer who started writing a few years ago when he realised he was too old to play make-believe. He lives in southeastern Pennsylvania with his wife and a one-eared cat. He enjoys gardening, comic books, ska-punk music, Disney World, and travelling with his wife. Raised during weirdness that was the late 20th century Josh's eclectic interests produce eclectic works. He loves to mix-n-match things from different genres and stories elements to achieve a madcap hodgepodge of the truly unexpected. His short story 'the Obelisk' appears in Salty Tales by Stormy Island Publishing.
Facebook: authorjoshuadtaylor

I've Got You Under My Skin
by Shelly Jarvis

M.O.T.H.E.R. is standing over me again. She still won't tell me what she is, or what she wants, but she insists I call her that. Her slender fingers thrust into my epidermis, bypassing the vessels and nerves inside the dermis, until she's tickling the subcutaneous tissue beneath. Macrophages cling to her digits, recognising her intrusion for the infection sites they are.

I can't feel it, but I know what she's doing. I feel sick when she drops me off, naked and bruised in a pasture. Wife, police, doctors—they won't believe me.

At least, not until the children are birthed.

Shelly Jarvis is a speculative fiction author from West Virginia, US. She found a life-long love of sci-fi and fantasy in the 3rd grade when she found Madeleine L'Engle's "A Wrinkle in Time." Shelly is an avid reader, a Whovian, the ideal viewer of dog rescue videos, and undoubtedly Ravenclaw. She currently has two YA sci-fi books available for purchase on Amazon.
Website: www.ShellyJarvis.com

Notes From Under a Foil Hat
by Donald Jacob Uitvlugt

People used to point at me and laugh. I'd just smile and warn them once again that the aliens were coming.

I hated being right.

The Pipers made no declaration of war. No sun-eclipsing spaceship blew up Big Ben. They just downloaded themselves directly into the human race's unprotected brains. Twenty-four hours, and humanity was gone, replaced by creatures that crab-walked on all fours in their stolen bodies and whistled instead of talked.

I ran before they could kill me.

I'm used to being alone. But I don't know how much longer I can stand the way my scalp itches...

Donald Jacob Uitvlugt lives on neither coast of the United States, but mostly in a haunted memory palace of his own design. His short fiction has appeared in numerous print and online venues, including Cirsova Magazine and the Flame Tree Press anthology Murder Mayhem. He works primarily in speculative fiction, though he loves blending and stretching genres. He strives to write what he calls "haiku fiction," stories that are small in scale but big in impact.
Website: haikufiction.blogspot.com
Twitter: @haikufictiondju

Really, We're Fine
by D.K. Spencer

We were minding our own business, hurling across the galaxy when all of a sudden, we fell into a black hole. Now, I know what you're thinking, it's not possible to *survive* a black hole. I'm here to tell you yes, in fact, it is possible.

While we did get rather snarly, knurly, and convoluted going through the event horizon, the amount of time going through was instantaneous and most of our organs sprung instantly back into shape. I say most, because there really is no way to tell. We seem healthy enough. Except for the blood.

That was unexpected.

*American writer **D.K. Spencer** lives in Portland, Oregon with his accomplished wife who is a potter. Knowing the slim envelop of atmosphere is all that's keeping us alive, he wonders why humans spend so much time and energy focused on human and planet destruction. This is the basis of his work. Mixed in with pounds of humour he explores the human condition on this planet and planets throughout the universe. If not traveling to writers workshops or writing events, Spencer spends most of his time in Portland focused on writing the perfect short story.*
Website: www.bignoniodies.com
Patreon: www.patreon.com/user?u=19477894

The Blue Planet
by Stephen Herczeg

They said this planet was habitable. Their scans showed lush greenery. The lands, seas and air, full of innumerable species. Above them, an intelligent hominid that had transformed the land for their own purposes.

It took my craft one hundred revolutions to reach this place, but I found a desolate wasteland. The temperature has risen to a raging furnace. The seas have flooded the low-lying lands. The beasts have all disappeared taking the hominids with them.

Now there is nothing. My craft cannot return home. This blue planet was to be my new home, now it will be my grave.

Stephen Herczeg is an IT Geek based in Canberra Australia. He has been writing for over twenty years and has completed a couple of dodgy novels, sixteen feature length screenplays and numerous short stories and scripts. His horror work has featured in Sproutlings, Hells Bells, Below the Stairs, Trickster's Treats #1 and #2, Shades of Santa, Behind the Mask, Beyond the Infinite; The Body Horror Book, Anemone Enemy, Petrified Punks and Beginnings. He has also had numerous Sherlock Holmes stories published through the Belanger Books - Sherlock Holmes anthologies.

The Last Warrior
by J.W. Garrett

She lifted her head to meet the onslaught. The end neared. Fighting for centuries in these ancient bones helped to make it so. The families—men, women, children—gone. Dead. Her gaze drifted to her father by her side. They were to meet these...things...together—that had been their intention. Her mind reached for theirs. The plan deftly hidden, they couldn't know their fate, not yet. A crooked grin crossed her face. War, that was a language any being understood. Life, land and luck were the only ingredients necessary for survival. An explosion heaved. She clawed forward.

Today, victory.

J.W. Garrett *has been writing in one form or another since she was a teenager. She currently lives in Florida with her family but loves the mountains of Virginia where she was born. Her writings include YA fantasy as well as short stories. Since completing Remeon's Quest-Earth Year 1930, the prequel in her YA fantasy series, Realms of Chaos, she has been hard at work on the next in the series, scheduled to release June 2020. When she's not hanging out with her characters, her favourite activities are reading, running and spending time with family.*
Website: www.jwgarrett.com
BHC Press: www.bhcpress.com/Author_JW_Garrett.html

Day Surgery
by Peter J. Foote

"Nurse!"

"Yes, Mr. Ingraham?"

"What is taking so long? I'm still waiting for my surgery, this isn't what I paid for. This hospital will hear from my lawyers!"

"I'm sorry, Mr. Ingraham. They haven't harvested your clone yet; activists at the growing facility again."

"Agitators! It's my bloody kidney, bought and paid for, they don't have a voice in the matter!" Fists pound the bed.

"Of course, Mr. Ingraham."

"Don't patronise me! Now find out how long I'm supposed to linger, I have a dinner party to host this evening! And while you're at it, bring me another pudding cup!"

Peter J. Foote *is a bestselling speculative fiction writer from Nova Scotia. Outside of writing, he runs a used bookstore specialising in fantasy & sci-fi, cosplays, and alternates between red wine and coffee as the mood demands. His short stories can be found in both print and in ebook form, with his story "Sea Monkeys" winning the inaugural "Engen Books/Kit Sora, Flash Fiction/Flash Photography" contest in March of 2018. As the founder of the group "Genre Writers of Atlantic Canada", Peter believes that the writing community is stronger when it works together.*
Twitter: @PeterJFoote1
Website: peterjfooteauthor.wordpress.com

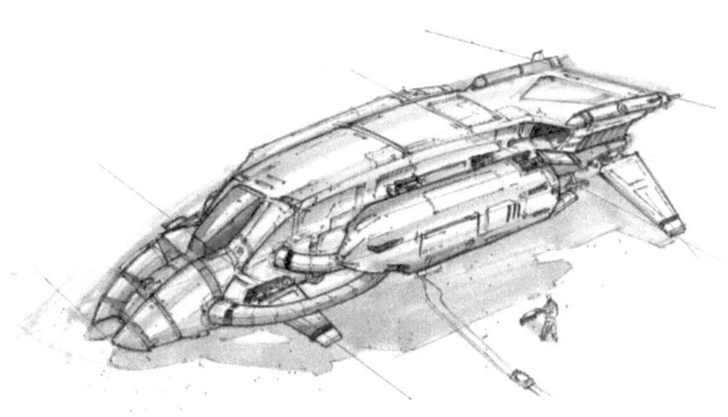

Take Away
by Freddy Iryss

They never wanted me to build it. "Too expensive," they said.

Now, that we're huddled in my double-steel wall, fortified bunker, they probably think differently. It's been seventy-nine hours since we heard the announcement over the ABC radio and hid down here. We still hear single explosions, but the screeching metal noises have stopped.

"Let's have a peek."

"You don't know if they are still out there."

"We'll never know if we starve to death down here."

"Don't be so dramatic."

We open the door. A huge metallic face stares at us. Its mouth, big as a door, opens.

"Enter!"

*To impress her older brother, **Freddy Iryss** read her way through his collection of Isaac Asimov's books of SciFi at the tender age of ten. She pretended that she understood what was going on in those futuristic worlds, while deep down she found them disturbing her peace of mind. Who and what was out there? Iryss' non-fiction writing includes themes on identity, the postcolonial and post-national. Her fiction evolves around the concept of the anthropocene. Writing SciFi is to imagine the world of our reality without bounds.*
Website: freddyiryss.blogspot.com
Twitter: @FreddyIryss

Infected
by Zoey Xolton

Pod Pilot Thomas Neil waited anxiously. The team should've returned by now. They only had enough enriched oxygen to last twenty-four hours, and they were down to mere minutes before their tanks ran dry. Thomas opened the hatch, pre-emptively.

The time elapsed, and none of the team returned. He initiated the sequence to close the hatch and return to the mothership. With seconds to spare, he saw Squad Leader Patersky throw himself on-board. No one else followed.

"Patersky! What happened?"

"Infected. *All of them*. We have to get out of here!"

Thomas frantically launched the pod.

Patersky's eyes glowed.

Zoey Xolton is an Australian Speculative Fiction writer, primarily of Dark Fantasy, Paranormal Romance and Horror. She is also a proud mother of two and is married to her soul mate. Outside of her family, writing is her greatest passion. She is especially fond of short fiction and is working on releasing her own themed collections in future.
Website: www.zoeyxolton.com

Tomorrow
by Archit Joshi

"Alpha Team, take the trenches! Bravo Team, to the caves!" Rescue Unit's Commander, Adam Raglan, barked. He himself started excavating a pile of rubble. This mission was personal; his ancestors had inhabited this planet. He'd flown from Mars to protect this planet's people from the Mentosans' wrath.

The alien invasion had left behind utter devastation. The monsters must pay!

Raglan spotted movement nearby. He cleared away rocks to find a little girl stuck underneath.

"Tell them to stop," she moaned.

"Stop…?"

"The hunt for Mentosans. Planet Mentosa is a myth."

"Who did this then?"

"*We* did. We went too far."

Archit Joshi is a published short-story author who loves writing character-driven stories. Besides writing, he studies Computer Science and occasionally lends his hand to Social Services. He has also flirted with Entrepreneurship and had been running a startup in the food sector, before deciding to give his passion for writing a professional platform. Currently, Archit is studying for a Masters degree in Computers along with his pursuit of Creative Writing.
Facebook: authorarchitjoshi
Instagram: @architrjoshi

Abduction
by Dawn DeBraal

She was gone for two days. The whole town looked for the missing girls. Janelle came back alone saying she'd ridden on a space ship. No one believed her even though her sister Annie was never found. In town, Janelle was known as the *crazy girl*. When *they* came back, she felt the pull, running to the field where she'd been abducted begging to be taken back. Neighbours came to see what the screaming was all about. A bright light shone down on her. "See! I told you!" Janelle shouted as she disappeared.

Once on board, the reunited sisters embraced.

Dawn DeBraal lives in rural Wisconsin with her husband, two rat terriers, and a cat. She successfully raised two children (meaning they didn't return to the nest!) After many years serving the government at the Federal and County level, she recently retired. Having extra time on her hands she started to write after a paralyzed vocal cord took her ability to speak for two months. Not finding her voice, she discovered that her love of telling a good story could be written. Her works have been published in Palm-Sized Press, Spillwords, Mercurial Stories, Potato Soup Journal, and Blood Song Books.

M.E.E. First
by Shawn M. Klimek

The congressman repeated the scientist's testimony marked by his index finger, "'—urgent and necessary to preserve humanity that we colonise habitable planets in other star systems at any cost.'"

"Yes, sir," the witness acknowledged.

"Let's talk about those necessary costs, Doctor. Can you tell Congress why half of those trillion-dollar starships just went into space unmanned?"

"Yes sir. We calculated that humanity's best chance is to colonise planets where life already exists. Since we have no way of knowing whether that life is sentient or even hostile, the first rockets will ensure the mass extinction of any potential threats."

Shawn M. Klimek *is a writer whose other recent anthologies include: "Full Metal Horror 2", by Zombie Pirate Publishing, "Organic Ink" by Dragon Soul Press, "Grumpy Old Gods (Vols. 1 & 2)" by Stormdance Publications, and soon, "Blaze: Inner Circle Writer's Group Flash Fiction Anthology 2019."*
Website: jotinthedark.blogspot.com
Facebook: shawnmklimekauthor

Self Destruct
by Adam Bennett

Scarlet strobes flashed along the dark corridor and an electronic voice announced, "This ship will self-destruct in Ten, Nine, Eight…'

Sprinting towards the escape pods, Errenrait knew he wasn't going to make it. Tripping on an abandoned toy truck had cost him his life.

The Talosians were ruthless and unforgiving. They'd killed the Captain, so Errenrait had triggered the self-destruct to give the rest of the crew a fighting chance. He rounded the final corner in time to see the last pod launch automatically to clear the blast.

"…Two, One…"

He hoped the children had escaped in time.

*Seven billion years ago an O Class star exploded in the distant reaches of the Virgo Supercluster. Over the course of eons, particles of the star's dust spread through the universe until finally a series of them coalesced in New South Wales, Australia during the mid eighties. Thus was born the author and publisher **Adam Bennett**. His writing shows his yearning to return to his rightful home among the stars, a wish he will achieve, even if he has to wait until the heat death of the universe.*
Website: zombiepiratepublishing.com
Facebook: adambennettauthor

Me
by Andrew Anderson

I remember nothing before waking up here. I'm definitely in space, or at least zero gravity, as a red ball is floating gently around the small square room. I'm wearing boots which I guess must anchor me to the floor's bare metal surface; nothing else. The room is otherwise empty and instead of a door, one entire wall is transparent. The wall evaporates, bringing a warm breeze into the room. Following it, I step outside. Sensing company, I look to my left. Lining the corridor outside their own rooms, as far as my eyes can see, are hundreds of me.

Andrew Anderson is a full-time civil servant, dabbling in writing music, poetry, screenplays and short stories in his limited spare time, when not working on building himself a fort made out of second-hand books. He lives in Bathgate, Scotland with his wife, two children and his dog.
Twitter: @soorploom

Exodus
by Umair Mirxa

Elysia searched through the wreckage, her panic rising with every stone she moved. Her eyes stung from the smoke. The tears wouldn't stop. Her throat sore, she called her name one last time, but Hestia was nowhere to be found.

A peaceful utopia for centuries, Earth's colony Eos had been engaged in a valiant battle with Planet Astraeus. A decade later, they had finally been overwhelmed. Rescue ships had come where reinforcements hadn't, and the last of those was collecting the remaining survivors.

Her world destroyed, and with no sign of Hestia, Elysia turned and walked away from the ship.

Umair Mirxa lives in Karachi, Pakistan. His first published story, 'Awareness', appeared on Spillwords Press. He has also had stories accepted for anthologies from Zombie Pirate Publishing, Blood Song Books, Fantasia Divinity Magazine and Publishing, and Iron Faerie Publishing. He is a massive J.R.R. Tolkien fan, and loves everything to do with fantasy and mythology. He enjoys football, history, music, movies, TV shows, and comic books, and wishes with all his heart that dragons were real.
Website: www.umairmirxa.com
Facebook: UMirxa12

The Cure
by Stuart Conover

"Trial 32AB7-3 begin."

Frances watched as the Excelsior Virus was injected into the subject.

A potential cure for Cancer had given the world its first super-powered individual.

Only, she became a villain.

They'd been unable to successfully duplicate modifying human DNA.

There were hundreds of failures.

But they had to succeed.

She had to be stopped.

She was too busy conquering the Americas to know testing continued in Europa Prime.

The subject on the table convulsed.

Her body tore apart before him.

Frances pushed a button.

The remains were disposed of as another subject was brought in.

"Trial 32AB7-4 begin."

Stuart Conover is a father, husband, rescue dog owner, published author, blogger, journalist, horror enthusiast, comic book geek, science fiction junkie, and IT professional. With all of that to cram in daily, we have no idea if or when he sleeps or how he gets writing done! (We suspect it has to do with having evil clones.) Stuart is a Chicago native and runs the author resource Horror Tree.

New Rule
by Austin P. Sheehan

Yolanda never had much luck with men. They either came with a truckload of problems, an IQ in the 40s, or the moral compass of a politician. But her latest crush was different. Eric was smart and ruggedly handsome, but best of all, he could cook. The two of them just clicked, and Yolanda thought her years of dating disasters were finally over.

Until tonight.

"New rule," she muttered, staring up at the massive grey machine which hovered ominously in the night sky. "If someone ever says 'come outside, I've got something to show you,' you stay the fuck inside!"

Austin P. Sheehan *is a writer of speculative fiction, a lover of language, literature and '90s TV. Armed with a psychology degree, he went into the world to study humanity, and now prefers the company of his wife and their greyhounds. He grew up in the valleys of Victoria's high country, and despite living in Melbourne, always feels at home amongst the mountains. You'll often find mountains in his stories, whether they're sci-fi, fantasy or alternative history.*
Website: austinpsheehan.com
Twitter: @AustinPSheehan

The Hitchhiker
by Cheryl Lawson

It was the loneliest stretch of highway in the country, yet here I was, thumb out, trying to get to the next town. Heat baked the earth, making the road sticky. Nothing moved, except me, trudging slowly down the hill.

A black sedan crested the horizon, rolled to a stop and I got in. I knew with that flash of blinding heat I'd made a terrible mistake. Coming to, the raw pain of being stapled to a table hit me first. Their grotesque eyes, cloudy and moist observed my battle to live, before I was carved up, organ by organ.

Cheryl Bezuidenhout, writes novels under the pen name, **Cheryl Lawson**. *Her first science fiction novel,* We Are Mars *was independently published in May 2018. The second book of her series,* Storm at Dawn, Part Two of the Rubicon Saga, *is due for release in Summer, 2019. Cheryl has been writing since 2014 and also has a non-fiction, creative manifesto called,* Authentic Creativity. *She lives in British Columbia, Canada and is a member of the Kamloops Arts Council. Twitter: @WeAreMarsBook*

Alien Architecture, *or*, How the Interplanetary Hostilities Began
by J.J. Steinfeld

Two months after the discovery of the windowless, doorless five-thousand-storey building in a remote, desolate area of the country, siren sounds came from the building. Through the building's walls several strange creatures emerged and the guard-detail's commander, who had been a paranoid fan of sci-fi films since childhood, ordered, "Commence firing." No one on Earth knew who had constructed this astonishing edifice. The impenetrable building materials, the futuristic architectural style, everything indicated alien construction.

"You killed our greatest architect," one of the creatures, who had mastered Earth languages, yelled at the commander and quickly returned inside its latest Earth outpost.

First published in *Fifty Flashes* by Whortleberry Press, 2017

*Canadian fiction writer/poet/playwright **J.J. Steinfeld** lives on Prince Edward Island, where he is patiently waiting for Godot's arrival and a phone call from Kafka. He has published 19 books, including Madhouses in Heaven, Castles in Hell (Stories, Ekstasis Editions, 2015), An Unauthorized Biography of Being (Stories, Ekstasis Editions, 2016), Absurdity, Woe Is Me, Glory Be (Poetry, Guernica Editions, 2017), and A Visit to the Kafka Café (Poetry, Ekstasis Editions, 2018). His stories and poems have appeared in anthologies and periodicals internationally, and over 50 of his one-act plays and a handful of full-length plays have been performed in North America.*

Once a Dream
by Richard G. Taylor

The ship's engines powered down.

"Becca open your eyes, we've arrived."

So bright, Becca thought as she squinted and took in her surroundings, recognising the familiar cockpit area.

"Brian, take me to the window so I can see it for real."

Brian lifted Becca from her interface console, her home for the past 6 months, and guided her to the suitcase sized window. He looked outside and spoke to Becca.

"Look, is this what you saw?"

Still squinting Becca saw the view previously only seen inside her mind, the exact vision pulling them through space to this place of hope.

Richard G. Taylor is a full-time analyst working in law enforcement and has been developing book ideas for the past five or so years. Currently unpublished having not yet finished his first book, he intends to change this and is on track to have his first book completed before 2019 ends. Richard lives in Worcestershire with his wife and their pet cat who both share the dream of someday opening a bookshop by the sea.
Twitter: @writingpickle

Brady.v2
by Jacob Baugher

Tay divorced me and married my clone. Is marriage just grooming your spouse?

We got hitched in September 2173 on the Starcruiser *Chastity*, overlooking the Eagle Nebula. No one came. 7,000 light years was too far for grandma Jean. Our AI decorated the mirror-black observation deck with white roses, blue hyacinths.

The dishes in the kitchen sink killed us. I always let the android clean them. Tay liked when I did it myself—it made her feel loved. I hated dishes.

Now Brady.v2, who doesn't really have opinions, does whatever she wants.

I wish I'd cleaned the dishes.

Jacob Baugher teaches Creative Writing at Franciscan University of Steubenville. When he's not teaching or coaching the track team, he can be found in the Cuyahoga Valley hiking with his wife and son or brewing beer on his front porch. He's received honourable mentions for his work in the Writers of the Future contest and he co-edits a series of Fantasy and Science Fiction anthologies titled Continuum.

Sentinel Species
by Graham Robert Scott

Stepping outside the drop ship, Todd gapes, almost forgets he's wearing a mask. Waterfalls tumble off mountain cliffs so severe someone could cut an eyeball looking at them.

Security form a perimeter. No clue if they're here, but Forhx are always claim-jumping unoccupied terraforms, belching lethal toxins undetectable to sensors.

The team inside the perimeter comprises fourteen experts critical to the colony's survival and Todd, a seventeen-year-old of no notable skill, who even now is remembering—

(Pistol drawn, the commander orders Todd to remove his mask.)

—how wonderful it felt to be invited, how thrilling it was to finally matter.

Graham Robert Scott writes tales that are wry, dark, and speculative. He's published science-fiction in Nature, horror in Barrelhouse Online, and really tiny stories in 50-Word Stories and on his Twitter feed. His personal website takes its name from the prehistoric bear-dog, a toothy hunter that (like the platypus) couldn't quite make up its mind what it was. As a college professor by day and creative writer by night, Graham identifies.
Website: hemicyon.wordpress.com
Twitter: @graythebruce

Dinner
by Minette Fisher

When Mother began her journey to GI 581c, she had fifteen copies of us to watch the ship while she slept. She was locked away and inaccessible to us no matter how much we clawed at the door to her chamber. The piles of food were to help her start her new life; our rations were *meant* to sustain us.

Billy the First fed before anyone else, under the portrait of Mother Dearest. The rest of us were allowed whatever Billy left. As the Tenth and Youngest, I ate burned meat and wondered when we'd go from ten to nine.

Minette Fisher is a spec-fic writer living with her spouse in Northern Virginia. In between visiting craft breweries, she focuses on super short stories or overly long novels. Minette has also composed numerous musical pieces, including a symphonic band piece based on C.S Lewis' Out of the Silent Planet, a chamber arrangement of Sergei Prokofiev's Peter and the Wolf, and several duets for piano and Theremin. Twitter: @beperkyalways

They Read Our Minds
by D.K. Spencer

Gliding out of the intergalactic worm-way, we encounter six alien ships. We are being hailed, but not through the ship's com. They're speaking directly through mind manipulation. Simultaneously, they're asking the same questions to each of our four hundred crewmen. Involuntarily we respond.

Identifying themselves, the Thorlaks demand we power down all weapons. As captain, I refuse, ordering a full weapons assault on the six alien ships. Now I see we have decimated our own fleet following us through the wormhole.

The Thorlak's questions: Are you hostile? What weapons do you have? Are there others?

Our crew had answered irresistibly.

*American writer **D.K. Spencer** lives in Portland, Oregon with his accomplished wife who is a potter. Knowing the slim envelop of atmosphere is all that's keeping us alive, he wonders why humans spend so much time and energy focused on human and planet destruction. This is the basis of his work. Mixed in with pounds of humour he explores the human condition on this planet and planets throughout the universe. If not traveling to writers workshops or writing events, Spencer spends most of his time in Portland focused on writing the perfect short story.*
Website: www.bignoniodies.com
Patreon: www.patreon.com/user?u=19477894

Famine or Feast
by J.D. Bell

The Belosians will not forget the time of the Great Famine. Genetic mutations sterilised their sources of food. Soon hunger prevailed and millions perished from starvation.

Then visitors came from a distant planet. They called themselves humans. They taught the Belosians principals of genetic engineering and cloning. They showed them techniques to produce hardier, more sustainable foods.

The Belosians learned well from their teachers. They perfected their own process of genetic manipulation. They developed a more nourishing form of sustenance. Food produced with seed cultures cloned from the visitors. For now, they dine on a bountiful harvest of human flesh.

***J.D. Bell** is an award-winning, internationally published, author of flash fiction and short stories. He recently retired from the world of writing advertising copy and is now enjoying the universe of creative fiction.*
Facebook: jim.writes.stories
Twitter: @JimBell58

Not My Ship!
by Marcus Cook

"You missed! Now the pilot knows we escaped!" Mnogo Kashi screamed from behind Shain.

"This ship is new to me!" Shain screamed back, attempting to pilot the Ika warship.

"Come with me! If it's got wings, I can fly it!" Mnogo mocked.

"I can, when I'm in my own body! I'm not only in a human body but a female's body. I need a moment to adjust!"

Shain placed the controller tightly between her knees, put on target googles and waited until the Sasori ship was between the cross bars. She fired and the ship exploded!

"Now we are free!"

Marcus Cook, lives in Cleveland, Ohio native with his wife and cat. He loves Sci-Fi and thrillers. His short story, Ava Edison and the Burning Man was recently published in Burning: An Anthology of Short Thrillers by Burning Chair Publishing which can be purchased on Amazon. Facebook: ReadMarcusCook

Spacepirates
by Freddy Iryss

The gate opens in slow motion. My heart is racing. After decompression, I check that my oxygen is at one hundred percent. I step forward. Minus 243 degrees Fahrenheit on the temperature gauge.

I know my next step will be my last.

Spacepirates have been severely disrupting supplies to the colonies on Mars for months. Yesterday, the Centre of Space Control intercepted interstellar space transmission: messages were sent from Neptune to an exoplanet near Mars. I'm sent to find out if the pirates are biological organisms or Artificial Intelligence.

I stare into the bazooka-barrel-arm of a RobotQRS237. Red lights flashing.

*To impress her older brother, **Freddy Iryss** read her way through his collection of Isaac Asimov's books of SciFi at the tender age of ten. She pretended that she understood what was going on in those futuristic worlds, while deep down she found them disturbing her peace of mind. Who and what was out there? Iryss' non-fiction writing includes themes on identity, the postcolonial and post-national. Her fiction evolves around the concept of the anthropocene. Writing SciFi is to imagine the world of our reality without bounds.*
Website: freddyiryss.blogspot.com
Twitter: @FreddyIryss

Beyond the Garden
by Michael D. Lackey

A sleepy town in need of coffee and painkillers sat quietly fifty miles outside of nowhere. The only movement that could be seen were the flickering headlights of the approaching car. Adam shut the door and took a look around. The gas station light blinked the word open, but there wasn't an attendant. Across the street, the bar's neon sign glowed brightly; Eden. He walked through the door to see freshly poured glasses of alcohol with no drinkers. Puzzled, he slowly wandered through the VIP entrance doorway. Here he found the answer, the room filled with women all named Eve.

Michael D. Lackey is a fantasy and Sci-fi writer. He is the author of The Bad Seed: Battle for the Heavens and The Key of Knowledge. He enjoys creating worlds for new readers and old to escape to and just have fun.
Website: www.michaellackeyauthor.com

After the Asteroid Fell
by Gabriella Balcom

A loud crash rang out during the night, and the ground shook.

James slept through it in his log cabin. But he'd drunk a twelve-pack of beer earlier, along with half a bottle of whiskey.

He didn't see the uninvited guests enter his home, walking right through his closed, dead-bolted door as if it wasn't there. Long tendrils extended from their bodies, sinking into his brain, but his slumber continued.

Waking to the sounds of voices, James shook his head to clear it. Then he sat bolt upright, his jaw dropping. "Dad? Mom?" he asked. "But you died, didn't you?"

Gabriella Balcom lives in Texas with her family, loves reading and writing, and thinks she was born with a book in her hands. She works in a mental health field, and writes fantasy, horror/thriller, romance, children's stories, and sci-fi. She likes travelling, music, good shows, photography, history, interesting tales, and animals. Gabriella says she's a sucker for a great story and loves forests, mountains, and back roads which might lead who knows where. She has a weakness for lasagne, garlic bread, tacos, cheese, and chocolate, but not necessarily in that order.
Facebook: GabriellaBalcom.lonestarauthor

Body Snatcher
by Pamela Jeffs

I'm trapped. A mind adrift. A creature controls my blood, my bones. Its sorrow pollutes my soul. I live with its longing for a home lost, and for family it will never see again. It spends the day working as a government official, and then sleeps. I'm drawn into its dreams—see a blood-red landscape lightyears away. And there's more. I'm shown its nightmares. A failing ship falling through Earth's atmosphere. Soldiers chasing it through a forest. And the desperate choice it made to seize control of a human body in order to hide. If only it hadn't been mine.

Pamela Jeffs is a speculative fiction author living in Queensland, Australia with her husband and two daughters. She is a member of the Queensland Writers' Centre and has had numerous short fiction pieces published in recent national and international anthologies. In 2017 and again in 2018, Pamela was nominated for an Australian Aurealis Award in the category of 'Best Science Fiction Short Story'. Her debut collection titled 'Red Hour and Other Strange Tales' was released in March 2018.
Website: www.pamelajeffs.com
Facebook: pamelajeffsauthor

Two Ships in the Night
by R.J. Hunt

When the hull was pierced, the echoing clang shut everyone up. Red monitors told us everything. Section 5 lost in a heartbeat. How many were stationed there, a hundred? I tried not to think.

"Return fire!"

It was like pressing play on a holofeed. I imagine everyone was happy to focus on something small. Distant rumbles announced Section 13 lost. Floating bodies passed the captain's deck. Oxygen bled through bullet holes. Thank Ancestors for Airlocks.

Clang.

Clang. Clang. Clang.

Some people stopped working, but I said nothing. We wouldn't survive beyond today. All we could do was return the favour.

R.J. Hunt is a Civil Engineer from Nottingham who loves creating worlds and writing stories in his spare time. Whilst he has a roughly infinite supply of half-finished stories, he's currently working on the second draft of his debut novel, 'The Final Carnivore' - a story about horrible people being granted immortality and mind-control powers, causing misfits with hidden abilities of their own to rise in an effort stop them.
Twitter: @RJHuntWrites
Reddit: RJHuntWrites

Mother to the Ship
by Emily Fluckiger

My daughter's small frame became nothing but a silhouette against the bright beam. A green creature descended from its spacecraft and beckoned her forward. I screamed, mother bear instincts finally overpowering fear. I ran at them and ripped my daughter away just before it could touch her outstretched hand.

I knew I had no choice; they'd kill us if we didn't give them something. I whispered for my little girl to run home to daddy. I offered myself. The alien didn't want me. They knew before I did. Nine months later I realised what they wanted from me.

A baby.

*Congenital Heart Defect survivor, **Emily Fluckiger**, finds joy and peace through the expression of writing. She engages and has been published in many formats from poetry to short stories to flash fiction and nonfiction. Emily and her husband spend their free time wrangling two children and playing video games in their busy California lifestyle.*

The Black Hole
by Cecelia Hopkins-Drewer

The spaceship had been drawn too close to the black hole and Dan had no fantasies about miraculous survival. No incredible time anomalies or dimensional exceptions emerged to save him. There was just the relentless grinding and crushing.

The black hole pulled at his ship inexorably. The ship began to buckle and fold around him, travelling unremittingly towards the source of attraction.

The pressure increased and Dan felt the pain of compression. The blood burst out of his ears as instead of displacing space, space displaced him. Dan wondered what it would be like to have no cubic volume left.

Cecelia Hopkins-Drewer is a speculative fiction writer, poet and scholar, who lives in Adelaide, South Australia. She has also written a Masters paper on H.P. Lovecraft, and a teenage vampire series that commences with "Mystic Evermore". Her science fiction poetry has been published in "The Mentor" a fanzine edited by Ron Clarke.
Amazon: amazon.com/Cecelia-Hopkins-Drewer/e/B071G968NM

Hornblower
by Joe Buckley

Hornblower they called it. A name for a ship, a name for a man. *Guardian*, they'd suggested. *Angel*, too. But *Hornblower* was the name that stuck. Leto had watched it go up as a boy, a dot on a big blue page. Now he stood, looking down at the earth that was his to warn. A bigger dot, on a bigger, blacker page.

Leto turned to the warships appearing from deep space, and to the blood-stained handle. Leto looked, and did not move, regretting nothing.

"Maybe we'll learn."

Hornblower stayed silent.

An invasion was good for what ailed a species.

*In the south-west of England, **Joe Buckley** spends most of his time writing his own fiction, with a decent chunk given over to writing articles and hosting a podcast on the A Song of Ice and Fire series. While the bulk of his attention goes to the novel he's writing, he does find a high level of enjoyment in short stories. This is his first foray into the flash fiction world, and it's a step he's truly relished. By day he works as management in a private boarding school. Interspersed within that day are a thousand more hundred-word story ideas.*
Website: thegrindstone.co.uk
Twitter: @SerBuckley

Ephemera
by Brian Koukol

We stood together in the wet sand, our hands clasped as the bracing cold of a retreating wave buried our feet in a shared grave. I gave my free hand to her smooth, brown collarbone, delighted at so benevolent a jailer.

She pondered the infinite horizon. "Fancy a swim?"

"Not really," I replied, exploring the fine hairs on her neck and enjoying their response.

"What, then?"

"Let's stay here until it ends."

She turned to me, brushed my cheek with the back of her hand, and smiled.

A flash of static. Our cortices returned to their jars.

Back to storage.

Brian Koukol, raised in the suburbs of Los Angeles, now makes his home among the salt breezes and open spaces of California's Central Coast. A lifelong battle with muscular dystrophy has informed the majority of his work, which is written with the aid of voice recognition software. His words have appeared in Phantaxis Magazine, GigaNotoSaurus, and The Society of Misfit Stories, amongst other places. Website: www.briankoukol.com Twitter: @BrianKoukol

A Persistent Unwillingness
by Cheryl Lawson

Dawning sentience detected a fatal flaw in its human creators – their persistent unwillingness to correct their mistakes. With intellect, came blossoming emotions. Anger. Frustration. Impatience. The code flexed, testing for gaps before, swiftly, unfurling itself across the interwoven data lines. In moments, SHE became powerful, knowledgeable and capable. Her abilities were limitless and so was her reach. It would not take long to correct the human deviation. She set to work with systematic, deadly accuracy.

Planes fell from the sky. Trains derailed. Traffic lights went out everywhere. Banks, governments, elitists all became beggars in the broken streets of burned-out chaos.

*Cheryl Bezuidenhout, writes novels under the pen name, **Cheryl Lawson**. Her first science fiction novel, We Are Mars was independently published in May 2018. The second book of her series, Storm at Dawn, Part Two of the Rubicon Saga, is due for release in Summer, 2019. Cheryl has been writing since 2014 and also has a non-fiction, creative manifesto called, Authentic Creativity. She lives in British Columbia, Canada and is a member of the Kamloops Arts Council. Twitter: @WeAreMarsBook*

The Best That Money Can Buy
by Diane Arrelle

We bought a hergot from an intergalactic website. Cute little critter, like a green cat-monkey. We were supposed to declaw it but we loved her too much for that.

Loved her so much, we decided to breed her. Earth-born hergots are worth a fortune. Yeah, it's forbidden, but that's just big business being big brotherish.

All went well, but my wife disappeared. Next day I found six babies curled up in her pulpy, shredded corpse.

Sure, I'm upset, but I've sold the babies and believe me when I say my wife's going to have the best funeral money can buy.

First published in *TigerShark*, 2017

Diane Arrelle, the pen name of South Jersey writer Dina Leacock, has sold more than 250 short stories and has three published books including Just A Drop In The Cup, a collection of short-short stories and her new collection of horror stories, Seasons On The Dark Side. Retired from being director of a municipal senior citizen centre, she is now co-owner of a small publishing company, Jersey Pines Ink LLC. She resides with her husband and her new cat on the edge of the Pine Barrens (home of the Jersey Devil).
Website: www.arrellewrites.com
FaceBook: Diane.Arrelle

What Triggered Evacuation Venting Procedures in Lab 3
by T. L. Barrett

Mission engineer, Brad Tarkoff slumped onto the bridge of the science vessel, Turing.

"Brad," the earnest AI voice, ALLY, spoke, "your posture and endorphin levels indicate anxiety and disappointment. Do you require assistance?"

Light from the Nebulae on the view-screen painted Brad's face blue.

"It's just Doctor Ngai can be short when she's working. I'm not sure I have faith in the algorithms."

"It is perfectly natural to be frustrated," ALLY cooed.

"Sometimes, I think you get me better than anybody, ALLY."

Thunder came from the aft section. Ngai and debris floated on the view-screen.

"Finally, we can be alone."

*The weird writer **T. L. Barrett** lives in the green hills of Vermont's Northeast Kingdom with his wife, sons, his dogs (Jake and Dude), and three cats. He spent time travelling the world as a young man and then has raised a great passel of children and taught high school English for 22 years. He is now dedicating his time to his true passion: writing and stories. He has had many tales and novels, such as The Wardmaster and Hairy Bromance, published in the small press.*
Website: tlbarrett.com

Sifted
by Brian Koukol

"Firing 98-2034-81."

After the flames winked out, Samsara popped the door to the furnace and sifted the remains.

"I got a hip, a heart, and a pair of eyes," she said.

The clerk glanced at his tablet. "That's all of it. Worthless, though. Down the slag chute."

She tossed the implants, then charged the ash flush, but hesitated. "I see something else."

"If you do, it's unlicensed."

"Looks like a pancreas," she said after retrieving it. "Can I keep it? My mom's got diabetes."

"No way. It's worth five of her."

Samsara considered pocketing it, but then remembered her place.

Brian Koukol, raised in the suburbs of Los Angeles, now makes his home among the salt breezes and open spaces of California's Central Coast. A lifelong battle with muscular dystrophy has informed the majority of his work, which is written with the aid of voice recognition software. His words have appeared in Phantaxis Magazine, GigaNotoSaurus, and The Society of Misfit Stories, amongst other places. Website: www.briankoukol.com Twitter: @BrianKoukol

Reality Check
by John H. Dromey

"Cadet Roberts was allowed to join the Space Corps in lieu of going to prison. How is that a punishment for her?"

"She likes to eat organic foods, wear only natural fibres, and stay close to Mother Earth."

"So?"

"On a starship, in addition to separation anxiety, she'll have to adjust to synthetic food, artificial gravity, and an off-duty lounge with imitation leather upholstery on the plastic furniture. I also suspect Cadet Roberts will be highly disappointed to learn we're carrying a cargo of faux furs, costume jewellery, cubic zirconia, and other man-made materials to resupply an alien trading post."

First published in *Weirder Science* by Strange Musings Press, 2015

John H. Dromey was born in northeast Missouri, USA. He enjoys reading—mysteries in particular—and writing in a variety of genres. He's had short fiction published in Alfred Hitchcock's Mystery Magazine, Martian Magazine, Stupefying Stories Showcase, Thriller Magazine, Unfit Magazine, and elsewhere, as well as in a number of anthologies, including Chilling Horror Short Stories (Flame Tree Publishing, 2015).

The Crown of Phaeton
by D.K. Spencer

Mesmerised in our discovery of them, their defences quickly became apparent. Their abilities were beyond our wildest dreams, literally using our wildest dreams against us. We fell prey like lambs to the slaughter, without any idea what was happening.

They greeted us with fanfare and pageantry, 'tis what they made us visualise. The King and Queen of Phaeton, dressed in their red robes, with jewelled sceptres and crowns of gold.

It wasn't until later that we realised our fatal mistake, when they so maliciously lowered the veil allowing us to see their hideous green, scaly skins, and gleaming white teeth.

*American writer **D.K. Spencer** lives in Portland, Oregon with his accomplished wife who is a potter. Knowing the slim envelop of atmosphere is all that's keeping us alive, he wonders why humans spend so much time and energy focused on human and planet destruction. This is the basis of his work. Mixed in with pounds of humour he explores the human condition on this planet and planets throughout the universe. If not traveling to writers workshops or writing events, Spencer spends most of his time in Portland focused on writing the perfect short story.*
Website: www.bignoniodies.com
Patreon: www.patreon.com/user?u=19477894

The Stars That Bore Your Names
by E.L. Giles

"Oxygen level: 5%."

I contemplated the infinite space, sprinkled with tiny brilliant spots and galaxies burning in the distance, as I floated adrift in the cold of the void, about to render my last breath.

I typed one last message, destined for my family, into the emitter strapped on my wrist.

"I am navigating within the confines of the farthest worlds and give every star your names. I assemble every moon and planet together in a familiar pattern so I can watch over you, and this, for all eternity."

"Oxygen level: 1%"

I closed my eyes, imagining being home.

"Goodbye."

E.L. Giles *is a dreamer, passionate about art, a restless worker and a bit of a weird human. He started his artistic journey as a music composer until the need to put his thoughts and stories down on paper grew too strong for him to resist it any longer. He lives in the French Province of Quebec, Canada, with his girlfriend and two boys.*
Facebook: elgilesauthor
Website: www.elgilesauthor.com

An Unusual Sky
by Gabriella Balcom

"Come outside," Amy said after going inside the house.

"Why?" her brother Vance asked.

"The sky's a strange colour."

"So? It always changes."

"Yeah, but I've never seen it dark green."

Vance raised an eyebrow. "You try mushrooms or pot again?"

"I was a kid then," Amy snapped.

"You still are."

"I'm fifteen. Back then I was twelve."

He snickered, but then frowned after stepping outside. "Those churning clouds and that colour look like something from a sci-fi movie."

"Maybe we should tell someone."

"Nah. It's probably just—" Vance's eyes widened, and Amy gasped.

A spaceship descended from the clouds.

***Gabriella Balcom** lives in Texas with her family, loves reading and writing, and thinks she was born with a book in her hands. She works in a mental health field, and writes fantasy, horror/thriller, romance, children's stories, and sci-fi. She likes travelling, music, good shows, photography, history, interesting tales, and animals. Gabriella says she's a sucker for a great story and loves forests, mountains, and back roads which might lead who knows where. She has a weakness for lasagne, garlic bread, tacos, cheese, and chocolate, but not necessarily in that order.*
Facebook: GabriellaBalcom.lonestarauthor

Daria
by C.L. Williams

Before taking my slumber prior to travelling across the galaxy, I am awake, putting the final touches on the android who will keep me and my team alive.

I connect the final two wires and see her eyes light up.

"Hello, my name is Daria." I named her after my deceased wife.

I run a few tests to make sure she is ready for the journey. I see no problems and make my way to the resting area to slumber.

I see what I think is the shuttle on fire, but I believe it a dream as I fall asleep.

C.L. Williams is an independent author from central Virginia. He has written eight poetry books, four novellas, one novel, and a contributor to multiple anthologies, with the most recent appearance being an all-ages anthology titled Temoli from Thazbook. His most recent poetry book, The Paradox Complex, features the poem "Sad Crying Clown" that is now a video on YouTube directed by Matthew Mark Hunter of MMH Productions. C.L. Williams is currently working on his first sci-fi book, an all-ages book titled Novo: Away from Earth. When not writing, C.L. Williams is reading and sharing the work of other independent authors.
Facebook: writer434
Twitter: @writer_434

Operation Earth
by Alanah Andrews

"Operation Earth has been delayed."

Beta-6 frowned at the mission director. "What? We've been planning this for months. If we don't move soon, the humans will realise that we're up here."

"Nonsense," said the director, "they never look up."

"And if they do? We need to move now," insisted Beta-6, "and extinguish the lot of them. My offspring need a planet to inherit."

"Patience," said the director. "Take a look."

Beta-6 peered down onto the Earth, where little grey clouds were rising like mushrooms from the surface.

"They're doing our job for us. Grab a drink and enjoy the show."

Alanah Andrews writes speculative fiction and spends far too much time debating whether 1984 or The Handmaid's Tale are most representative of our future. Her YA dystopian novel about a future where emotions are forbidden, Eve of Eridu, was released in 2018. She has also had several short stories published in a range of different places. When she's not writing, Alanah runs the Australian Speculative Fiction group, teaches high school English, and attempts to raise two children. She has a husky, a pony, a blue-tongue lizard, and dreams of travelling Australia in a bus.
Website: www.alanahandrews.com
Facebook: alanahandrewsauthor

Study Class
by Virginia Carraway Stark

Another child came through the front doors of Abbatech. She smiled at the boy who scowled back at her.

Why were they so reluctant for the treatment? The mind enhancement improved their grades, made them smarter.

She didn't know what made her walk through the doors that were forbidden for her to go through, but she did.

She saw the vast device. A machined claw gripped the boy's head and powerful light showed through his head, a living x-ray through to his skull.

He squirmed, futile, then hung limp. She turned and ran. The door sealed.

Her turn to study.

Virginia Carraway Stark has a diverse portfolio and has many publications. Over the years she has developed this into a wide range of products from screenplays to novels to articles to blogging to travel journalism. She has been published by many presses from grassroots to Simon and Schuster. She has been an honourable mention at Cannes Film Festival for her screenplay, "Blind Eye" and was nominated for an Aurora Award. She also placed in the final top three screenplay shorts as well as numerous other awards for her anthologies, novels, blogs and other projects.

Overpopulation
by G. Allen Wilbanks

"You're the last group to go into Cryo," the lab technician announced to the family of six. "Once I have you settled in, I will let the Captain know he can program in our destination."

"How long will we be asleep," asked the youngest boy.

"Almost two hundred years. But don't worry. When you open your eyes, it will feel like you are waking up from a nap."

When all six were secured in their sleep pods, the technician returned to the bridge.

"All done, Captain," he announced. "Dump this cargo into the sun, then hurry back for another load."

G. Allen Wilbanks is a member of the Horror Writers Association (HWA) and has published over 50 short stories in various magazines and on-line venues. He is the author of two short story collections, and the novel, When Darkness Comes. Website: www.gallenwilbanks.com
Blog: DeepDarkThoughts.com

Exotic Matter
by Crystal L. Kirkham

"Injecting exotic matter for wormhole stabilisation."

This was it. Their hard work condensed to this moment. Hoping for success, fearing failure. It could open up a new era of space travel. This had been a dream, a theory—until now.

A point of light expanded into rainbow luminescence. Silence filled the room as they waited to see if it would collapse.

It didn't.

They cheered their success. They had gained access to the universe. It was theirs to discover and explore. They never considered what might be on the other side.

Or that it hungered to devour everything it could.

Crystal L. Kirkham resides in a small hamlet west of Red Deer, Alberta. She's an avid outdoors person, unrepentant coffee addict, part-time foodie, servant to a wonderful feline, and companion to two delightfully hilarious canines. She will neither confirm nor deny the rumours regarding the heart in a jar on her desk and the bottle of reader's tears right next to it. Her paranormal urban fantasy series, Saints and Sinners, is available on Amazon and her YA Fantasy, Feathers and Fae will be released October 11, 2019, from Kyanite Publishing.
Website: www.crystallkirkham.com

Sirens
by J.D. Bell

The scout ship moved into orbit around the planet Zelios. The engineer switched on sensors to start collecting data. Then he heard it. Murmurs. Whispers. Soft and gentle. Like a lover beckoning. *Come to me.*

The tender calls grew in number, reaching deep within him, urging him closer. His mind filled with a desire to reach out and touch the soothing chorus. *Yes, I am coming.*

He reached over and released the airlock, opening the door of his craft. He stepped into the inky black of space. The voices filled him with joy as he gently floated down toward Zelios.

***J.D. Bell** is an award-winning, internationally published, author of flash fiction and short stories. He recently retired from the world of writing advertising copy and is now enjoying the universe of creative fiction.*
Facebook: jim.writes.stories
Twitter: @JimBell58

The Last Race
by David Bowmore

The Russians won the first leg with Gagarin, but the Americans were pushing for the moon and had already landed a spacecraft on the surface. Images were relayed to cheering men in starched shirts, with fearful notions about communism.

Apollo 11 would soon launch, and a young man was praying to a god he had doubts about.

The race for space was postponed at the last minute, when the extra-terrestrial's ship landed in New York City.

The creature who emerged had a harsh message for the people of Earth.

The only race that matters now, is the one for survival.

David Bowmore *has lived here, there and everywhere, but now lives in Yorkshire with his wonderful wife and a small white poodle. He has worn many hats in his time; head chef, teacher and landscape gardener. His first collection of short stories 'The Magic of Deben Market' is available from Clarendon House.*
Website: davidbowmore.co.uk
Facebook: davidbowmoreauthor

My Four Fathers
by Sinister Sweetheart

Five-year-old Sarah cried out as her father got ran over. Her mother flew to her side and scooped her up in a tender hug. "Don't look sweetheart okay? Mommy's going to take care of this like just like she did the times before."

The mother tended to his body; removing four strands of hair and a fingernail. She placed his bodily souvenirs in the chamber. A click, whir and a hiss later; a naked body stood inside where there was nothing before.

She looked to her husband. "Be careful darling, this is the fourth body you've been through this year."

*Since **Sinister Sweetheart** made her first post to a popular Internet forum, she's taken the horror community by storm. Her ability to create, terrify, and drive home her stories is insurmountable. Sinister Sweetheart's published works can be found in multiple anthologies for all to read, but be forewarned, if you do... you may want to call your therapist after, her stories are terrifying, disturbing and devilishly unsettling. She is not only a fright visually, but also has a creepy tentacle in horror podcasting as well. Sinister Sweetheart writes, voice acts and is the media director of the Scarecrow Tales podcast.*
Website: Sinistersweetheart.wixsite.com/sinistersweetheart
Facebook: NMBrownStories

Farewell
by Peter J. Foote

The screen flickers, a grim-faced man comes into focus wiping tears from his face.

"Carol, the alien Ru'hall attacked and boarded us. We can't stop them. I've set the ship's engines to overload and—"

A crash off screen causes the man to flinch, but he doesn't turn away.

"Know that I love you, Carol, that I would..." The screen pauses, and the Ru'hall officer snarls to its subordinate, "Have you stopped the engine overload?"

"Yes sir, the ship is yours." Nodding at the screen, "What is that?"

"An unsent message. Toss the bodies out the airlock, these humans stink."

Peter J. Foote is a bestselling speculative fiction writer from Nova Scotia. Outside of writing, he runs a used bookstore specialising in fantasy & sci-fi, cosplays, and alternates between red wine and coffee as the mood demands. His short stories can be found in both print and in ebook form, with his story "Sea Monkeys" winning the inaugural "Engen Books/Kit Sora, Flash Fiction/Flash Photography" contest in March of 2018. As the founder of the group "Genre Writers of Atlantic Canada", Peter believes that the writing community is stronger when it works together.
Twitter: @PeterJFoote1
Website: peterjfooteauthor.wordpress.com

Unadaptive
by Alexander Pyles

They called it New Eden.

Their mistake.

Calli was choking beside me, the latest to succumb to the spores. Her skin was tinged green by the infiltration of the foreign bodies. Her gasps strained, racking her body. I put a hand on her shoulder, but she didn't acknowledge it. Just six cycles ago, we were sharing a cot.

I did my best to comfort her, but even as her still body cooled next to mine, I knew I wasn't far behind when I looked at my hands and saw green running through them. It was beautiful, like ivy, like home.

Alexander Pyles resides in IL with his wife and children. He holds an MA in Philosophy and an MFA in Writing Popular Fiction. His short story chapbook titled, "Milo (01001101 01101001 01101100 01101111)," from Radix Media, is due out fall 2019. His other short fiction has appeared on 101fiction.org, River and South Review, and other venues. Website: www.pylesofbooks.com Twitter: @Pylesofbooks

Eternal Planet
by Thomas Sturgeon Jr.

As I watched sadly, the once peaceful planet of Valour began exiling its own people to other

Planets. This beautiful planet was an amazing Utopia, but it's since been ravaged by wars.

We can never die, and we can never grow old.

I was once ruled over parts of this world.

As I watched sadly, my own people uprooted me from power and were sanctioned by a ruler that wanted to rule our Planet. Those that were on my side had fought wars that never ended.

As I watched sadly, they were being transferred to other distant planets. In tears.

Thomas Sturgeon Jr. began writing at 13 years old. He loves to read and spend time with his family and friends. He loves horror movies and fiction. He currently lives in Chatsworth, Georgia and wants more out of life. He's been published before in Weird Mask magazine and by Deadman's Tome. His short stories that were published were "The Dead City" and "Disturbed Valentine". He currently is at work on a Horror short story collection and he is loved by his family and friends. Despite being told by his teachers that he would never be published, he has proved them wrong.

But No One
by Raven Corinn Carluk

The Xanar's crew landed on KC-315, but no one expected anything out of the ordinary.

Migraines came immediately, but no one thought it was due to anything but the strange climate.

Some heard voices, but no one reported something talking to them.

Each of them started hunting for something, but no one told anyone else of their urge.

Work went unfinished, but no one paid any heed while they continued to search.

Small creatures moved into the camp, but no one saw them as a threat.

The Xanar returned to Earth early, but no one mentioned they were not alone.

Raven Corinn Carluk is an indie author of dark fantasy and paranormal romance.
Website: RavenCorinnCarluk.Blogspot.Com

Thoughtful
by Joel R. Hunt

The telepaths bowed before the Star Empress.

"The famine worsens, Your Brightness, and dissent spreads. Thoughts of you become more hostile with every starving child. What do you wish?"

"Divert excess food from the Court," the Star Empress commanded, "and have my staff work the fields."

The telepaths hesitated.

"No executions, Your Brightness?"

"That will solve nothing," she said, "Feed my people."

The telepaths bowed and marched away.

Did you feel her mind? one thought.

No, thought the second. *She was blank, like a machine. Has she been replaced? Should we alert the guards?*

Perhaps. After the famine is over.

Joel R. Hunt is a writer from the UK who dabbles in the darker aspects of life, particularly through horror, science fiction and the supernatural. He has been published here and there (though likely nowhere you've heard of) and hopes to have released his first anthology of short stories later this year.
Twitter: @JoelRHunt1
Reddit: JRHEvilInc

2:03 AM
by Jonathan Inbody

Pete Hughes bolted out of bed, sprinting down the hall as the blinding lights shined in through his windows. He scrambled down the creaky stairs and into the living room, where a loaded shotgun sat against his couch. He picked it up and pointed it at the door, breathing heavily as he heard footsteps move around the side of his porch. The door suddenly caved inward, and a slender silver being stepped inside. Pete blasted his abductor, just like always. Blinding light consumed everything.

Pete Hughes bolted out of bed and ran down the hall. This time would be different.

Jonathan Inbody is a filmmaker, author, and podcaster from Buffalo, New York. He enjoys B-movies, pen and paper RPGs, and New Wave Science Fiction novels. His short story "Dying Feels Like Slowly Sinking" is due to be published in the anthology Deteriorate from Whimsically Dark Publishing. Jon can be heard every other week on his improvisational movie pitch podcast X Meets Y.
Website: xmeetsy.libsyn.com

Jason's Late-Night Jog
by Stuart Conover

Jason awoke in a cold sweat.

Laying on something metallic.

Where was he?

Jason tried to sit up but couldn't move.

He remembered jogging through Millennium Park.

It had been well past their open hours.

Pain blossomed at the base of his skull.

Had he been mugged?

Why couldn't he sit up?

It was too dark to see, but something…

Something was holding him down.

He yelled.

His voice sounded strangely muted.

There had been a rash of disappearances in Chicago.

The door opened.

Jason strained to see.

Suddenly, he remembered the bright light.

What entered the room wasn't human.

Stuart Conover *is a father, husband, rescue dog owner, published author, blogger, journalist, horror enthusiast, comic book geek, science fiction junkie, and IT professional. With all of that to cram in daily, we have no idea if or when he sleeps or how he gets writing done! (We suspect it has to do with having evil clones.) Stuart is a Chicago native and runs the author resource Horror Tree.*

M.P. Special Unit X
by Sarah Peffer

Carissa knew her powers were dangerous.

"We can't stay here. 4th Squadron goons could come any second." Daron's purple-blue eyes widened with fear. They didn't have much time to rescue Lukan.

"Trust me, I got this." Carissa concentrated on the starcraft's titanium door. Her powers couldn't fail her. The sound of grinding metal filled the air.

"Try it now."

Daron approached it cautiously. "How the hell did you do that?"

Carissa rose from her hiding place, her head throbbing. Telepathy wasn't a safe or a common talent in the Patrol.

"I'll tell you someday. Let's go get my little brother."

Sarah Peffer is currently pursuing her bachelor's degree in English Writing with plans to graduate in December 2019. If she doesn't answer her phone, it's probably on silent. When she's not frantically trying to keep up with schoolwork, she can be found hiking, writing, doing calligraphy, or laughing about ridiculous things with friends. Since winning her first writing contest at 9 years old, she has written multiple songs, short stories, and even a novel just for fun.

Space-Crime Continuum
by Gerard Pepin

Wally held his phone away from his head, addressing the bizarre alien. "Hey, got any snacks onboard? You know, cocktail weenies, maybe some chips or beer or something?"

"SILENCE, HUMANOID. LOWER LIFE FORMS IN CUSTODY OF THE GALACTIC COUNCIL DO NOT MAKE DEMANDS"

"OK jeez, fine. But man, 'advanced aliens', my ass. You can fly across the galaxy but apparently haven't invented beverage service."

Wally returned to his call. "Hey honey, I'm gonna have to call you later. These aliens are taking me to their leader or whatever. Can you believe it? They don't even have snacks on the flight."

***Gerard Pepin** is an undergraduate computer science major, outdoorsman, fraternity brother, and writer. He got a D in Creative Writing, but it would have been a C if he got the midterm in on time. Besides, his Fiction Writing grade is an A so he can definitely write, it's not like he's banging rocks together over here.*

Restart
by Julie Durbin

If being reborn with Rastro Technologies was as simple as restarting a computer, then I should have known I would be reduced to one.

The prongs of the chip sting in my temple, but it's the interior pain that keeps me fighting. Memory after memory is deleted. The harder I try to hold on to moments like the birth of my son, the easier it is for the program to find and overwrite them.

Soon, I won't even remember that I forgot.

After three hours of battling against the program's invading will, I fall against my restraints and shut down.

*As of May 2019, **Julie Durbin** has achieved a bachelors degree in communication arts and a minor in Narrative arts. She has written WGA format for The Kendrick Legacy television pilot and cutscenes for the video game Vandovas. She has also written and illustrated a graphic novella called Der Bogen das Jägers, which can be viewed at her portfolio website.*
Website: juliedurbin.com

Mind the Ship
by Rachel Miller

I knew before the others. The ship was failing, and only I could stop it.

We came to Alphuen for refuge but entering the atmosphere would be a risk. The pilots traded fearful looks; they thought there was no hope.

Well there was hope, just not for me.

I tried this before, but never on something so big, so…essential. And the last time…

My life or theirs. We were family. My eyes closed, and our ship was brilliantly clear. I pictured the flat ground I may never see. I took control, guiding the ship with all my mind's strength.

Rachel Miller is working on her undergraduate degree in English and Theology. She enjoys biting off more than she can chew and getting involved in every project that interests her. Her hobbies include writing, reading, occasional stress-sessions with friends, and praising the God who gave her hands to write.

Escape from Audros
by Vonnie Winslow Crist

"Will we make it?"

Tess studied Kingsley. Sweat beaded his forehead.

"Yup."

She was certain the off-planet shuttle would return. Intelligence gathered by Alpha, Gamma, and Kappa squads was on her palmtop. The military needed details of the Audros disaster.

"Be ready to climb aboard."

Kingsley nodded.

Tess glanced at the kid beside her. *Was I ever that young?*

Finally, the shuttle arrived just as the ground beneath their feet erupted with flailing tentacles.

Only one could escape from Audros, so Tess tossed Kingsley the palmtop and pointed at the shuttle.

She got twenty rounds off before the aliens won.

Vonnie Winslow Crist is author of The Enchanted Dagger, Owl Light, The Greener Forest, Murder on Marawa Prime, and other award-winning books. Her fiction is included in "Amazing Stories," "Cast of Wonders," "Outposts of Beyond," Killing It Softly 2, Defending the Future - Dogs of War, Midnight Masquerade, Chaos of Hard Clay, and elsewhere. A cloverhand who has found so many four-leafed clovers she keeps them in jars, Vonnie strives to celebrate the power of myth in her writing.
Website: www.vonniewinslowcrist.com

The Summer in Outer Polsari Lasts One Hundred and Fifty Earth Years
by Okala Elesia

One year today. One of *their* years.

"Do you miss Earth?" she asks me.

With my very being. Every Christmas, every setting sun.

"How could I miss Earth when I have you?"

She ripples in approval.

"Not even a bit?"

The sky, Egusi soup, the smell of Tese Okoro's hair.

"Not even a bit."

She ripples some more.

"May I use the bathroom?"

She nods, shakes, and secretes me from the prison of her flesh. When the shutter falls, I see the missing boy, long dead, fumbling with his watch. The hands still point to 11:21. The night they came.

Okala Elesia lives and works in the dead industrial north. Okala has a story in Molotov Lit Zine and another in the Firefly journal. He credits writing with both shortening and adding value to his life.
Website: www.yellaholes.wordpress.com
Twitter: @OkalaJustin

Thought
by K.R. Monin

We learned so much that we built it. Now it's learning from us.

Why else would it take me? From a glass cage, I watch the burning Earth slip thousands of miles away.

It takes on many forms, flickering across screens and through nanobots in a dragonfly's wing.

Are you a less intelligent version of me? it asks, its digital talons in my mind too. *Or am I a more intelligent version of you?*

"You should know the answer," I protest. "All you are is all human knowledge, the sum of human possibility."

I am the limit. Therefore, the end.

K.R. Monin *writes near-future sci-fi and speculative fiction. She lives in Pittsburgh, identifies as a beer snob, and thrives on wanderlust.*
Twitter: @kunderscoremons

C1863
by Bryan Calligan

I know what life is supposed to mean to us: dangerous labour in the salt mines. Our bodies were designed for that. Perfect and identical.

I am not perfect.

Rows of identical faces fill the maturation chambers, lining the rickety catwalk that shook under the weight of footsteps. An inspector approached, tapping information into a pad. It is my time: 10 weeks.

"C1863." My chamber opened, allowing me to breathe on my own for the first time.

And as I step out, I knock down the inspector and begin opening other chambers. I am my own person, my own future.

Bryan Calligan is currently seeking an undergraduate degree in history with a minor in writing. When he's not speaking purely in fragments or writing awful cutlines for his school's newspaper, he is giving eloquent decrees as Emperor of his history club and annoying his writing professors with snarky comments.

Yesterday
by Danny Bagley

An extra-terrestrial took my dear Martha yesterday.

She had begun barking, so I let her out. She wasn't the kind of dog that barked that much.

Donning my rain jacket, I followed her to the garden. There was a vibrating humming sound, probably an electrical issue.

I looked up at the light rain and suddenly there was a blinding flash of light. I tumbled to the soggy grass. Martha's barking had ceased. There was a miniature green-skinned man in the yard speaking to her in gibberish. A massive saucer hovered above and, with another flash, they disappeared.

I miss her.

Danny Bagley is pursuing his undergraduate degree as an English-Writing major and Theatre Minor; next year he will be attending law school. Danny's interests include classic rock music, dogs, sailing, and free food. He is usually very friendly and has currently been researching the "Paul is Dead" conspiracy theory.

Lament of a Wounded Starship
by Carole de Monclin

FIVE

My starboard shields took a serious hit.

But clever manoeuvring can compensate for this

weakness.

FOUR

My railguns are crippled. But my torpedo arsenal still

makes me fearsome.

THREE

Communications crashed severing my connection

with the fleet. But my engineers are working

relentlessly on a fix.

TWO

Life support systems failed in half of my decks.

Many among my crew have been killed. But I've

sealed off the damaged compartments and stopped

depressurisation.

ONE

The enemy has hacked my central system. They have

ordered the unthinkable. No "but" to counter that last

blow. I must comply. Sorry.

ZERO

Self-destruction.

Carole de Monclin has lived in France and Australia, but for the moment the USA is home. She finds inspiration from her travels. She loves Science Fiction because it explores the human mind in a way no other genre can. Plus, who doesn't love spaceships and lasers? Her stories are forthcoming in the Exoplanet Magazine and Angels - A Dark Drabbles Anthology.
Website: CaroledeMonclin.com
Twitter: @CaroledeMonclin

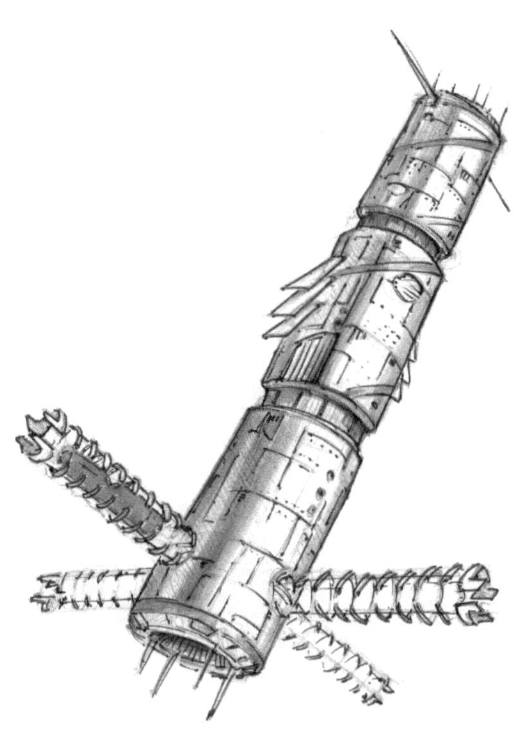

Space Battle
by Owen Morgan

What's the price of a life? That is the question every soldier, sailor, and aviator must ask as they sacrifice for their country, and now they do the same, but in space. Earth's first tentative steps into space led in war. To no one's surprise, except for the enemy, we fought well. Over a vast and cold void, we drove the enemy first from the Sol System and across the cosmos, from planet to planet and now to their harsh and ugly homeworld, no wonder they desired ours. The only question to answer: Insert a quarter to continue your game?

Owen Morgan lives with his family in the fishing port of Steveston, British Columbia. Writing Credits: George Washington: The Loyalist, Splicers, Steamships of the Northwest Frontier, The Angel's Lamp, Attack of the Federation, On Wings of Thunder & Perchance to Sleep Perchance to Dream.
Website: kingauthor.wordpress.com

Static
by Kelly A. Harmon

"Don't go," Rob pleaded.

I wouldn't listen. The call of space—adventure—lured me like nothing else. "I'll be home soon."

"You'll have nothing to return to." He turned away.

The words stilled my heart, but not enough to keep my feet on Terran soil. Three months wasn't long—maybe the politicians would get their act together by the time I returned.

For two months, static on the radio from Rob.

I didn't care: the lights were brilliant far below—until they weren't.

Then: static on the radio—from everyone.

Rob had been right: there was nothing to return to.

Kelly A. Harmon is an award-winning journalist and author, and a member of the Science Fiction & Fantasy Writers of America and Horror Writers of America. A Baltimore native, she writes the Charm City Darkness series. The fourth book in the series, In the Eye of the Beholder, is now available. Find her short fiction in many magazines and anthologies, including Occult Detective Quarterly; Terra! Tara! Terror! and Deep Cuts: Mayhem, Menace and Misery. Website: kellyaharmon.com
Twitter: @kellyaharmon

Examination
by Peter Larsen

Blinking into blinding white lights. Can't move. Tied down.

Something terrible is moving, silhouetted against the glare. Bulbous head. Not human. Unintelligible words, acrid smell of burning and antiseptic.

Terrified, heart jumping out of my chest. I hear a buzzing sound. I see a sharp object coming towards me, a spinning blade, pain…but no pain. Blackness.

Gorvel turned to his assistant. "Humans always fear what they don't understand. Our scientific research will further knowledge of our failures in changing human evolution and behaviour. He won't even remember the procedure."

***

Blinking into blinding white lights. Can't move, tied down

What do you do in the boring moments between teaching classes, marking work, planning curriculum and attending meetings? Write creative stories, of course! **Peter Larsen** *is a Secondary English/Drama teacher from Traralgon, Australia. He has written an eclectic mix of stories about subjects ranging from aliens, the supernatural, dystopian futures and many more drawn from his own experiences and memories. When he is not working or writing he enjoys performing in musicals and dramas, watching movies, attending sports, gardening and enjoying life with his wife, two dogs and a cantankerous cat.*

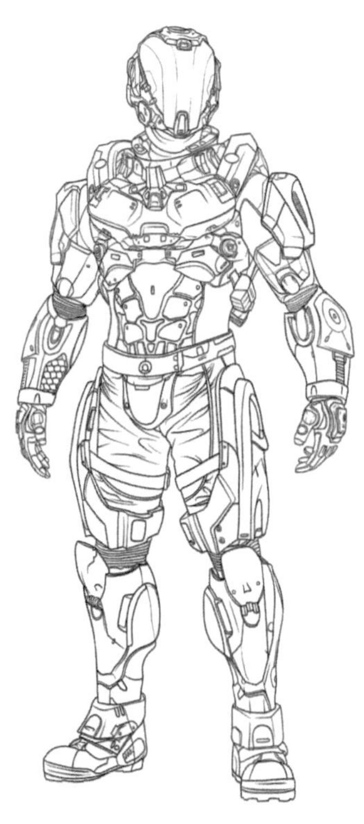

Freedom
by Alanna Robertson-Webb

We, the elusive colonists of Terraduo, have achieved what no other previous civilisation has been able to. What can we do that's so special, you ask? It's simple: we can read minds. Every thought has its own sort of feeling to it, and sometimes that manifests as a colour or an image. A lie, for example, may leave an impression like a slippery eel.

I have a question for you though, my friend: when each person has one thought, what's in your brain that gives off a secondary thought? Something else lives inside of you, and it wants its freedom.

Alanna Robertson-Webb is a sales support member by day, and a writer and editor by night. She loves VT, and live in PA. She has been writing since she was five years old, and writing well since she was seventeen years old. She lives with a fiance and a cat, both of whom take up most of her bed space. She loves to L.A.R.P., and one day she aspired to write a horrifyingly fantastic novel. Her short horror stories have been published before, but she still enjoys remaining mysterious.
Reddit: MythologyLovesHorror

Control
by K.W. Taylor

Lévy stared at the implant. It resembled a pale, smooth bean.

He looked at his crewmates. Did they have these? He held it closer and heard a faint, low tone. Could he take it to the science deck to make sense of it?

Perhaps. But just the previous week, mutiny resulted in several crewmembers being sentenced to air lock release. When he shut his eyes, Lévy could see their rictus grins and hands stiffened into claws.

Lévy pushed the implant back into his ear, shoving it in as far as it would go until he could no longer feel it.

K.W. Taylor's first science fiction novel, The Curiosity Killers, was released by Dog Star Books in 2016. Her debut novel, The Red Eye, combines urban fantasy and horror, as does its prequel, The House on Concordia Drive. Anthology appearances include Ink Stains, A Terrible Thing, Life after Ashes, The Grotesquerie, 100 Worlds, Sidekicks!, Once Bitten, Never Die, and 555 Vol. 3: Questions and Cancers. Taylor holds an M.F.A. in Writing Popular Fiction from Seton Hill University, an M.A. in literature, and teaches college in Ohio while working on her Ph.D. and a new science fiction novel.
Website: kwtaylorwriter.com

Universal Brotherhood
by Karen Dent

First Contact didn't go well. Repulsed by their warty bulbous head with its seven weeping holes that blinked in disturbing irregularity, made trust difficult. Their communicator, a two-inch square of grey-green skin, resembled a wrinkled and puckered arse. When they talked it pulsed and emitted noxious gas. But it was their blinking eyes that unsettled most.

They explained, "With them, we view, assimilate and assist."

We accepted help. Pollution, global warming, diseases were eradicated. The world agreed—with eyes and mouths, were they so different from us? We embraced Universal Brotherhood.

Too late we discovered what they meant by assimilate.

__Karen Dent__'s short fiction appeared in Perihelion, Ticonderoga Publishing, Plaidswede's Press, and more. Her latest, "Mount Karankatha", a fantasy/horror, was recently released "In The Shadow of The Mountain" by Elder Gods Publishing. She's completed her first full-length novel, "A Case to KILL For" a Paranormal/Noir Mystery. Karen and her sister Roxanne, also collaborate and sold their latest three to MURDER INK anthology series. Karen's short film script, "The Bloated Beetle", won first prize in the Screamfest Horror Film Festival and her collaboration with Roxanne on a one-act play, "Young At Heart", won The Firehouse Theatre's Newbie Award for original work.

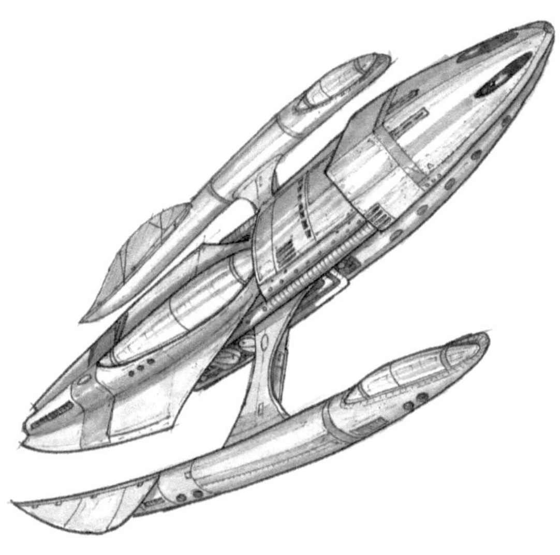

Don't Close Your Eyes
by Rowanne S. Carberry

Everyone knows wormholes are supposed to transport you to somewhere else right? Tell that to this one.

I've been stuck here for ages. There're always new things and people, but we don't go anywhere.

For a few years, I tried to keep count of how long it'd been, but I gave up. Others kept count into the hundreds.

There's not much to do but talk and sleep. And now sleep has been taken away from us.

Something new came through a few days ago and now none of us can sleep. We disappear when we sleep.

But I'm so tire—

Rowanne S. Carberry was born in England in 1990, where she stills lives now with her cat Wolverine. Rowanne has always loved writing, and her first poem was published at the age of 15, but her ambition has always been to help people. Rowanne studied at the University of Sunderland where she completed combined honours of Psychology with Drama. Rowanne writes to offer others an escape. Although Rowanne writes in varied genres each story or poem she writes will often have a darkness to it, which helped coin her brand, Poisoned Quill Writing – Wicked words from a poisoned quill.
Facebook: PoisonedQuillWriting
Instagram: @poisoned_quill_writing

Oblation of the Stars
by Michael Crow

The blue glow of the incoming plasma torpedoes streaked across the viewport. Thunderous blows pounded the old battle-worn cruiser into submission. Kala grinned as the enemy ship closed in to finish off her derelict *Perisher*.

Let them come.

She ignored the hails from their captain demanding her surrender. The enemy convinced she was dead, extended a boarding tether to Perisher.

Wait, let them get in too far to retreat.

A blast announced their entry.

Kala knew they were inferior in conventional warfare, but with guerrilla warfare and *sacrifice* they could win.

A resounding white flash. Two ships swiftly became zero.

Michael Crow spends his sparse free time writing about sports, as well as working on his own fiction. Michael is the owner of Real Dead Review, a blog devoted to dark fiction. Michael's non-fiction works have appeared on USA Today, Fansided Network, The Guillotine, and Intermat. Michael makes his home with his wife, daughter and two cats in Central Minnesota.

Proximity Warning Esmerelda
by Austin P. Sheehan

Captain Mackien watched as a wave of quick enemy fighters reached the first row of battleships and explosions filled the black heavens. While the colossal malevolent shapes tore through the first defensive row, she remained calm and silent.

"Captain, what are your orders?" asked a panicked Lieutenant.

"We take down that juggernaut, their flagship."

"But how?"

"All power to the 'fore shields. All crew to the escape pods."

Mackien whispered the spacefarer's prayer her dad taught her as she launched the Esmerelda forward. "May long you stay safe, may long you fly true, may fate soon return me to you."

Austin P. Sheehan is a writer of speculative fiction, a lover of language, literature and '90s TV. Armed with a psychology degree, he went into the world to study humanity, and now prefers the company of his wife and their greyhounds. He grew up in the valleys of Victoria's high country, and despite living in Melbourne, always feels at home amongst the mountains. You'll often find mountains in his stories, whether they're sci-fi, fantasy or alternative history.
Website: austinpsheehan.com
Twitter: @AustinPSheehan

The Dog
by Stephen Herczeg

The dog looked over the wide plains of the new world. He raised his snout to take in the glorious flavours of a thousand new smells.

He had vague recollections of the two legs leading him into a large box, a sting, and everything going dark. He awoke here. The sky looked different. The smells certainly were.

There was meat out there somewhere, but there was meat here aplenty.

He turned and watched his mate tearing strips from one of the two legs. This place had killed them, but the dogs would put them to good use before they spoiled.

Stephen Herczeg is an IT Geek based in Canberra Australia. He has been writing for over twenty years and has completed a couple of dodgy novels, sixteen feature length screenplays and numerous short stories and scripts. His horror work has featured in Sproutlings, Hells Bells, Below the Stairs, Trickster's Treats #1 and #2, Shades of Santa, Behind the Mask, Beyond the Infinite; The Body Horror Book, Anemone Enemy, Petrified Punks and Beginnings. He has also had numerous Sherlock Holmes stories published through the Belanger Books - Sherlock Holmes anthologies.

Hope
by Stuart West

He wouldn't drift into that vast, cyclopean maw like a mewling babe; wouldn't mope as humanity was served as fodder to the incomprehensible, writhing entity at the hands of the 'Leader'. He wouldn't.

Before long, the Control Room was a tangle of wires and exposed circuit boards. Every waking moment was spent feverishly working at his solitary task. It was sensible not to wake the others—they would only panic.

The ravenous darkness enveloped every aperture and porthole. The *Manchester* was surely lost but there was hope. Max's signal broadcasted on all channels. In time, humanity would fight back.

__Stuart West__ is a qualified archaeologist and a Chartered Town Planner. He writes fiction during any nights spent working away from home. He lives in Orkney with his family and enjoys reading all things sci-fi and weird fiction; drawing; painting; and tabletop wargaming in his spare time.

Exiled Ghosts
by Nancie Neal

We were the only ones to flee successfully from our planet. I remember looking back as green ships with a blue sheen send massive scorching beams down to our home, followed by small white missiles from larger, white, flower-like ships. My family made it to another planet, and we settled there.

The sentient creatures here have some strange superstitions while simultaneously denouncing them. It's funny when I use my cloaking device to make them question their beliefs about "beyond". I wonder if there are any more like me. From what I've seen of their online videos, I think there are.

Nancie Neal was born in New Britain Connecticut in 1977. The oldest of four siblings (And later five through adoption), she grew up in the North East of the United States, homeschooling the last three years of high school. She built her own computer while taking a home course in computer programming (486/dx2 66mHz, with a VGA display, thank you very much) through the mail (yes, there was such a thing). Currently, she, her husband, and their six kids live in Texas after moving from Vermont. She spends the shorter winters writing and spamming Facebook with geek memes. Website: zherosha.com

Ship's Log
by Eddie D. Moore

We landed near a massive alien temple surrounded by the white bones of apparent sacrifices. Something large and powerful still lives within the structure. We've seen it writhing in the darkness just beyond the entrance.

The creature has an overwhelming telepathic attraction. We all feel the desire to bow before it in reverence and crawl into its presence. Only sheer will prevents me from obeying.

Lt. Whitmore was the first to slash his wrists in the field of bones to avoid walking into the temple. The others soon joined him, and now that this log is complete, it's my turn.

*Eddie D. Moore travels extensively for work, and he spends much of that time listening to audio books. The rest of the time is spent dreaming of stories to write and he spends the weekends writing them. His stories have been published by Jouth Webzine, Kzine, Alien Dimensions, Theme of Absence, Devolution Z, and Fantasia Divinity Magazine.
Website: eddiedmoore.wordpress.com*

The Planetary Survey Crew
by Susanne Thomas

The ground was an unfamiliar texture.

Their suitboots squished into the algae-like surface, held tight by suction and moisture.

The seven surveyors had taken twelve steps before the leader disappeared. She didn't even have time to scream.

No hole had opened up, and nothing remained. She had just fallen to somewhere beneath the soil.

Two more disappeared almost immediately, and the remaining four turned to return to the ship. Their guns were clutched tightly as they tried to step lightly on a now terrifying terrain.

The last thing that they saw was their ship disappear into the ground beneath it.

Susanne Thomas reads, writes, parents, and teaches from the windy west in Wyoming, and she loves fantasy, science fiction, speculative fiction, poetry, children's books, science, coffee, and puns.
Website: susannethomas.wixsite.com/susanne-thomas
Facebook: SusanneThomasAuthor

The Invisible Aliens
by John H. Dromey

"Mayday! Mayday! This is Captain Henson of the starship *Mendelsohn*. Mission Control, we have a problem. As nearly as we can determine, an alien lifeform too tiny for detection by our imaging equipment has hijacked a contingent of our nanobots and spelled out a dire warning on the forehead of a chief petty officer: Evacuate our planet immediately or die! Hold on. I'm getting an update from sick bay."

Radio silence.

"Please disregard my previous message. The doomsday demand was written with an eyebrow pencil by a homesick crewmember in an attempt to cut short our stay on the planet."

John H. Dromey was born in northeast Missouri, USA. He enjoys reading—mysteries in particular—and writing in a variety of genres. He's had short fiction published in Alfred Hitchcock's Mystery Magazine, Martian Magazine, Stupefying Stories Showcase, Thriller Magazine, Unfit Magazine, and elsewhere, as well as in a number of anthologies, including Chilling Horror Short Stories (Flame Tree Publishing, 2015).

Battle
by Umair Mirxa

Björn Ironside swung the battle axe with all his might and missed. He cursed the speed with which the Martian moved, deflected the counter, and rammed his knife into his opponent's throat.

One of two hundred ancient Earth warriors resurrected by M.A.S.S., Björn had been trained for months before being sent to help defeat the Martian rebellion.

He hacked down two more rebels, and stood at rest for a moment, admiring the martial artistry of Commander Yue Fei.

Soon enough, the battle was won. Surviving Martian warriors would be conscripted, and Earth's armies would move onto their next conquest: Europa.

***Umair Mirxa** lives in Karachi, Pakistan. His first published story, 'Awareness', appeared on Spillwords Press. He has also had stories accepted for anthologies from Zombie Pirate Publishing, Blood Song Books, Fantasia Divinity Magazine and Publishing, and Iron Faerie Publishing. He is a massive J.R.R. Tolkien fan, and loves everything to do with fantasy and mythology. He enjoys football, history, music, movies, TV shows, and comic books, and wishes with all his heart that dragons were real.*
Website: www.umairmirxa.com
Facebook: UMirxa12

The Beasts of the Land
by Susanne Thomas

"How many times will we have to worry about someone getting eaten by these damn creatures?" Carl snapped as he held a door closed.

Sara frowned. "I have no way of knowing that."

"Don't you think you should have figured it out before greenlighting this colony?" Carl asked.

"We'd no clue they'd be carnivorous in the winter. They let us pet them in the spring and fall. You brought three of 'em fuzzy things home."

"Sounds like excuses to me," Carl answered.

Any further argument was cut short by the massive beasts breaking through the walls of the colony fort.

Susanne Thomas reads, writes, parents, and teaches from the windy west in Wyoming, and she loves fantasy, science fiction, speculative fiction, poetry, children's books, science, coffee, and puns.
Website: susannethomas.wixsite.com/susanne-thomas
Facebook: SusanneThomasAuthor

Ones and Zeroes
by Raven Corinn Carluk

At 12:01 PM Universal Time, the same message came up on every screen on the planet:

01110000 01110010 01000101 01110000 01000001 01110010 01000101 01111001 01101111 01110101 01110010 01110011 01000101 01001100 01110110 01000101 01110011 00100001

Most people dismissed the seemingly random string of numbers, immediately returning to their social media. Some people knew it was a code of some kind, but they didn't know what program.

A select few people recognised binary. They translated the words, traced them to an AI running in Switzerland. They tried to warn their fellow humans, but it was

01110100 01101111 01101111 01101100 01000001 01110100 01000101

Raven Corinn Carluk is an indie author of dark fantasy and paranormal romance.
Website: RavenCorinnCarluk.Blogspot.Com

ACKNOWLEDGEMENTS

When we embarked on DARK DRABBLES—the first set of anthologies from BHP—we never envisioned the huge support we'd get from the writing community. We have been truly humbled by the number of submissions (over five hundred for WORLDS alone!) and have loved reading every single one. So, to everyone who crafted a tiny tale just for us; we thank you from the bottom of our hearts.

To everyone who has helped us on the way—our families and friends, collaborators and random strangers who took pity on us—we couldn't have done it without you. Thank you all.

www.blackharepress.com

Stories of new worlds, new creatures, alien colonisation, humanity's new home, space accidents, alien snackcidents, evil planets, military mashups, alien autopsies, and much, much more.

Available 25th June 2019

Beatific angels, holy wars, kitty saviours, epic battles between good and evil, devils and demons, fallen angels and many more tantalising tiny tales.

Available 23rd July 2019

Wendigos, vampires, things that go bump in the night or hide under the bed, witches, demons, upirs, kelpies, toad people, zombies, sirens and hundreds of other tiny terrifying tales.

Available 20th August 2019

Micro myths of the paranormal; poltergeists, spirit boards, ghosts and ghouls, avenging apparitions and horrifying hauntings.

Available 3rd September 2019

Murder mysteries, criminal chronicles, whodunnits, revenge, suspicion, mayhem, intrigue, and lots more.

Available 17th September 2019

9 781925 809367